Blue Mountain Wolves - Awakening

By

S.C. Macklin

For Jasmine and Montana

**This book never would have happened if not for you two!
xx**

Chapter 1

Langdon stepped out of the classroom, three things on his mind: Brooke, food and getting home after an afternoon sitting in the detention room to finish his week. Striding down the hallway, his eyes scanning for his best mate, Tom, he paused and scrunched his nose in distaste. *Fucking Beau Vandenberg. Scrawny, nerdy, little shit, look at him-head down, not looking where he's going. Then, an idea came…*

Beau shuffled down the corridor, balancing his books and belongings high in his lean, wiry arms. His head was down, avoiding other students filling the area with the roar of excitement and chatter. His eyes refused to make contact, too aware of judgmental peers. His palms were sweaty, his heart pounded louder than the surrounding voices. He just wanted to get home, far away from his anxiety-causing peers.

'Ugh,' Beau tripped over something and fell onto the hard concrete ground, his books flying in all directions.

Beau didn't even see that Langdon was smugly waiting two feet away with his left leg extended.

Getting slowly to his feet, he looked up to see what had caused him to fall. 'Langdon! Damn it, I'm so sick of you picking on me!'

Langdon scoffed, 'Nerd, watch where you're walking.' Then he burst into a fit of laughter.

Sighing heavily, Beau tugged at his wavy brown hair, now noticing his belongs strewn across the walkway. He cringed seeing people stepping on his beloved physics book. Dropping to his knees, he scrambled to collect his books, calculator and pencil case that had made their way across the corridor.

Small crowds of students from their Year 11 cohort had stopped to take on the entertainment. Beau was still gathering up his books and scowling at Langdon, whose laughter travelled through the long hallway, encouraging onlookers to have a chuckle.

Tom came from the opposite direction and saw Beau picking up the last of his books. Then he glanced opposite Beau and saw Langdon paying out on him.

'What's wrong, nerd? Did you trip over your goofy feet? Ha-ha.'

'Langdon!' Tom yelled over the noise. 'Come on mate, stop being a dick.'

Langdon looked away from Beau and saw his best mate, *oops caught out, don't know why Tom hangs out with that loser.*

'What's up?' Langdon acted blasé, as if he'd just been standing there minding his own business.

Tom shook his head and strode over to Beau and mumbled something before they walked off together.

Langdon ignored them, and his grin grew when Brooke walked out of the classroom, her long brown hair hanging loosely around her shoulders and her light blue eyes lit up when she saw him. *God she's beautiful.* His eyes couldn't help roaming and landed on her short shorts that barely covered her thighs, he smirked, imagining running his fingers up, right up to the apex of her thighs. Langdon grinned as she sucked on her bottom lip, knowing his effect on her.

'Hey Baby,' Langdon cooed as he swung an arm around her shoulders.

Brooke looked up at her boyfriend and smiled, 'Hey,' she replied, falling into sync beside him as they walked towards the school buses.

'So, coming back to mine this afternoon?' he asked, hoping she would say yes. He'd asked her at lunchtime, but she had needed to organise a ride home from his place if she was coming over.

'Yeah, okay, my sister said she can pick me up from yours when she finishes work.'

Langdon smirked and held her closer, pausing to lean down and kiss her gently on the lips. *So soft,* he wanted to kiss her, taste her, push himself up against her, but he pulled away, too aware of the crowds of students heading towards their buses. Instead, he dropped his arm from her shoulder and linked his fingers with hers; he knew she loved holding hands, so he gently caressed his thumb across her fingers, loving the softness of her skin.

Arriving at the bus pickup zone, the area looked crowded with students waiting. Noisy chatter of weekend plans and cars revving engines and streaming past had Langdon moving behind Brooke so she could lean back against his torso while he leaned up against the pole, slightly away from the commotion. Wrapping his arms around her waist, he held her close, and she rested back against him, her head on his chest. Langdon could smell vanilla strongly in her hair, he breathed in enjoying the aroma.

When the bus finally arrived, students scrambled on, relentless in their pursuit of claiming a seat. Langdon pushed his way through, not caring about bumping into people as he went ahead with Brooke following closely behind, his hand still gripping hers.

Grabbing a seat at the back near Tom and Beau, he pushed Brooke in first so he could extend his long legs out to the side. He nodded a hello to Tom, who returned the greeting, then went back to talking to Beau. Langdon scrunched up his nose; he couldn't stand Beau—tiny, weak, all books and no muscle. *I'm on the rugby team, all he does is sit in class thinking he's smarter than everyone, sucking up to the teachers.*

The ride home jostled the students, and with each turn, Langdon deliberately moved his hand higher up Brooke's thigh. She didn't seem to mind as she chatted to her friend sitting across the aisle. Langdon glanced around, inwardly scoffing at the weaker kids, and nodded in time to the beat of pop-rock tunes played loudly from a phone nearby.

The bus slowed to a stop, so Langdon glanced up to see Tom and Beau getting up for their stop.

'Ready for the game tomorrow?' Langdon projected his voice at Tom.

'Yup,' Tom nodded and grinned at Langdon as he walked past.

Once the bus resumed the journey, Langdon settled back, his attention now on Brooke, asking about her day.

Soon, the bus finally arrived at Langdon's stop, and he watched as his younger sister, Hayley, climbed down before him, and he followed behind Brooke.

Along the way out, Zane and Quinton bumped fists with him as a hello. He heard them discussing the other team they would verse this Saturday. Langdon grinned and yelled out, 'We'll crush 'em,' earning himself cheers from his teammates.

Hopping off the bus, Langdon put his arm around Brooke as they walked.

His sister Hayley stopped to readjust her heavy backpack. 'Ugh! Wait up!' then she hurried to catch up with them.

There was a short walk from the bus stop to their house, but they still had a few streets to cross. Hayley ran to catch up. 'Brooke!' she called out.

Brooke slowed, much to Langdon's annoyance.

'Hey Brooke, I love your nail polish, where'd you get it?' Hayley asked, half skipping and half jogging beside them to keep up with their long strides.

Langdon groaned inwardly. He was in a hurry to get home and spend some time with his girlfriend.

Brooke giggled, Langdon loved that sound, 'Oh, just from that chemist at Wentworth Shopping Centre.'

'Ooh, I love it! Does it come in glittery pink too?'

Ugh, Langdon tuned out while his sister continued to ask Brooke questions.

Arriving home, he unlocked the front door and took Brooke through to the kitchen. 'What do you feel like, babe? Muesli bar? Biscuit?'

He opened the pantry cupboard to show her some options. Grabbing himself a muesli bar, he raised his eyebrow, waiting.

'Oh, I'll have the same as you,' she replied shyly.

Langdon handed her a muesli bar and opened the fridge for a can of soft drink, grabbing out two cokes he passed her one and walked toward the staircase leading up to his room. 'Come on, babe, we'll have that up here.'

Langdon knew his parents wouldn't be home for another hour and wanted to make use of this time. He wasn't allowed to close his bedroom door with her when they were around. This made any alone time together even more potent with possibility. Thinking about how far he could get with her he wanted to make the most of their time alone. Not worrying about his parents barging in.

Brooke walked in and sat in his office chair, swivelling around to rest her chilled Coke on the desk. She hungrily ripped into her muesli bar and started eating as Langdon sat on the bed drinking his coke, he'd already scoffed his snack and was waiting for Brooke to finish hers.

'How's your English assignment going?' she asked between bites. She'd been struggling with hers but didn't want to admit it, not to her boyfriend, anyway.

Ugh, English? I don't want to talk about school. 'Yeah, okay, can't stand Mrs Hills though, I hate how she drones on, she puts me to sleep.' Langdon rolled his eyes at the thought of his English class.

Brooke giggled and wiped her mouth after chewing her last bite. She glanced around the room as she sipped her drink.

Langdon's room was large, with a king single bed up against the wall, a large window covered the wall partly beside his bed and extended further along. The dark blue curtains were pulled to the side, allowing enough light from the afternoon sun.

Posters of rugby players and the NSW State of Origin team were pinned sporadically around his room. A few dirty clothes were thrown haphazardly around, as if he couldn't be bothered to toss them into the bathroom laundry basket. The second door, which was closed, was an interconnecting door to the shared bathroom with his sister.

Langdon finished his drink and moved off the bed to toss it in the bin. He closed the bedroom door and then sat on the bed with his back against the headboard. Then he glanced across at Brooke watching and made a show of flexing his muscles as he adjusted his position. Brooke took a sip of her Coke, and he wished she'd hurry and join him.

'Come here,' Langdon spoke softly and beckoned her with his hand out to guide her.

He watched as she placed her Coke onto his desk and then gracefully climbed off the chair, her shorts had scrunched up revealing more of her thighs. *God, she's hot*, thought Langdon as he admired her body. She took his hand and climbed onto the bed beside him. Sitting this close to him, she stared into his deep blue eyes as he gazed back. His eyes would pierce everyone when he glared. Now, though, his pupils had dilated as he drank in her features.

Langdon's eyes wandered over Brooke's chest before finding her gaze again. He lifted a hand to move some hair that had fallen onto her face and pushed it back behind her ear. Brooke licked her lips as she stared back, making Langdon inwardly groan with need. The sight of her tongue tracing her lower lip pulled him closer until he finally pressed his mouth to hers, while resting his hand on her exposed thigh. Brooke leaned into him, responding with a soft urgency that sent a rush through him.

Langdon caressed her tongue with his, dominating, yet careful, while his hand slid from her thigh to her waist. Brooke moaned softly into his mouth, and he could tell she enjoyed the feel of his tongue moving against hers. He softened his touch, tracing her arm and leg, up and then down, to reassure and soothe her.

She'd seen him get into fights and bully Beau. But he was always so kind to her. She placed her hand gently on his chest, feeling his muscles as his chest rose and fell.

Langdon moaned into her mouth as he held her closer. Her lips were so soft against his. Withdrawing his mouth from hers, smiling when she whimpered, the soft noise that came from her was almost his undoing. He placed gentle kisses along her jawline and down onto her neck. Then, running his tongue over her earlobe and biting gently, he could feel her rapid breaths against his skin.

He inhaled her intoxicating vanilla scent, continuing to kiss under her earlobe and down her neck again. Moving his hand from her waist, his fingers travelled slowly up towards her chest, firmly cupping her breast, and he squeezed gently. Brooke moaned against his mouth.

He could tell she was feeling aroused as she gently grabbed his face and brought his lips back to hers, thrusting her tongue into his mouth. Langdon moaned loudly at her possessiveness. She caressed her tongue against his, groaning, and pulled gently at his hair. Feeling turned on, he leaned into her, and moaned when finally, her hand travelled lower, then lower still, down his toned stomach, then lower still to the bulge in his shorts.

'Like this, babe,' he cooed as he undid his shorts. Guiding her hand, his breath grew uneven, and he kissed her with more urgency, their lips moving in a deep, hungry rhythm.

Brooke followed his lead, her touch making him groan softly against her mouth. His hand slid up to her chest, his touch lingering as he pressed closer.

Langdon's breathing quickened, his forehead resting against hers, 'Baby!' he whispered urgently, his voice breaking on the edge of his control.

The intensity between them built until his body shuddered, his arms tightening around her. For the next few moments they stayed wrapped in each other, hearts racing, before he finally relaxed away from her embrace as his breathing steadied.

When he composed himself, Langdon eased off the bed, 'Back in a sec, babe.'

He wasn't embarrassed and headed toward the bathroom. He opened the door and closed it halfway to change his shorts to a pair sitting on top of the laundry basket. Then he came back to lie beside her.

'Now, where were we?' Langdon shifted his body around and guided Brooke to lie half on his chest, his hand gently stroking up and down her back.

'Don't know,' she replied quietly in his ear.

'Hmm, time for me to repay the favour I think,' grinning, he moved his hand around to her front.

Langdon's lips found her neck, and his other hand stroked her gently. As Brooke moaned, he continued to touch her, guided by her sharp breaths and the tight grip she had on his arm.

Langdon knew how to please her. His experience with girls had taught him to ease into it, speak softly, caress them. He enjoyed pleasing her and urged her to relax.

He was great with words of encouragement. 'That's it, baby,' he whispered. 'You know I love your body.'

Brooke always responded to his words, his touch, he felt as though he had full control, and he puffed his chest as she ran her fingers across him.

With a few more words of encouragement and a kiss on her cheek, he drifted his mouth to hers, breathing her in until she pulled away, gasping. 'Langdon!' Brooke gripped his shoulder, and he loved the feel of her fingers digging into his upper traps.

Her hand caressed down his biceps as her head came to rest on his shoulder, while her breathing slowed.

'That's my girl,' Langdon cooed, drawing her closer to him. He embraced her, holding her close.

He looked down at her, wondering when they would progress in their relationship. They'd been dating for almost three months now, and this was as far as she would allow him to go.

Hearing her phone buzz, Brooke quickly checked the message. 'My sister is on her way, she'll be here in five minutes, we better go downstairs.'

'If we must,' Langdon grumbled, slowly rising from the bed to follow her down the stairs.

Langdon flopped himself onto the lounge, 'Come here,' he beckoned, grabbing her hand, and pulling her onto his lap.

Brooke squealed as she lost her balance and fell onto him. Langdon began kissing her neck. 'There's a lot we can do in five minutes,' he whispered into her ear.

'Stop it,' Brooke scolded, 'my sister will be here any minute.'

'How can I when I find you so irresistible?' he cooed, kissing her neck, while his hands roamed.

Brooke exhaled and relented, running her hands through his hair.

Just as she reached down, touching him through his shorts, there was a loud knock on the door. Brooke smiled and climbed off his lap. 'That will be my sister.'

Langdon groaned and followed her to the door. He pulled her by the arm to face him and kissed her before opening the front door.

'See you tomorrow babe, I'll save you a seat on the bus.'

Brooke grinned, 'Bye.'

Langdon watched her walk away, then closed the door and pulled out his phone. He had felt it buzzing in his pocket. Glancing at the screen, he read the text from Tom.

Hey Langdon, we're going camping next weekend, it's going to be awesome.

Who's we? Langdon texted back.

U, me and Beau.

Nooo, not nerdy Beau! Langdon wrote.

Don't be such a bully, he's done nothing to U

He's breathing. Langdon sent the text with a smirk, knowing he was riling Tom up. *I don't want Beau coming! He'll ruin it for all of us!* He waited for Tom to respond.

Stop it!

Fine. Where?

Great spot I know in the Blue Mountains.

The following week at school, Brooke came to him crying, saying that her family was moving to Queensland, and she only had two weeks remaining at this school.

Langdon felt as though his world had imploded. He'd only dated Brooke a short time, even so, it was practically three months, his longest relationship.

To save himself from the hurt he knew was imminent, he began pushing her away with each day that her move became closer. By the end of the following week, she was sick of his attitude and refused to speak to him which was fine by him. He didn't need to pine over her.

'Don't worry,' said Tom, on the bus ride home that Friday afternoon. 'Plenty more girls vying for your attention.'

Langdon grinned, 'Yeah, I know,' he said, cocky as ever.

'Maybe this camping trip will take my mind off it all.'

Tom laughed 'That's the spirit, might change your life.'

Langdon didn't know how much truth was in his words that day.

Chapter 2

The werewolf howled as lightning struck the dead tree trunk. Sound reverberated for miles, causing the forest to freeze in anticipation.as the midnight storm continued to rage, wild and fierce, through the overgrown wilderness. Tree branches swayed this way and that, controlled by the piercing wind.

Nearby, a magnificent old castle stood tall and uninviting against the darkness of the eerie night. Its majestic outline was strikingly visible through the light of the radiant full moon which seemed to shine directly above. It was built from once smooth, even, and square light grey stone, but now, the walls and tower looked pitted and scarred.

A little distance away, Beau, Langdon, and Tom froze as the sounds around them echoed.

'What the hell was that?' whispered Tom.

'Not sure,' answered Langdon, 'but I certainly don't want to find out!'

'It doesn't sound too close,' Beau added, trying to sound brave.

But Langdon could hear the quiver in his voice. 'A bit scared, are we?' he taunted, grinning but trying to hide his own mounting fear.

Tom intervened, 'Come on, let's just keep going, there must be a clearing soon where we could set up camp and at least get off this wet ground.' He glanced down at his soggy joggers and flicked a long, spiky strip of a plant that had attached itself to his ankle socks.

They had started out early enough in the afternoon for a boys' camping trip in the Blue Mountains forest and had enjoyed a short hike to an area they thought was perfect for camping.

Unfortunately, they had not been aware of the ravine they had accidentally wandered into, and when the rain started–heavy and unrelenting–the area had become soaked within minutes. Water cascading down the small hill had infiltrated their campsite, wet their sleeping bags, and extinguished their fire within minutes. They had quickly gathered everything up and stuffed their small sleeping bags into their large waterproof backpacks and began walking under Beau's direction using his phone navigation. They walked and walked, heads down, cold and wet, in places they did not wish to mention. They were all silent - their moods had become as grey as the night sky.

Another roll of thunder hit loud and close, the sound pulsating through the tall trees. A howl was heard moments later, off in the distance. Beau jumped and looked around cautiously, trying to see through the darkness.

The rain had eased to a light drizzle, allowing them to hear the surrounding noises better. Every rustle caused the boys to walk quickly and glance around often. The moonlight, though imposing strikingly above the castle, strangely, only provided a fraction of light in their current location. The boys could see far enough to a dead tree stump five feet away, along with spiky protruding plants, shrubs, and trees of all shapes and sizes meshed together - a haven for the slithering snakes, lizards, and frogs.

They were exhausted, as they had been walking for hours since having to move on from their first attempt at a campsite. They were lost—had been lost since leaving the ravine. Fear had crept further under their skins, but none of the boys dared speak of it. Fatigue was setting in, and their bags now weighed heavily on their backs.

Beau looked at his phone again, squinting his fatigued olive green eyes intently at the unreadable directions. His brow furrowed, and he tried to still his shaking hand so that Langdon would not criticise him. He couldn't understand what was happening. The navigation app had indicated north, then moments later, south, contradicting every direction he tried to follow. Biting his lip, he knew he had to let Tom know he was failing in his role of navigator.

Stopping in his tracks, he spun to face Tom, looking up into his calm blue eyes, then taking a breath and whispered, 'I think we're lost.'

Langdon overheard and took two giant strides before grabbing the phone off Beau as he was handing it to Tom. 'What!' he growled, glaring with his piercing icy-blue eyes and clenching his fist.

Some time ago, their compass had gone crazy, driving them off course, rendering Beau's direction skills useless.

'Beau, you idiot!' he hissed. 'It's your fault we're lost out here!' In frustration, towering over Beau, he lunged forward and shoved him, making Beau stagger and fall to the ground.

'Ugh!' Beau's slight frame landed painfully, but he quickly got to his feet, pushing his wet hair out of his eyes, and cautiously moved away from Langdon. The two had never been friends, and Langdon had taken it upon himself to ridicule and push Beau around since he had met him two years ago.

Beau stared back to see Langdon fuming, nostrils flaring, his fists curled at his sides. It looked like Langed wanted to hit him. Beau stood as tall as he could, but still only came up to Langdon's shoulders. Langdon was only two feet away, he could take a swing and Beau would not even be ready for it.

Tom, also seeing the aggression from Langdon, took a step in front of Beau to prevent him from further hostile actions. Keeping his tone cool and with an air of authority, Tom called out, 'Hey, Langdon!' Looking directly into Langdon's eyes, he said, 'We'll just keep heading in this direction. At least this path is fairly clear. We just need to get out of this rain for a bit, come on.'

Tom began walking in the direction he had suggested. He did not need to look back to know that Langdon was right behind him and that Beau was leaving a considerable gap at the end. Tom rolled his eyes, and with a slight shake of his head, he walked onwards, pushing any wayward branches out of his way.

Rain poured down harder, it was unrelenting. The boys scurried in their search to find cover with any foliage that could provide some relief. Spotting a large tree nearby with many tall ferns overlapping, they scrambled underneath. It provided some relief, although droplets were dancing off the leaves and landing on them like fat kisses on their already damp clothes. Huddled shoulder to shoulder, Beau felt uncomfortable being so close to Langdon. At least he had scrambled in ahead of the idiot to be closer to Tom, who always stood up for him.

Tom looked around at their surroundings. With limited vision, he shone his torch around, spotting the dense foliage and trees surrounding them. He then looked towards his friends. He had planned this camping trip to bring his two closest friends together in the hope they would find a connection. So far, it had not gone well.

On many occasions, he had navigated his way through the vast Blue Mountains National Park and was familiar with some of the area. This time, however, it seemed everything was going wrong. He had even checked the weather forecast, and it was supposed to be 19 degrees and clear. Tom looked out from his covered position and watched the heavy, pelting drops land on the leaves, then drip down onto the ground that had become muddy.

Beau began vigorously rubbing his hands up and down his skinny arms to create warmth. His tan arms had puckered with goose bumps, but no amount of rubbing eased the frigid cold. Rain had soaked through his shoes, and his feet felt as though they were icicles! He pulled his hoodie tighter, but although covered, his head was mostly wet as the rain had soaked through. His normally wavy brown hair was sticking flat and unruly at the sides. He looked menacingly at Langdon, whose burly build made him feel inferior. Beau was so sick and tired of being pushed around. He glanced then at Tom; Tom always made him feel included. He was happy to be asked along on the camping trip, but when he found out Langdon was coming, he had refused to go at first. But Tom had told him *it will be good opportunity for you to get to know him. He's not so bad once you get to know him.* Beau rolled his eyes just thinking about it. He sighed quietly, 'Brrr, it's so cold!'

'I know,' replied Tom, his teeth chattering. He glanced down at his knee-length shorts and wished for loose tracksuit pants. He pulled his hoodie strings tighter, trying to keep some warmth in. His short, light brown hair was saturated underneath. He looked at his two friends, thinking back to when he had first met them. He had been friends with Beau longer, ever since he had moved in next door ten years ago, they had hit it off well over a game of *Grand Theft Auto*.

Beau was small framed and had worn glasses until he was fifteen years old, which made him an easy target for bullies. Now, he wore contacts.

Tom had looked out for Beau ever since another kid had tried to beat him up in year three on the school playground. Tom didn't tolerate violence and despised bullies who picked on smaller kids. This year had been particularly tough on Beau after his parents separated, so Tom tried even harder to include him.

At seventeen, Tom was tall for his age and had filled out to tower over most kids in his year eleven cohort, much like Langdon. This made it easier for him to stand his ground.

Langdon was quite the opposite of Beau. He was a confident, cocky, seventeen-year-old whom Tom had met two years ago at karate. Langdon's dad had made him sign up and commit to the martial arts because he was always getting into fights and needed a place with discipline to control his anger.

Tom had just never been able to get both Langdon and Beau in the same room without Langdon uttering a derogatory remark. The only thing they had in common was being friends with Tom.

Langdon, ignoring his companions, could feel his quad muscles burning in his squatted position. *Oh yeah, all those weighted squat presses at the gym yesterday,* he thought. He glanced down to admire the definition in his legs, a smile lifting the corner of his lips. Turning his torch away from the small area they were crouched in, he shone it out further in all directions and spotted a path a few feet away from them.

'Hey guys, let's head in this direction, I can see a pathway. There must be something up ahead.'

'Righto,' agreed Tom.

They each cautiously crept out of their undercover shrubs and merged onto the pathway. Fortunately, the rain had eased to a light drizzle, allowing better vision with their torches. They had not been walking for long when Tom noticed the shape of a building or house of some kind in the distance.

'Hey, check that out!' he called with mild excitement, the exhaustion and hunger dimming with his relief.

The boys continued walking in the direction of the building, and as they approached it, they noticed it was not just a house, but an old-looking, slightly decrepit castle.

The group quickened their pace and within a few minutes; they had arrived at the entrance of the out of the way castle.

'Oh wow, what a find,' Beau said in awe, his wide eyes showed he was clearly impressed.

As the boys approached the castle, they saw what looked to be a moat surrounding it, with a wide timber drawbridge that was long enough to span the entire width of the moat. Tom and Langdon shone their torches in and saw that it was mostly dry and about three feet deep, so the trio walked across the drawbridge to the front door.

Beau tried the door, and it creaked open. He raised his eyebrows in surprise and turned to look at Tom for his reaction. Tom smiled and gave a slight nod, urging Beau to go inside.

Langdon looked at Tom and grinned, 'Cool! Let's check it out.' Langdon pushed past Beau, shoving the door wide open, and walked inside.

Tom and Beau cautiously followed. Who knew what they were going to find? The foyer was too dark to see anything clearly, so they crept in further to see an open lounge room. Langdon sniffed the air 'Ugh, smells musty,' he scrunched up his nose.

They could not see much except for the outline of furniture due to the moonlight glow. The boys edged in further and began to poke around. Seeing the fancy-looking loungeroom, they were happy to be out of the storm. They sprawled themselves on the floor and pulled snacks out of their bags.

Finally able to remove their wet hoodies, they felt relieved to gain some comfort.

Loud crunching and mild groans filled the silence. Each focussed on eating and passing the junk food until they finished a large bag of M&M's and two packets of chips between them.

Glancing around, Tom announced, 'Let's check this place out.'

The lower part of the castle had a generously sized lounge room with sheets covering the couches. Tom lifted the edge of one to feel what was underneath, and his fingers touched the softness of velvet. The walls and anything on them were not visible due to the lateness of the hour, and they could not find any light switches. They could only see what the soft glow of their torches illuminated, which was just small bits of their surroundings.

Tom and Beau found a dining room, a large kitchen, and a sitting room of some kind with a tall bookshelf and decanters of liquor locked in a huge glass front cabinet. Two bottles of Jack Daniels and a bottle of Port stood alongside five glass decanters. Some were nearly full, and others were halfway filled with what seemed to be alcohol. 'Let's not tell Langdon about that,' whispered Tom as he pointed at all the bottles. Beau nodded and smirked in amusement.

Langdon, not wanting to stay near Beau, had walked over to a winding staircase. He could see a light flickering in one of the rooms above, so he climbed two steps at a time to get to the top, the stairs creaking with each step. Once he arrived, he looked around and shone his torch to see three rooms and a bathroom.

He was drawn to one room in particular, which seemed to have light cascading out of it. As he slowly walked toward it like a moth drawn to a flame, the door slammed shut, making him jump. *Probably just the wind*, he thought. Curious, Langdon walked forward to check it out. The door handle turned, and he pushed the door wide open, cautiously stepping into the room. Looking around, he realised that there were no light switches on; it was the strong glow of the full moon penetrating through the open window. Langdon stared longingly at the bed, he felt so tired.

Suddenly, the room grew chilly. Goosebumps erupted on Langdon's arms, and he felt the strange sensation of being watched. He turned around slowly, expecting to see something. Out of the corner of his eye, he saw a white misty figure, but by the time he turned around, it had faded. With his heart hammering in his chest, Langdon quickly dashed out of the room and raced back downstairs as fast as he could, eager to tell Tom about what had just happened.

'Guys, are you down here?' Langdon called breathlessly. *Shit, man, get it together,* he scolded himself.

'Over here,' Tom called out.

He was talking quietly with Beau by the window. They had been discussing the oddness of finding a fresh loaf of bread on the kitchen table and a small amount of food in the fridge. They were also surprised at the large layout of the building. The lounge area where they first walked in seemed to have a two-seater lounge and two armchairs. Judging by the generous kitchen, foyer and dining room, Tom could tell it must be owned by a wealthy person. They weren't sure what was upstairs. It was as if someone were living there. Well, sort of, because there were coverings on the furniture, and the castle did not exactly smell stale, as if it had been years since someone had been there. Looking around, Tom thought the place looked generally habitable.

Beau agreed, 'Someone has definitely been here recently.'

Langdon walked over in the direction of Tom's voice. 'Shit man! I was just upstairs and saw the creepiest room! I'd say if that had been you upstairs, Beau, you would have wet yourself!'

Beau looked away, sick of Langdon's pathetic put-downs. He would not give him the satisfaction of a reaction.

'That's enough,' Tom sighed, glancing at his watch, the torchlight showing him the lateness of the hour. 'It's after two in the morning.' He was feeling the day catch up with him. 'Look, guys, at least we're indoors and out of that storm and whatever the hell it was that howled before. I say we sleep here on the floor and make our way out in the morning.' His tone, sharp and cranky, was not to be messed with.

'Right-o,' agreed Beau.

'Fine,' said Langdon, although he didn't think he would get much sleep in this creepy castle. Eyeing the sofa, he moved to flop down and stretch out his long legs, only to have them hang over the edge. He placed one arm behind his head and the other on his lean stomach, getting comfortable. Staring through the darkness, he focused his eyes on the large bay window, squinting, trying to see better. He listened intently for any ominous sounds. He still had a prickly, eerie feeling and urged sleep to take over so that he could wake up to the morning.

'Good on you, Langdon!' Tom growled at the way Langdon had made himself at home on the only couch while he and Beau were stuck with the hard floor. The armchair was too squishy.

Langdon grinned arrogantly, at least he'd be comfortable. Beau and Tom lay uncomfortably on the floor, using their backpacks as a pillow and fell into a light, restless sleep, exhausted from their late trek into the forest. Tom had curled his tall athletic body into a foetal position for warmth. Beau, also curled up, had his skinny arms tucked under his armpits.

*

A few hours passed before Langdon was woken by a scratching noise coming from the large bay window. It was still dark, with just a glimpse of moonlight shining through the window. He lay still, wondering what the noise could be. At that moment, a loud howl came from outside. It sounded so near! Instantly, Beau and Tom's eyes sprang open.

'Shit! That scared me,' whispered Beau. He'd been dreaming of striking back at Langdon for once, and the noise startled him wide awake.

'Sounded too close for my liking,' Tom responded, looking around with anxiety rising in the pit of his stomach.

In another part of the castle, they heard glass shattering. Time seemed to stand still as they listened cautiously. Tick, tick, tick, went the old grandfather clock, along with creaks and groans from inside the castle that rattled the three boys.

Just then, a loud growl came from one of the other rooms. The boys slowly rose to their feet and moved away from their sleeping area. Beau's heart was beating fast like a freight train, he looked up at Tom to anchor himself. He was about to ask Tom what he thought they should do when Langdon interrupted his thoughts.

'Tom! Where are you?' Langdon whispered loudly.

'I'm right here,' Tom beckoned Langdon to join him and Beau.

Langdon hurried over from the other side of the lounge room. The three boys stood huddled together in the middle of the foyer. Their eyes darted left and right, and right at this moment no one cared who pressed up against whom.

Another loud noise came from upstairs. Simultaneously, a howl was heard from the next room. The growl was growing closer and louder. The boys looked towards the staircase, then snapped back to the sound of the growl.

Anxiety was growing in each of the boys, and fear grew like a fire between them. They waited, frozen, all senses alert and ready for the fight-or-flight response their bodies would take. Seconds seemed to drag, and yet no time seemed to pass.

'Over there!' screeched Beau. 'Look!'

The other two looked on in disbelief and saw a huge, dark-haired, menacing wolf creeping threateningly across the room. It was so large that it would have come up to Langdon's thigh if he had been standing next to it. The wolf was as black as the night sky outside.

The boys simultaneously stepped backwards towards the front door. Their hearts were beating fast, Beau shook with fear, unknowingly he stepped behind Tom.

The wolf growled and walked closer, its sharp teeth dripping with saliva, and its canine fangs bared behind the pulled-back muzzle. Each enormous paw tapped its claws across the ground with each step, breaking the silence. It sat back on its haunches, ready to attack.

Langdon clutched Tom's shoulder as Tom did the same to him. Beau whimpered, clinging to the back of Tom's shirt. Langdon was the closest, trying to edge the others backward.

The menacing wolf growled again. Suddenly leaping forward, it attacked, latching its sharp teeth into Langdon's arm, and threw him across the room in one swift, violent move. Langdon screamed as his tall, muscly body slammed onto the floor with a sickening thud.

Screams erupted from Tom and Beau, still huddled near the door.

'Ahhh!!' Langdon screamed again from the force of the attack. He quickly curled his body into a protective position, cradling his injured arm and whimpering quietly. Blood seeping out in a steady flow from the vicious attack had begun to soak his shirt. Turning his light blue cotton material to a dark red.

Tom and Beau were frozen with fear. Langdon lay helpless in the corner and looked on in horror as the wolf crept closer to the other two, who had backed away closer to the front door. The boys, unable to think or move, stood clutching each other by the arm.

This is it for me, thought Tom, as he stood facing off with the wolf. Too afraid to move a muscle, all he could do was stare into the wolf's brown eyes which were narrowed into terrifying slits. It snarled, sharp teeth bared ferociously, gums exposed. Langdon's blood was dripping from its mouth onto the slate flooring.

Just then, the sun, which had begun to rise in the midst of the scuffle, now shone its first rays through the many windows on the lower level where they all were. The early morning light shone over the wolf just as it leapt at Tom and Beau, and instantly it fell with an almighty thud to the floor.

It lay motionless for a moment before it began making pained howls; the sounds punctured by what seemed like the cracking of bones, as its form shrunk smaller. The wolf's howl was cut off into a gurgled cry as a fully formed man emerged from the mess of limbs.

The three boys stared in horror and amazement at what had transpired before them.

Langdon, still holding his arm, sat up and looked from the man to his friends.

Beau and Tom glanced from the man to Langdon to each other.

'What the fuck just happened?' whispered Langdon, holding his arm protectively, the pain momentarily forgotten.

The man, on his knees and naked, quickly rose and grabbed a sheet from one of the nearest armchairs to cover himself. 'Oh, my God! I am so sorry, did I hurt anyone?' his voice was a low, gravelly sound as he frantically looked around.

The boys shook their heads dazedly, unable to speak, They stared incredulously, looking the man over. He was attractive and appeared in the prime of his adulthood with cropped dark brown hair, brown eyes, and a toned, muscled body. Dirt covered his face and arms, and he looked around in anguish as he took in the boys before him. He seemed like he had never seen people near his castle before and stood, stunned, almost as surprised as the boys.

Langdon, feeling brave, grabbed the two backpacks nearest him. He slowly rose and staggered over to Tom. 'Let's get the fuck out of here,' he said in a strangled whisper.

The three boys backed towards the front door, and just after Tom turned the handle, the man called out to them.

'Wait! I bit one of you. I have something important to tell you! The curse! I have to tell you…'

But the boys had already run out the door.

Once they were outside, under the solace of the morning sun, the boys all made a run for it. They ran until they were at the top of the clearing where they had first noticed the pathway to the castle Breathing heavily, they all started talking at once:

'Geez!'

'Fuck!…'

'Shit, Langdon, your arm!'

Langdon winced, 'Shit!' He had forgotten about his injury in the terror of what he'd seen. But now, he sucked in a breath as he looked down at all the blood. The wolf had torn the skin on his right forearm. There was a piece of skin hanging off, and, seeing the flesh and blood covering his arm, he suddenly felt lightheaded. The pain all of a sudden screamed up his arm and through his body. He flopped down onto the grass, head back and eyes closed, his face wincing in anguish.

Tom was quick to open his backpack, and he pulled an old, faded shirt out. He tore a long strip in a frantic rush and grabbed Langdon's arm, wrapping the material around it with a tight grip.

Feeling thankful, Langdon gave a slight grin at his friend. He had blocked out the pain with all the adrenalin racing from the castle, but now pain spread throughout his whole body The tight bandage seemed to help, and he took this moment to gather his thoughts. Breathing deeply, he did his best to appear calm.

Beau shrieked, 'Oh my God! Did that wolf really turn into a man?!' The gravity of the situation hit him like a ton of bricks. He felt his stomach rise into his mouth and doubled over and vomited. He sank to his knees, one hand pressed against the earth for support.

'Eww! Beau! Keep it together,' cried Langdon, scowling at the weak nerd.

'Shit, Beau!' Tom rushed over to see if his friend was okay. 'You all right?'

'Yeah,' he mumbled weakly, slowly rising, and wiping his face on his shirt. Still a bit dazed, he tried focusing on the nearby assortment of ferns that had mushrooms and fungi thriving next to a decaying tree. *Breathe*, he told himself, *in to the count of four, out to the count of four. Nice and slow. Breathe long and deep.* This breathing technique he had learnt from the school counsellor often helped him ground himself. He felt a hand gently tapping his back in concern and looked over his shoulder at Tom.

Tom sent him a quick half-smile before turning to look at Langdon. 'Fuck! That was unbelievable!' he exclaimed. He glanced at Langdon's forearm and the makeshift bandage he had fumbled to make.

'I know, right,' Langdon agreed. Thoughtful, his brows furrowed. 'What do you think he wanted to tell us?' He looked up at Tom and Beau from his seated position, his blue eyes full of worry and concern.

'Don't know,' said Tom. 'But no way am I going back there.'

Langdon stood carefully and wiped the sweat from his brow.

Beau, clutching his backpack, looked to see that Tom was holding onto his backpack, but Langdon was missing his. 'Hey Langdon, where's your backpack?'

Langdon felt around his back with his good arm, expecting to feel a small weight. 'Oh shit,' he cursed, 'I must have left it behind! I could only grab the ones nearest me, and I wasn't sure which ones I got.' His face crumpled at the realisation and he smacked his forehead with the palm of his hand in frustration. 'Well, I'm definitely not going back to get it!' he declared, looking solemnly back at Tom and Beau.

Once they'd had a moment to collect themselves, Langdon said, 'Let's get out of here.' He glanced down the hill toward the castle and wanted to get as far away as he could.

Nods of agreement followed.

The three boys walked silently back in the direction where they had left their bikes at the start of the journey. As they walked, Tom placed his hand tentatively on Langdon's shoulder. 'Are you okay, mate? Do you think you'll be able to ride back?'

'Yeah, I'll be okay,' answered Langdon, trying to sound as if he was handling everything fine.

'Hey!' exclaimed Beau. 'The compass works fine now!'

Tom shook his head at the irony. 'Yeah, that'd be right.'

After a two-hour hike, the boys reached the clearing to find their bikes where they had left them. They stood and faced each other with grim expressions.

Langdon, giving a half-smile, said, 'Let's not tell anyone about this, hey?' His furrowed brow spoke volumes about his plea.

'Yeah, sure, man, no worries.' Tom said reassuringly, giving him a light thump on his good arm.

'Yeah, no worries,' agreed Beau.

They turned to their bikes, giving each other a quick grin, and rode off.

Langdon, still wincing in pain, could not extend his arm to put both hands on the handlebars. He managed to ride one-handed, his other arm tucked protectively at his side. All he wanted right now was to be at home and forget all about this camping trip from hell.

*****

Eric was at the castle, sitting fully dressed in his t-shirt and cargo shorts in his loungeroom. He'd showered and cleaned the mess off himself, relishing the cleanliness and relief he felt now that he was back in human form.

He sat with his hands over his face, his elbows resting on his knees, and felt miserable. He shook his head; *how could this happen? I bit a kid! I can't believe this is happening,* he thought to himself. He was mortified. It made him feel sick to his stomach.

Looking up, he noticed a dark backpack sitting near the fireplace. He slowly rose and walked over for a closer look. Picking it up, he could feel the weight of its contents, and he brought it back to the couch to take a look inside. He sighed heavily at the realisation of what he had to do. Somehow, he had to contact the boy that he bit. *What were those boys doing in my castle, anyway?* He thought crankily, *this is private property*!

'Well, at least one of them left his backpack, maybe this will lead me to one of the boys.' He searched through the bag and found a boy's wallet with a student ID and provisional driver's licence. *Yes, that's the face I remember.* This was the boy he had bitten. The licence showed that the boy was a seventeen-year-old kid—who was in the wrong place at the wrong time. *The poor kid will experience his first transition next month*, Eric thought regrettably.

'Langdon Core,' he read off the Licence. 'Lives in Wentworth Falls.' *That's a fair hike from here*! he thought.

Eric got up from his comfortable position on the recliner and strolled over to his office. At his desk, he pulled out a piece of paper from the second drawer. Taking a pen from the holder, he began to write.

When he finished his letter, Eric folded it neatly and addressed the envelope to Langdon. He would purchase a postal sachet and post the letter with the wallet when he headed back to Sydney.

Chapter 3

A week later, Langdon collected the mail as he walked into his driveway after getting the bus home from school with his sister Hayley.

Glancing at his arm as he lifted the lever, he was pleased with how fast it had healed. By the time he had ridden home that fateful morning, the bleeding had stopped. By the afternoon, his skin had pulled together and sealed. By the following day, a scar had formed, and he didn't need the bandage. Now, the scar had faded.

The only problem was that his licence was IN the backpack he'd left at the darn castle! The wallet he could easily replace—but he licence? Not so easy. He'd needed to make excuses for not wanting to drive his parents' car on the weekend, claiming he preferred to use his bike.

He pulled out some letters and noticed a parcel stuck further in; he reached in and dragged it out. It was addressed to him. *Hmm, who could this be from?* he wondered as he walked inside the house.

He dropped his parents' mail on the kitchen bench and continued to his room. Leaping up the stairs, two at a time, he was eager to get to the privacy of his bedroom to open the package. Peeling it open, he was surprised and elated to see his wallet; flipping it open, he was even more pleased to see that everything was still in there. There was also a letter.

Langdon's fingers trembled as he opened the paper, spreading the creases out. He knew who it was from. *He knows where I live!* As Langdon began to read, his heart pounded.

Langdon,

This note is for you, the one I bit that night you were in my castle. Here is your wallet.

I'm so sorry for biting you, and it must have been a terrible shock seeing what happened to me.

I need to speak with you about this and what it could mean for you. It is the full moon that triggers the curse. If it happens to you, you need to contact me, and I need you to know you are welcome here at this castle when the full moon is upon us.

You cannot stop the change, nor will it just go away. I will leave you my phone number, and you can contact me anytime. I know you will have many questions.

Yours faithfully,

Eric

Phone: 0400 711 711

Langdon inhaled a shaky breath as he put the letter down.

What the fuck is he on about? he thought angrily. *What curse? A full moon? This guy must be crazy.* Langdon scrunched the letter up and tossed it in his bin. *I don't need him.*

He didn't tell anyone about the letter; he wanted to forget all about it. So, he tried his best to get his mind on other things.

Langdon spent his time focused on practising his pattern for his blue belt in karate. It was difficult, and just the distraction he needed. The eight patterns he needed to learn were a series of kicks and punches, and there were certain fitness components he needed to meet. The class needed to be fit to do push-ups on the toes, run two kilometres, and other strength exercises.

He and Tom had been practising together an extra afternoon a week and also hitting the gym to build his pectoral muscles.

His body thrived on pushing himself harder every day. All the exercises that Langdon pushed himself to do triggered hypertrophy. He was once tall and lanky, with skinny arms that he hated and had worked hard over the past few years to build muscle. Even though he had filled out, only minor muscular definition had formed; however, recently, the definition had become more defined.

The obsession with exercise kept his mind off the letter, and he revelled in the exhaustion that put him to sleep as soon as he hit the bed each night. But little did he know that there was no escaping fate and soon he would have to face the inevitable life-altering outcome.

Chapter 4

Eric

Three weeks later.

Eric had told his girlfriend of eight months that he had a meeting in Melbourne. He was a computer programmer and could do most of his work from home, but at times, he had to go away for conferences. He'd met Summer at one such conference a year ago, after which they had crossed paths at other events a few times.

He had tried to fight the attraction, believing he couldn't be in a relationship. The curse, as he saw it, affected so many aspects of his life. Changes to his body, his stamina and emotions had taken time to adjust to. Still, near a full moon, his emotions would get out of control if he wasn't careful. Eventually, he gave in, unable to function properly without seeing Summer every day, and he asked her out when she was there catering an event he was at.

35

The full moon was less than 24 hours away. He had timed it right with his story. The perfect excuse to get away for the change that was imminent.

Every month that he had been dating Summer, he had come up with a reason to be out of town or working late and unable to see her any said night of a full moon.

Two months ago, they had decided to move in together and agreed on a small but stylish apartment in Sydney in the central business district area. It had been an ideal location, close to public transport, coffee shops and restaurants that they frequently visited. The area had a bustling energy that suited Eric and Summer.

Since moving in together, their relationship had intensified on all levels. Eric loved that he could talk to Summer about everything. Almost. He could never tell her about his curse that possessed him every full moon. He had to continue with the excuses of having conferences to attend, or a family matter down south.

Sometimes, he would simply feign working late so that he could arrive home in the early hours of the morning. She had never suspected anything, trusting his every word, and he hated that he was lying to her. It was for her own good because he feared if he ever told her the truth, she would think he was crazy. And if she ever saw the monster he became every month, she would run screaming and never look back.

Eric was all packed for his "conference". An overnight bag was waiting by the door. He ran a hand through his cropped dark-brown hair as he strode to his girlfriend sitting on the couch, looking at her phone.

Hearing him approach, she lowered the phone to look up at him, her light brown eyes shimmering with delight, seeing his athletic body stride toward her. He lowered himself to her, sitting close to put an arm around her shoulder.

'Bye, babe,' Eric kissed her tenderly on the lips. Summer hung onto Eric and stared into his sweetly intense brown eyes. 'I'm going to miss you,' she whispered, holding on a bit longer.

Eric liked her hands on him, feeling his hard biceps with her small hands. He wanted to feel the lines of her body and caress parts of her before he had to leave. Kissing her, his thoughts went to their lovemaking that morning, and again when he arrived home from work. Eric seemed to have a hunger that pushed her to climax more than once.

'Oh, babe,' he smiled, one dimple prominently displaying itself. 'I'll see you in a couple of days.' Kissing Summer more passionately, he ran his fingers through her long brown hair. He loved the feel of the silky waves that cascaded over her shoulder. He smiled again and untangled himself from her caress.

He had to leave now—or there would be consequences.

Eric waved as he walked out of their Sydney apartment and down to his car. He had a two-hour drive ahead of him west on the M4 highway to the Blue Mountains. Eric loved the Blue Mountains, especially the ruggedness of the region. He had often gone there on camping trips as a kid growing up in Sydney, and he knew the area well.

Twelve months ago, Eric had inherited this castle. It had been in the family for generations, but he did not know about it until inheriting it from his uncle. No one in the family spoke of it. On his first visit to his new ownership, he had gone out to inspect the so-called 'castle' and see if it was worth anything. He had thought perhaps he could sell it.

The castle, situated in the lower Blue Mountains of Faulconbridge, was in a state of disrepair. Parts of the archways had deteriorated, and it had appeared as if it were in the dark ages. However, Eric loved a challenge and had spent many weekends using his renovation skills to fix up what he could.

Over the months, he had made positive changes to the interiors and fixed some of the structural stone walls outside. His uncle had already renovated the kitchen and bathroom, and the slate floor was still in good condition.

As he was driving, Eric thought back to his first visit to the area. The visit changed his life forever. Eric shivered at the memory.

The weekend had started without a hitch. He had just broken up with his girlfriend at the time, Belinda. She had been a full-on drama queen who thankfully agreed with his decision to call it quits on the relationship. So, he thought it was a perfect opportunity to get out of town to check out his inheritance. He had arrived in the late afternoon on a Friday and stood in awe, taking in the majestic, but ancient castle that appeared before him.

The first night was creepy, to say the least. Sheets covered the furniture, and dust, and cobwebs were scattered around in the corners and under tables.

During the night, tree branches scratched on the windowpane and an owl hooted, making him jump. He had gone to bed in the main bedroom and felt uncomfortable the whole night. The shutters knocked with the wind, and the moon shone brightly, illuminating much of his room. A few times, he thought he heard footsteps.

The next day, he had taken advantage of the daylight and explored the surrounding area. He had gone further than anticipated, so the trek back took longer. Twilight was upon him, so he quickened his pace. Night would fall quickly and the moon, round and full, was shining brilliantly, illuminating the area. He remembered being a couple of hundred feet from the front door of the castle when he first heard the howl close by, making him freeze on the spot.

Out of nowhere, a beast had leapt out of the bushes and pushed him to the ground. The wolf had bitten his torso before racing off into the forest. Eric, stunned and bleeding, crawled to his feet and staggered back to the castle. He pulled off his shirt once inside and inspected the damage. A small tear from his midsection to his hip seeped with blood. He grabbed his flannel shirt and held it against his tender, bleeding skin. Breathing heavily, he stood slowly and made his way to the kitchen. By then, spots had been blurring his vision. His heartbeat was pounding in his chest. He managed to run some water and wet another shirt to place on his wound.

He remembered… *sweating profusely, lying on the couch. He'd fallen asleep, in and out of consciousness, until the morning when he had driven home in agony and went to the hospital for stitches for his wound. He was amazed at how quickly it had healed. The following day, the stitches had dissolved, and the wound was barely a scar!*

Coming back from his reverie, Eric refocused his attention back on the road. He was now on the outskirts of Sydney, well on his way to his destination. He drummed his fingers lightly on the steering wheel in time with the music on the radio.

His thoughts went to Langdon and how he was certain the boy would go through his first transition the next night. Worry and concern filled his mind, recalling what it had been like for him during his first transition.

Since the fateful attack twelve months earlier, he had been coming back to his castle, knowing what the full moon would bring. Unfortunately, this was not the case for his first transition…

He had felt extremely hot, sweating profusely, and screaming in agony as his body betrayed him and turned him into a werewolf. He had been alone in his apartment when the change happened. Luckily, at the time, he was not in a relationship, so he didn't have to explain the wreckage that resulted from his thrashing about, out of control of his own thoughts or actions. The lamp had smashed onto the tiles, the dining table had been destroyed, and it looked as though his apartment had been ransacked.

He had awoken the following morning, lying naked on the kitchen floor, with the cuts up and down his arms and torso healed before his eyes..

The transformation had been very traumatic for him, and he sat, shaking, shocked by the whole experience. Once he recovered his equilibrium, he slowly dressed. Trying to make sense of what had occurred, he went to the old, fraying box holding the diaries and paperwork of his late uncle, hoping there might be something in one of his uncle's diaries that could explain what had transpired.

Eric had then found a diary of his uncle (whom everyone thought had gone crazy) amongst the paperwork of his inheritance. Everyone in his family had thought the uncle had made up some rambling story and put it down to schizophrenia. No one had visited him, as he had become a bit of a recluse. While reading his uncle's ramblings of 'changing', he understood what was happening to him. His uncle had written that no one had believed him when he told them about the attack he was a victim of all those years ago. Now, Eric understood why his uncle had led such a solitary life towards the end.

Driving onto the property, he slowed and parked his HiLux Ute. He gathered his overnight bag, walked across the old drawbridge, unlocked the front door, and walked inside. After opening some windows to let fresh air in, he threw the cover off the couch. A routine he was used to after all this time.

Eric then settled himself in for the evening, getting comfortable on the couch after pouring himself a glass of wine. He would relax and enjoy the peacefulness of the night, as the following night would be a different story.

It would be the full moon, and he would succumb to the curse he had endured for the past 12 months every full moon. *And now,* he thought to himself, *that poor kid is going to have his first transition and not know what the hell is going on.* He sighed at the ominous events he knew were about to occur.

Chapter 5

Langdon

The last few weeks went by in a blur for Langdon. His arm had healed quickly, and luckily, he had been able to hide it from his parents. His friends had said nothing about their failed camping trip, and he just wanted to forget about it. He had not even told his parents about the lost backpack. It was only an old spare anyway, no one would even notice. At least he now had his wallet and licence back.

However, Langdon could not get the letter out of his mind. He had so many questions, and none of them made any sense. After much deliberation, he decided to confide in Tom that he had received a package from the man at the castle. Tom was level-headed and easy to talk to, and Langdon knew he could confide in him.

Ugh, finally, it's Friday! thought Langdon as he climbed out of bed that morning. It had been an intense week completing three of his assignments. He was feeling on edge, and his temper seemed to explode in an instant.

He thought back to the camping trip, which was one month ago now. *The next full moon is nearly here. I guess we'll find out if I got that curse!* He opened his drawer and roughly pulled out a t-shirt and another drawer for his shorts. He slammed the drawers shut aggressively.

He dressed quickly for school and stood looking in the mirror, admiring how ruggedly handsome he looked. His piercing blue eyes looked back at him from his reflection, and seeing his hair looking messy, he roughly added some gel to his unruly blond hair. He flexed his biceps, admiring their definition, smiling back at himself. He had been able to lift heavier weights recently, and the workouts had helped with his bad moods.

'Are you finished with the bathroom yet?' yelled his thirteen-year-old sister, Hayley. She had been holding on for five minutes while her annoying brother had been preening himself. Flicking her long blonde hair over her shoulder, she pounded her fist on the door for the third time. 'Now, Langdon!' She stood hopping from foot to foot.

Langdon opened the door, 'Here you go, princess! All yours,' he grinned, towering over her. He gave her a light punch on the arm on his way past.

'Ow!' she whined, rubbing her arm. 'That hurt!'

'What?' Langdon asked mockingly. 'I didn't feel anything.' He grinned and swaggered away from her.

Hayley scowled at her brother and walked into the bathroom.

Langdon raced down the stairs, jumping past the last five steps in one giant leap. Walking into the kitchen, he saw his mother making coffee. He saw she was dressed for work, wearing long black pants and a blue blouse with a small white flower print. Her hair was the same colour as her children's, dark blonde, and was neatly plaited down her back.

'Morning, Mum,' he greeted

'Oh, good morning, love.' His mother always greeted him with such terms of endearment. He didn't mind… except when his mates were over.

Grabbing a bowl of cereal, he ate quickly and was off to catch the bus to school.

'Hurry up! Hayls,' he called out. 'I'm heading out the door.' He smirked, enjoying annoying his sister by pretending to leave without her.

'I'm coming!' Hayley yelled angrily, running down the stairs and grabbing her bag, stopping to say goodbye to their mum.

'See you later, sweetheart, have a good day,' their mum said to Hayley as she skipped towards the open door.

'See ya, Mum!' Langdon called as they both headed out the door.

'Bye, love,' his mother called back.

His school bus stop was a five-minute walk from where he lived, passing the park that was up the road. Further up the street, there was a primary state school at the top of the hill. The bus stop was right beside it. There was always a fight to get a seat. Kids from other schools also got on at this stop, making every ride crowded and noisy.

The bus arrived, and he was quick to push past the smaller kids to the back of the bus where his best mate, Tom, was sitting with

Beau. They had secured the seats that were in the third row from the back.

Beau—what did Tom see in him? Langdon thought Beau was an annoying little nerd, although after their camping trip last month, he was tolerating him better. He still did not understand what Beau was talking about most of the time, and he always felt like Beau was showing off how smart he was. *Little know-it-all*, he thought.

'Hey, bro!' Langdon greeted Tom. 'Hey nerd,' he nodded at Beau as he slipped into the seat across from Tom.

'Hey Langdon, how's things?' Tom asked, shifting his body to face him with his eyebrows raised.

'Yeah, good,' Langdon replied, feeling fired up with unexplained energy. Receiving that letter and his licence weighed heavily on his mind. He wanted to talk to Tom about it. He glanced at Beau and saw that he was engrossed in his phone and his AirPods were in.

'Hey, Tom…' Langdon started, but wasn't sure how to progress the conversation.

'Yeah?' Tom asked.

'You'll never guess what that freak at the castle did,' he paused for dramatic effect, looking at his friend.

Tom stared back, waiting.

'He mailed my wallet to my address, and everything was still in it. My cash, my licence and my student ID.' He hesitated, 'And a letter,' he added, looking for Tom's reaction.

'Well, that was nice of him. Wait, what? A letter? What did it say?'

'That he was sorry for biting me and something about the full moon and a curse, and he even put in his phone number!'

'Shit, that must be what he wanted to tell us back at the castle when we ran out.'

'Yeah, I guess.'

'So, are you going to call him?'

'What for?' Langdon frowned.

'I don't know, thank him for returning your stuff?'

'Fuck off. I'm not calling him!'

'Well, do you reckon anything will happen with the next full moon?' asked Tom.

'Nope, and honestly, I just want to forget it all ever happened.' Langdon was adamant that he was going to be fine.

'Okay, fine.' Tom knew Langdon well enough to know that once he'd made up his mind, there was no changing it and that it only made Langdon angrier if he was pushed.

'Don't tell anyone about the letter,' Langdon said emphatically.

'What about Beau?'

'No,' Langdon growled.

'Come on, he was out there with us. He's part of this now,' Tom persisted.

'Oh, fine, you can tell him,' Reluctantly, Langdon gave in.

'Good.' Tom nodded, noticing Langdon's frown and rude behaviour. His friend had spread himself out, taking up the space of two seats. Langdon was flexing his long muscular legs into the aisle, ignoring the younger kids standing.

Tom turned back to Beau to tell him about the letter as the bus moved along slowly, making further stops along the way with more rowdy kids getting on.

The noise was getting to Langdon. There were no more seats available, so now even more kids were standing. He and his sister were lucky to get on when they did.

Langdon searched his backpack for his AirPods, which were nowhere to be found. He tugged on the strings attached to his bag in anger, and a kid standing next to him gave him a quick glance which made Langdon grunt. The footy-boys at the back of the bus played loud rap music with their speakers which always vibrated through the seats, and no one could ever hear the bus radio. A couple of other kids were blasting music on their phones. It was when a younger boy fell against Langdon's leg when the bus turned sharply around a corner that he snapped, 'Hey! Watch it!'

The boy immediately apologised. Seeing the look on Langdon's face, he quickly shifted his footing so he wouldn't lean his way when the bus went around another corner.

Langdon made it through the day but couldn't help feeling more on edge as the day went on, and he wasn't sure why. Math class had been almost unbearable. He couldn't focus on the board or the teacher. Miss Roberts was going over the previous night's homework, but Langdon hadn't done it and tried his best to avoid her eye. He couldn't sit still, his left leg bounced rapidly, and he felt agitated. He started tapping his pen on his notebook - a nervous twitch he couldn't control.

Tom was sitting at the desk next to him and kept shooting him glances. At his friend's obvious agitation, he mouthed, 'What's up with you?'

Langdon just shook his head. He would not be able to explain what it was he was feeling. Hell, even he didn't understand himself.

Langdon looked at the clock again - 2:55 p.m.-five minutes until the bell went. Tick, tick, tick, he watched the minute hand go around.

Every second seemed to drag. A full minute felt like torture.

DING! The bell rang just as he felt like he was about to lose control. *Finally!* He raced to his bag, shoving his tall, athletic frame past the other students. He didn't care. He just wanted to get out of the school grounds. Striding purposefully to the front of the school to wait for Tom, he folded his arms and couldn't stand still. Then, as soon as Tom joined him, they both went to meet Beau for the bus ride home.

Immediately after he arrived home from school, Langdon dropped his bag on the floor before going into the kitchen for some food. Gosh, he sure was hungry. Going straight to the pantry, he grabbed a medium tin of baked beans, tore the tin lid off, and shook the contents onto the pieces of bread in front of him. Slapping the top slices on, he quickly moved it onto the hot sandwich press.

A minute later, he had two hot toasted sandwiches in front of him. *Yum!* he thought as he hungrily ate every last bit. Licking his fingers, he went back for a packet of chips and a Coke.

'It's the thirteenth of October. Ooh, it's a full moon tonight!' chirped Hayley excitedly. She was sitting at the breakfast bar reading a magazine. 'With Mercury in retrograde, that makes everyone's emotions heightened and you need to ground yourself to stop the effects of the planets ....'

'What are you going on about, Hayls?' Langdon interrupted as he ruffled her hair on his way past.

'Ugh,' she grumbled, fixing up the bun she had tediously coiled on top of her head. She glared at him for a moment before responding, 'I'm reading Mum's women's magazine. The section by Yasmin Boland about star signs and what the planets are doing and how they affect us,' she answered, trying to sound like an expert.

'Oh, better watch out then, all the crazies come out on a full moon, and they'll be all emotional,' laughed Langdon, changing his voice from mysterious to sad in an exaggerated way, dodging a swat from his sister. He continued laughing, walking up to his bedroom. Once inside, he plopped down on his bed to listen to some music.

As the evening went on, Langdon felt more and more unbalanced and moody. Throughout dinner, he was quiet and scarfed the takeaway pizza his parents had bought.

Finishing before everyone else, he raced back up to his bedroom. Langdon saw that it was just after six, and he decided to go out for a run. Feeling fired up, he threw on his gym shorts and singlet, laced up his joggers, and ran out the door, calling, 'Going out for a run!'

'Okay,' he heard his father call back.

Langdon ran across the road and onto the pathway behind the park opposite where he lived. He had a good pace going and ran for an hour before heading back to the park.

He was sweating more than usual; the droplets running down his face. It was a cool night, with barely a cloud in the sky. The bright full moon was beaming down on him, even though the sun was still setting.

Langdon sat on the park swing, wondering why he was feeling so fired up. His body felt hot like it was a furnace, and it was only getting hotter, with his heart pounding rapidly in his chest, his breathing turned rapid.

Before he knew what was happening, he was on all fours, dry heaving. He sat back on his haunches, hands on his lap, panting, trying to get more air into his lungs. Anxiety swept over Langdon as his back arched. He felt so hot, yet cold at the same time. Beads of sweat had dripped down his face, and it felt as though his skin wanted to stretch further over his body. All his muscles were on fire. Excruciating pain was ripping through his body like nothing he had ever felt before. He screamed in agony as his body began to change. First, his hands changed to giant paws, limbs lengthened and reshaped themselves, and fur sprouted all over his body. His whole body shook until the transition was complete.

Langdon, now a wolf, looked at the world with fresh eyes. *Food, water, run* ... these thoughts were running on a loop in his mind. The wolf raced towards the creek behind the park and drank swiftly before crossing to the paddock beyond it. He loped ahead, darting around trees, and brimming with energy. Under the light of the full moon, the wolf felt free, no longer burdened by human worries. With no more thoughts plaguing him, he gave in to his animal instincts.

***

The next morning, Langdon woke up feeling cold and uncomfortable. He was curled into a ball, his knees hugged tightly to his chest, and something seemed to dig into his skin. He stretched out as he peeled his eyes half-open, and he was shocked to find daylight was upon him.

Looking around, he realised he was lying next to the swing in the park — naked. The scratchiness he felt was the sand underneath the swings, and it was early, very early.

Langdon could hear something, it was what had woken him from his peaceful sleep. The thumping sound came closer. It was a man running on the pathway. He hadn't noticed Langdon and was too focused on his dog, who had caught the scent of the boy's supine form. 'Come on Banjo, keep going,' the man cooed, and soon they had moved further along the pathway and away from Langdon.

Langdon slowly began to rise. Sitting up and blinking lazily, he touched his fingers to his lips. There was something wet on them, and when he moved his tongue around, there was a foul taste. He put his finger in to see what it was and cringed when he saw that there was blood and pieces of short brown hair. 'Ew, gross!' Langdon groaned as he spat at the ground.

He looked down at himself, suddenly achingly aware of his bare form. 'Oh, my God!'. After a frenzied glance around, he spotted his clothes, ripped to shreds, lying a few meters away. Dashing through the sand, he grabbed what he could and held it against himself. *What the hell had happened?* Wasting no more time, he gathered up what he could and raced home.

Langdon snuck around the back and crept in through the laundry room. *Good, no one is up yet,* he thought, glancing at his watch that he had found beside his clothes with the snapped band.

He grabbed a pair of jeans from the dirty basket — wrinkled, but wearable and took a quick sniff, *yup, they'll do*. He put them on swiftly in case he saw anyone on his way to his bedroom. Firstly though, he needed to get rid of his ripped, bloodied clothes and ducked back outside to place them in the wheelie bin.

Walking back inside quietly, he crept to the staircase and up to his room. Grabbing a fresh shirt and jocks, he moved to the bathroom. A shower washed away the grime and the blood around his mouth, and the water felt so good on his warm skin. He gave his hair a quick wash it so desperately needed, and then he stepped out and quickly dried and dressed. Now that he was clean and clothed, the exhaustion hit Langdon like a ton of bricks, making him stagger back to his room. Flopping onto his bed, he was dead to the world in seconds.

He was woken by the clamour in the bathroom he shared with his sister. Hayley was in the shower, singing at the top of her lungs. Langdon rubbed his hand over his eyes, trying to focus on his side table to check the time - 7:20 a.m. He sighed. Placing one arm behind his head, he lay stretched out on his bed and stared at the ceiling.

His thoughts took him back to the previous night. He remembered going for a run, and feeling sick - *was that a dream then? No,* because he had woken without any clothes in the park, and there was blood under his fingernails and smears of it over his mouth and torso. With a shocking revelation, he thought back to the man at the castle and the words he had spoken.

Langdon froze at the memory of the man yelling, "I have something important to tell you", as they were running out of the castle. The man had even said something about the full moon and a curse in that letter. And Langdon had witnessed the stranger change from a wolf to a man. *What if that happened to me?* He had to find out. With quiet resolve, he decided to find the letter.

Rising slowly from the bed, he walked over to his rubbish bin, sighing about the disgusting, yet important task. Luckily, he only emptied it when it was practically overflowing, so he scrounged around until his fingers found the scrunched-up paper. It was near the bottom and had a stain he could only think resembled Coke from a can he had tossed in there. He smoothed the letter open and then re-read what Eric had written. *Damn it!* Now he needed to contact the man and ask him some questions. After the night's freaky experience, Langdon knew he would have to find out more. *Hopefully, that man will give me some answers,* he thought with mild apprehension.

Taking a deep breath, he picked up his phone and dialled the number. Then, listening intently as the phone rang, his leg bounced up and down nervously.

'Hello?' a man's voice answered, sounding rough and tired.

'Uh, hi, this is Langdon.'

'Langdon!' Eric sounded surprised. 'How are you?'

'Yeah, I'm all right.' Langdon suddenly wondered why he bothered calling Eric, second-guessing himself.

'Are you okay? What happened? Did anything happen with the full moon?' Eric seemed like he was stumbling over his words.

'Yeah, I think so. I don't know. It was weird.' Langdon bit his lip, still feeling unsure.

'I'm still at the castle, so do you want to come out here to talk?' Eric asked calmly.

'Yeah,' Langdon replied. For some reason, Eric's voice calmed him. He didn't understand why he was agreeing to go back to the castle - the place he said he would never return to again.

'Okay, are you right to get out here?' Eric asked gently.

'Yeah, I'll ride my bike.'

'Ride? What?' He paused, 'How about I meet you at the park entrance and drive you?' offered Eric.

'Nah, that's okay, I think I need the hike to clear my head. Do you mind if I bring a mate with me?'

'Not at all. All right then, I'll see you when you get here.'

Langdon hung up and stared at his phone. *I'm really doing this.* Thoughts of heading out to that ominous castle again caused butterflies to swarm in his stomach. First, he needed to bring Tom up to speed.

Grabbing his phone from his side table and bringing up his friend's number, his fingers flew over the letters, feeling adrenaline course through his body. *I think it happened.*

What? Tom texted back.

Langdon quickly replied, *You know, the curse.*

shit, Tom replied.

Yeah, "shit" sounds about right, thought Langdon.
I've rung Eric, going out to see him. Wanna come? Langdon waited, hoping Tom would go out there with him.

Sure...
I'll tell Beau, the two texts came through almost simultaneously.
K. Langdon thought for a moment before typing again. *I'll be at yours around 9.*

K Tom texted back agreeing to the plan, and Langdon fell back into his bed, wondering exactly what he had gotten himself into. Stretching his body, he closed his eyes, exhaustion taking over.

Chapter 6

A noise startled Langdon awake. He groaned, rubbing his eyes and glanced at his phone, *Shit, it's nearly 8, better get up.*

When he stepped out of his room and was about to head down the stairs, he could hear his parents talking in the kitchen.

'Did you hear Langdon come home last night, Mitchell?' Langdon's mum asked his father.

'No, he must have gone for a run to Tom's house, he sometimes ends up there when he goes for a run. It wouldn't be the first time, Lee.' Although her actual name was Leah, Mitchell always called Langdon's mum Lee instead.

Hearing this, Langdon raced back to his room and grabbed his phone to text Tom.

If my parents ask—tell them I was at yours last night.

A quick response came in the form of a thumbs-up emoji.

Smiling and tucking his phone in his pocket, his stomach growled, alerting him to his hunger. Running down the stairs and he saw both parents in the kitchen and greeted both of them tiredly. 'Morning Mum. Morning, Dad.' Langdon yawned again and rubbed at the sleep in his eye.

'Oh, good morning love, what time did you get in after your run last night?' his mum asked, concern showing in her voice. 'I didn't hear you come home.' She walked past, holding her coffee, still in her nightdress.

Langdon glanced at his mum. Her shoulder-length hair, usually tied back, was out and half blocking her face. 'Yeah, I ran for a bit, then remembered I needed to study for our science exam, so went to Tom's and we studied, so I got in late. Everyone was already in bed when I got home.' He went straight to the cupboard to grab a cup and filled it with cold water from the fridge, he felt so thirsty.

'Oh, that's good, love, want some pancakes?' His mum smiled up at him.

'Sure, thanks.' Langdon sat at the breakfast bar and glanced at his dad, who was quietly drinking his coffee and reading the morning paper.

Langdon was tall and burly, like his father, and people always said he looked like him.

After a huge stack of pancakes was placed in front of him, Langdon added a heavy amount of maple syrup to it. He ate hungrily, enjoying every bite, moaning in satisfaction as he chewed his last bite. He finished just as Hayley joined them in the kitchen.

'Morning, Mum,' Hayley strolled into the kitchen and held her arms open wide for her morning cuddle.

'Good morning, sweetheart, did you have a good sleep?' Leah held her close for a few seconds before gently brushing the fringe away from Hayley's eyes and looking lovingly at her daughter's beautiful face.

'Yup,' Hayley nodded, as she stepped away from her mother's embrace. 'But I had the weirdest dream! I was running away from ….'

Langdon stopped listening then and turned his attention to his phone, checking Instagram. After a few minutes, he went back to his bedroom.

He really needed to study for his science exam, so he reluctantly spent the next half hour going over diagrams and definitions. After his brain started thinking more about heading to the castle, he checked the clock - 8:40 a.m. *Good, it's time to go meet the guys.*

*

When Langdon arrived at Tom's, Beau was already there.

'Hey Langdon,' greeted Tom. He looked eager to get moving. 'Can't wait to see the castle in the daylight! I hope it will offer some explanations.'

'Hey Langdon,' Beau greeted Langdon with a quieter voice, looking at the ground.

'Hey guys,' Langdon responded glumly. He ignored Tom's enthusiasm and begrudgingly acknowledged Beau with a nod. Staring at Beau's shy behaviour, he thought that even though he used to find him annoying, lately, since their camping trip, he had found Beau easy to talk to. He had also kept their camping trip on the down low, much to his surprise. Beau was normally one to boast about events that happened.

'So, the change happened, hey Langdon?' Tom asked with wide eyes and a grin. It was obvious to Langdon that his friend was keen to hear about the events that had transpired during the full moon.

'What change? What's he talking about, Langdon?' Beau was staring at him, and then he looked over at Tom, frowning.

Langdon merely looked at Tom, who stared back. He knew Tom was waiting for an answer. Langdon had to tell them. He had to tell someone.

Taking a deep breath, he answered, 'Okay guys, what I'm about to tell you is gonna sound made up, but you've gotta swear you won't tell anyone.' He looked both Tom and Beau directly in the eyes, waiting for confirmation so he could go on.

Both of them nodded in agreement and waited for him to continue.

Langdon explained as best as he could. He went over how he had felt on Friday and how he had gone out for a jog. By the time he got to the part of waking up naked in the park, Tom and Beau were looking at him with a mix of fear and surprise. Beau's mouth was gaping open.

'Shit, man!' exclaimed Tom, staring back at him with concern.

'Yeah...' agreed Beau, still feeling lost for words.

They were both staring intently, not saying anything.

Langdon wasn't sure what his friends were thinking.

Tom was the first to speak. 'It's okay mate, we're here for you. No matter what,' he lightly slapped Langdon on the shoulder, showing his support.

'Yeah, me too,' said Beau, smiling up at Langdon.

'Do you know what exactly you want to ask that man at the castle? What's his name again?' asked Tom.

'His name is Eric. Um, I guess I just want to know more about the wolf thing, maybe it won't happen again. I'm hoping he might have some advice, you know, like he's got a bit more experience with this than me.'

'Yeah,' Tom nodded. 'Holy shit.' He stared at Langdon. 'I just can't believe it, mate, I mean, shit!'

Langdon rolled his eyes. 'Yeah, I know.'

'Good thing you kept that letter he wrote you,' Beau said.

'Yeah, I guess,' said Langdon. He hadn't told either of them about throwing it out. He felt somewhat glad that Tom had filled Beau in about the letter.

'Okay, guys,' Langdon began seriously, 'We've got a thirty-minute bike ride to the start of the Blue Mountain trails, then a two-hour hike. So if we head off now, that should get us out there by midday.'

Tom nodded. 'Let's go then.'

The boys jumped on their bikes and rode quickly, using a couple of shortcuts they had picked up over the years, which kept them out of the traffic. Riding single file, Langdon led the way.

They made it to the start of the mountain trails in good time and set up their navigation on Beau's phone like the last time. They had all remained quiet once they got off their bikes, but upon starting their trek, they all started talking at once.

'Wonder what we'll find at the castle this time,' Tom thought out loud.

'Hope this navigation doesn't get us lost like last time,' blundered Beau, anxiety creeping into his voice as he thought back to last month when they walked this trail.

'Yeah, maybe I should navigate this time,' Langdon stared pointedly at Beau. Then he smiled and said, 'Nah, you've got this.' He truly was trying to make an effort to be nicer. Beau had kept quiet about the attack, and he felt he owed him a solid.

Familiarity of the overgrown forest hit their senses. Tall eucalyptus trees were in abundance, and the pine mixed with menthol and honey provided a bold, fresh aroma to Langdon's sensitised nose. He sniffed absentmindedly as his senses were ensnared. The mild scent of eucalyptus was pleasant to Tom and Beau as well.

They trudged past natural vegetation; the various shades of green displayed thickly and from time to time the boys came across cutty grass–the tall various plants that inflicted minor cuts across their shins thanks to their sharp leaves.

'Glad I'm wearing long cargo pants!' Beau gloated.

'I'm wishing I did now too,' Tom rubbed at his leg.

Focussed on the man at the castle, Langdon didn't even notice any cuts. Any that appeared disappeared a minute later.

They talked most of the way, asking Langdon more questions about Friday night and wondering about what he would do if the change happened every month.

Langdon shook his head. In a resigned breath, he said, 'I seriously don't know.' Then he laughed, 'Looks like I'll be sleeping at your house every four weeks Tom!' He grinned at his friends as he pushed a tall scraggly bush out of his way.

Tom had always been there for him. They had been friends for two years after being partnered up at karate. Their sensei had been a hard arse on everyone, but especially Langdon–probably due to his cocky nature, since he was known to be sarcastic to other students at the centre.

'Honestly, that's easily done, Langdon. Mum doesn't care who I have over,' said Tom.

Langdon smiled at the two boys next to him. It was good to have real friends. 'Okay, but all this stays between us, yeah?'

'Sure,' said Beau. 'Stays between us,' he nodded his support at Langdon.

'Absolutely,' agreed Tom.

'At least it's not raining this time!' Beau quipped with a touch of excitement. He looked between the two of them with a broad grin.

Langdon ignored him. That was the least of his concerns.

As they continued walking, Beau said in a quiet voice, 'I love the clean mountain air, but I'm still wary of rustling noises,' his eyes darted across the path.

Determined to get to the castle faster, Langdon started jogging, making Tom and Beau increase their pace to keep up. Along the track, they dodged the rocky boulders sticking out in different parts of the pathway.

After about ten minutes of running, Beau gave up, he wasn't as fit as Tom and Langdon. 'Ugh! I can't run anymore,' Beau gasped out in between big gulps of air, trying to feed his lungs the air they craved.

Tom looked at his friend kindly. 'That's okay, Beau, I don't feel like getting all hot and sweaty anyway, and we've still got a way to go.' He waited a beat, then asked, 'How is that navigation going?'

'Yeah, we're on track, it just says to keep going in this direction...' his voice trailed off as Tom yelled, pointing near his foot.

'Snake!' Tom, who was standing two feet away from Beau, pointed at a brown snake that had just slithered onto the path and had raised its head, ready to strike at Beau's ankle.

Beau looked to his left, where Tom was pointing, and froze. His heart started racing, and his breathing became shallow.

The snake inched closer, flicking its long tongue as it picked up the scent of prey.

Having heard Tom's cry, Langdon swung around, moved at an accelerated speed, leapt two giant steps, and dived at the snake. He grabbed it by the tail and sent it flying in the opposite direction.

Time seemed to stand still. Beau, mouth still open, his body frozen in fear, slowly raised his head to meet Tom's surprised look as Langdon did a quick roll and was standing again before anyone had a chance to say anything further.

'That was fucking amazing!' Tom cried, with surprise plastered all over his face. 'I've never seen you move so fast, Langdon! Not even in our rugby games!'

Beau, still recovering from what he would be calling his 'near-death experience' for the whole of next year, stood in awe of Langdon. 'Langdon just saved my life!' he mumbled to himself.

'Was nothing, don't worry about it,' said Langdon, bashfully shaking his head and moving back into the lead.

Cautiously, Tom and Beau followed Langdon. Beau's eyes darted left and right every few minutes, afraid that something else would jump out at him. Every rustling noise in the shrubs and surrounding trees had him on edge. Beau's heart still raced as he looked back at his phone to check the navigation.

'Hey Langdon,' Beau called, 'we need to turn right in fifty metres.'

'Okay,' answered Langdon, somewhat distracted by his jungle skills of diving after that snake. *Shit! I cannot believe I did that,* he thought to himself.

The next hour went by quickly, and this time, they had no navigation issues. By midday, they had reached the driveway of the castle.

'Hey! Look. Nice ride, that must be his,' said Tom.

They all stood admiring the newish black Toyota HiLux parked in front of the castle.

Beau let out a low whistle, 'Very nice,' The mud and dirt encrusted along the sideboards of the car was evidence of driving on the dirt roads leading to the castle.

The three boys continued to stare, admiring the vehicle, before Langdon spoke up. 'Right-o, let's do this, come on.'

Nodding, the boys quickly caught up with Langdon, who had already started walking towards the castle. Langdon looked gratefully at his companions. He felt much braver having company going back. He needed answers. That was what Langdon was looking for today. He thought about the wolf who had turned into a man, right in front of their eyes - Eric. The man had bitten Langdon on the arm, and he did hear him say that he had something important to tell him. Anxiety was building in the pit of his stomach with each step he took closer to the castle.

They walked across the drawbridge, the three boys were still in awe of the moat surrounding the castle, although dry, it was still a spectacular sight. Langdon knocked three loud raps to announce their arrival.

They heard footsteps, loud and purposeful, drawing closer before the door opened, revealing a tall, muscular man, with his short dark hair styled to the side. Despite his broad frame and menacing build, he had a kind face. He smiled back at them.

'Hi boys,' the strange man greeted them. 'I'm Eric, and I'm glad you came back. Which one of you is Langdon?' he asked, looking at the boy himself.

Langdon answered boldly, 'I'm Langdon.' He stared at Eric, his blue eyes staring daggers, unwilling to let his guard down around the stranger.

'Look, I'm so sorry about what happened. I know you must have plenty of questions, yeah?' Eric held his palms out flat, emphasising his sincerity.

'Yeah, I do,' agreed Langdon. Tom and Beau nodded as well.

'Come on inside, boys. I'll get us some drinks.'

Eric smiled and strode away from the front door, through the foyer, and looked over his shoulder to make sure they were still following him. Making his way into the lounge room, he felt nervous but also determined to inform the boy about what he had become. Eric had arrived two days ago to open the castle up and had lifted the sheets off the furniture and bought a small supply of food and drinks. 'Who wants a Coke?' he turned to face them.

'Yes, please,' answered Tom.

'Sure,' replied Langdon.

'Okay, thanks,' answered Beau.

Striding toward the kitchen, he called out, 'Make yourselves at home,' then he dashed to the fridge and grabbed three Cokes and a large bag of chips from the bench. Eric walked back out to see the boys cautiously standing in the lounge room, their eyes darting around the large sitting room.

'Come on in, I'll pop these on the table for you.' Eric walked over and placed the open packet of chips on the coffee table. The boys followed Eric but stood cautiously to the side.

'Okay, boys, here you go,' he handed them their drinks. 'What are your names?' he asked as they all stared back at him. He looked at Beau and Tom.

'I'm Tom,' Tom answered, still cautious.

The boys glanced around the living room, recalling how different it had looked on the night of the storm.

The sun shone brightly through the bay windows, kissing the faded creamy rug underneath the couches and coffee table. The interior was clean, and the large grey stone blocks showing their age had cracks and small holes but were in better condition than in places on the outside.

Langdon noticed the dark timber grandfather clock standing boldly along the wall and a stone fireplace, looking well used, dirty with old timber scattered in the bottom amongst piles of black ash. It looked as though it had not been used for months. He guessed Eric only used it sometimes during the winter months, depending on how much time he had in human form while he was out there.

'I'm Beau,' said the smaller boy, introducing himself quietly.

'Okay, come and sit, please.' Eric wandered over to the lounge and sat down on the recliner so the boys might feel more relaxed.

Tom and Langdon sat in the two-seater, and Beau reluctantly sat in the recliner that was furthest away.

Eric stared kindly back at them. He drummed his fingers against his knees as he glanced from one boy to the other.

'Okay, so, what I have to tell you is very serious,' Eric paused, unsure how to articulate the critical information about the curse. 'So, if you boys remember the last time you were here, you saw something that didn't make sense, right?'

He looked to see if the boys were still okay and keeping up. 'Well, that night, I became a werewolf due to the full moon, and while I was in that shape, well, I bit one of you.' He looked directly at Langdon. 'Once bitten, you will succumb to the curse of every full moon as I have done for the past twelve months.'

Eric looked at Langdon, who looked very confused, so he tried to clarify further. 'Langdon, you will transition into a wolf every full moon,' The look on the boy's face was heartbreaking, he still looked like he either couldn't or wouldn't understand. 'I'm sorry to say that there is no cure and that, for each full moon, you are best to find yourself a location that is safe for not just you, but also everyone around you.' He looked each boy in the eye, and seeing that they all looked afraid, he smiled and paused before asking, 'Do you have any questions?'

'I don't understand. What do you mean there is no cure?!' Langdon asked, frustrated.

'Well, after it happened to me, I first thought it was my imagination, but it kept happening. Every month. Every full moon. Plus, I found some old diaries of my uncle who owned this castle, and he wrote that it happened to him as well, although none of my family knew.'

'How did this happen?' Langdon asked, still trying to understand.

Eric frowned and after a heavy sigh, explained how he had been cursed twelve months ago after inheriting the castle. How a walk around his property had him returning to the castle late and thrown to the ground and bitten. Eric told them how he thought the wolf was going to kill him, and how his wound healed quicker than he expected. At this point, he looked at Langdon and asked, 'Did your wound heal quickly?'

'Yeah, it was gone the next day,' answered Langdon. 'But it may not happen to me again, right? I mean, what did it feel like for you to transition?' Langdon was curious if his experience was different.

Eric explained that he also believed that after turning once, it would never happen again, only to realise how wrong he had been. He left no detail out, describing what he felt when he changed form and how he coped, if only to help the boy understand what he had to deal with. He had been talking awhile and looked at Langdon once more to see if he was okay. Apart from his hand nervously running through his hair, making it dishevelled, he only saw Langdon glance up a few times in between, studying the Coke can he was holding. Eric continued in a soft tone, offering his castle to Langdon for every full moon, 'It's the least I can do,' he said. He raised his eyebrows, waiting for any response from the blank faces looking back at him.

Langdon stared back at Eric, a million thoughts running through his head. He noticed how muscled Eric was, he could see the muscles of his arms and wondered if he worked out or if turning into a beast each month had bulked him up.

He shook his head slightly to get back on track, bringing his attention back to Eric's offer. 'I think I'll be all right. I can look after myself,' he said, nodding as if to convince himself. He wasn't about to accept help from someone he'd just met.

'That's fine, but just know that you are welcome here anytime. I travel here every month, and it allows me space and privacy. This is private property, all 400 acres of it. The change can be messy, and it's good to have somewhere you can hang out before it happens. I usually strip before I transition, so that I don't go through so many clothes.' He chuckled softly to lighten the mood.

When none of the boys made a sound, he cleared his throat, asking Langdon, 'Did you find yourself getting moody leading up to the full moon?'

'Yeah, a bit,' Langdon still couldn't make eye contact with the man.

The sound of a loud crunch made everyone stop talking and look at Beau. Poor Beau had taken a handful of chips and sat staring back, his green eyes wide. He paused mid-crunch, and said, 'Ahh, sorry.' He ducked his head down, surprise and embarrassment plastered all over his face.

Eric smiled endearingly at Beau, 'You're right, buddy,' he paused, retracing his thoughts. 'So Langdon, that's kind of the warning sign that you need to prepare for what's coming. The afternoon will be harder, and by nightfall, you will be tearing your walls down if you don't get out of your house. What did you do on this full moon?'

'I went for a run, and I don't remember what happened after. But I woke up at the park near where I live.' Langdon left out the part about waking up naked. At this point, he shot a glance at his mates, who seemed like statues just sitting there listening to everything.

'Well, you have my number, but take this anyway.' Eric said as he handed over a business card. 'Call me anytime. As I said before, you are welcome to come out here, Langdon.'

A few more moments passed, whereby the boys continued to stare around the room, not saying anything. Eric wanted to help the boys feel comfortable in his presence. 'How was the hike out here today, boys?' He glanced at each of them.

'Yeah, it was all right,' said Tom.

'A snake nearly bit me!' cried Beau. 'But Langdon got rid of it,' he added, beaming.

'A snake! Wow, good job Langdon.' Eric looked impressed as he glanced across at the boy, noticing that he looked strong and athletic. 'How'd you get to the walking track?'

'We rode our bikes from home and left them at Jackson Park. Then we came through Sassafras Gully and followed the walking track,' explained Tom.

Eric whistled softly and said, 'That's a bit of a hike! What's that, nearly two hours?'

'Yeah, we did it in under two hours, with a bit of a run at the start,' boasted Langdon.

'Okay, well, next full moon, feel free to ring me and I can pick you up from the park and save you the energy.'

'Okay,' Langdon thought about it. It would make it much easier for the next one. He was still dubious and wondered whether it would even happen again. 'I'll think about it,' he mumbled, his mind whirling with questions and fears.

Eric smiled, 'No worries. You've got my card. Now, can I offer you boys anything else to drink? Hungry?'

Unanimous answers of "no" came from the boys.

Tom looked at his watch and saw that it was already after two o'clock. His stomach had growled, and he shifted his body on the couch to cover the noise. 'We should probably get going,' Tom looked at Langdon expectantly.

'Yeah, we have to get back,' Langdon slowly rose to his feet, willing the feeling back into his long legs.

'Well, why don't I drive you three back to the park where you left your bikes?' Eric could see the hesitation in Langdon's blue eyes and even though he had tried his best over the last two hours to make him feel comfortable and feel that he could trust him, he knew it would take time.

Deciding to be bold, Langdon nodded and looked to his friends for support. Both Tom and Beau nodded at Eric and smiled.

'All right then, let's go.' Eric led them out to his black Toyota, locking the front door on his way out. The boys climbed in, Langdon in front and the other two in the back. The engine purred to life, and Eric eased out of the driveway and down the road. Within forty minutes, they arrived back at the park. Eric could see a few bikes sticking out from behind a bush.

'Nice meeting you, boys,' said Eric. He looked back at Tom and Beau as they were exiting the vehicle.

'You too, Eric, and thanks for the ride,' Tom nodded in gratitude.

'Yeah, thanks, Eric,' repeated Beau.

'Thanks for the ride,' Langdon glanced at Eric, making eye contact for a moment before he exited the vehicle. He was still unsure of the man and trying to gauge whether meeting him was the right idea.

'Anytime you have a question or need help, please don't hesitate to call or text me, Langdon.' Eric glanced at the boy, his brown eyes narrowed in concern.

Langdon nodded and looked away. He stepped out of the vehicle and walked over to his friends.

Tom, Beau, and Langdon stood by their bikes and watched as Eric drove off down the road. Then, Tom and Beau looked at Langdon, waiting for his reaction.

When none came, Tom asked, 'Well? What'd you think?'

'Seems like an okay guy, don't know if I'll come back out or not though,' answered Langdon.

'It's always an option, and you can always tell your parents you're staying at mine,' offered Tom.

'Yeah, I guess.' Langdon was hungry and just wanted to get home and eat. 'Come on guys, let's get back, I'm starving.'

'Same,' his mates agreed.

The guys rode in silence, with Langdon in the lead. His head whirled with everything Eric told him. Langdon pedalled fast, keen to get home and process what he had learned.

Langdon parted ways with Tom and Beau at the intersection where they had to go separate ways to get home. He picked up speed, easily flying past houses, and arrived home quickly.

As Tom and Beau lived next door to each other, they rode side by side on the journey home.

'Shit, did you notice how fast Langdon moves now? I could barely keep up riding there, his pace was too fast for me,' quipped Tom as he looked across at Beau.

'Yeah, same. I had trouble keeping up before he had the transition. Now he's faster, and I think he hears things before us,' Beau voiced as he turned to look at Tom.

'Yeah, I think you're right,' Tom went on, 'Can you believe this is happening to him?'

'Nope, although I've noticed he's easier to talk to now, at least for me anyway - you know, like, he doesn't pay out on me much anymore.'

'Yeah, I've noticed that,' agreed Tom.

'Do you believe in all this? You know, curses and full moons?' asked Beau.

'I didn't before, but now, well, we've all seen it. Remember our camping trip - we saw Eric change in front of our eyes. One minute we're standing there thinking we're about to die, and then as soon as that sunlight hit him, he changed into a man. Like, how crazy is that?' Tom shook his head at the strangeness of it all.

'Yeah, I know. It looks painful.'

'Sure does. Look, I think Langdon really needs us now. He's trying to come to terms with what's happening to him.'

'Mmm,' Beau agreed, deep in thought about Langdon's predicament.

The two boys turned onto their street and said their goodbyes as they parted ways.

Chapter 7

Langdon arrived home tired and hungry. He glanced at his watch and saw it was 3:15 p.m. He pushed his bike into the carport and walked inside, straight to the fridge to make a ham and cheese sandwich. Grabbing a Coke to go with it, he sat at the breakfast bar and was soon lost in his thoughts from the last twenty-four hours.

Is this real? Will this happen to me every month!? Maybe he's just a freak and is making this all up. Maybe I didn't turn into anything, I could have just fallen asleep at the park. I was tired...

'Langdon? Langdon!' his mum's voice pulled him back to the present.

'Yeah? I'm in the kitchen,' he called back.

He glanced up as his mum walked into the kitchen carrying a basket of laundry.

'Oh, hi sweetheart! I need you to take Hayley to her dance class on Monday after school because I'll be stuck at work. Your father is driving me and picking me up so that you will have the Subaru.' Langdon's mum was a teacher and always worked long hours marking schoolwork, especially around exam time.

'Oh Mum, no, I was going to hang out at Tom's!'

'Sorry, hon, your dad and I won't get home until after five,' his mother's voice was stern but still gentle.

Although he felt disappointed, a thought occurred. *I'll have the car*! Having passed his driving test last month and gaining his provisional licence, he looked for any opportunity to drive. *Maybe I could even drive to school that day!*

'Fine, I'll do it if I can drive to school that day.' He could pick up Tom on his way, and Beau as well, as he lived next door to Tom.

'Okay, but drive carefully, please.' His mum stared at him sternly, her eyes deep blue - a darker shade than Langdon's. Her face was serious, still flawless, and pretty. He couldn't help but smile at her endearing concern. 'Hayley's class starts at four-thirty, so if you're driving to school you can drive Hayley as well. Make sure you leave here by four so that she can be a few minutes early.'

'Yeah, yeah, I know,' he drawled, his attention going back to his phone. He needed to text Tom.

'Thanks, honey!' His mum wandered off to fold her basket of washing.

Langdon nodded absently, focusing on his text message.

Hey Tom! Monday, I'm driving—have to take Hayley to dance L8r. Tell Beau as well. I'll pick you up at 8.

A reply came seconds later - **K**

Langdon, his hunger finally sedated, trudged up the stairs into his bedroom and closed the door before he flopped onto his bed. *What a day,* he thought wearily. The events were taking their toll on his body. He was glad he had friends with him while meeting Eric, even though he had seemed cool. His eyes felt heavy, starting to close, and he drifted into a light sleep…

BANG, bang, bang. The loud knocking at the door jolted Langdon awake. He glanced at his phone - 5:42 p.m.

'Langdon!' yelled Hayley.

'What,' he growled back, still groggy from being abruptly woken up.

Hayley poked her head into his room, 'Mum's asking if you want to do a pizza and movie night?'

Oh God, really? His Mum loved those. Actually, he thought, they aren't half bad, especially if it means getting pizza… as long as we don't watch a soppy movie.

'Okay, sounds good,' he finally answered.

His sister nodded and closed the door. She had just started walking away when Langdon shouted, '*GET MEAT LOVERS!*'

'Okay,' she called, sounding further away.

Langdon lay on his bed listening to his favourite playlist for the next hour, and different theories played out in his head about turning into a werewolf, and of possible cures. He wondered what the next full moon would bring. That was his biggest concern right now.

His foot tapped along to a popular rapper called Juice WRLD, whose song 'Lucid Dreams' was blaring out of his AirPods. Soon, he became engrossed in listening to music.

Bang, Bang. Another loud knock sounded over his music just as another song ended. 'What!' he called out.

'Pizza's here,' called Hayley as she poked her head through his door.

Langdon removed his AirPods, but he could hear a small thump, thump, thump, outside his door. He got up and opened his door to see his sister jumping around, practising her hip-hop dancing, her long blonde hair swaying as she moved.

'Oh, hey!' she greeted with a grin and danced off down the hall and continued down the stairs.

Langdon shook his head. His sister was crazy. Hayley always danced around the house, she loved moving and sometimes could not just sit still. He quickly followed, remembering there was pizza waiting.

***

The next morning, he woke up feeling amazing and energetic. Langdon checked his phone to see that it was just a little after six. *Sunday*, he thought and decided to go for a run. Langdon usually went for runs every weekend and could go between five and eight kilometres depending on his mood. He quickly changed into his running shorts and t-shirt, then laced up his joggers. Taking a quick bathroom visit and checking his appearance in the mirror, he was out the door.

He ran straight to the pathway across from his house and began jogging. As he was running, he felt different, stronger, and more aware of his surroundings. He became much more aware of the sounds of birds, the breeze, and trees swaying; everything seemed louder than normal. He jogged further and stopped to look at a tree with overhanging branches, noticing all the distinct lines in the leaves, and felt as though he saw everything clearer. He reached up to feel its softness.

Hearing voices coming, he quickly dropped his arm and looked behind him to see who they were. He peered all around, but didn't see anyone for another thirty seconds. Yet, the closer they came, the more he could hear every word.

Shaking his head, he started running again, and before he knew it; he had arrived at North Point Retail, a shopping complex–seven kilometres away. *What*! Langdon stopped and looked around—this was the furthest he had ever run! He wasn't even out of breath! *Cool!* he thought, then turned around and ran home. He couldn't believe he had just run fourteen kilometres.

When he arrived back at the park near his house, he still felt like he had loads of energy, so he stopped at a grassy patch near the swing set and did three sets of twelve push-ups on his toes. Then he stood and looked at the park's jungle gym. He curiously eyed the climbing rocks and other playground equipment aimed at the younger kids. Then his eyes fell upon the section for older kids. His eyes widened seeing a giant slide, monkey bars, and a big playground climber. Langdon had attempted pull-ups before but had barely been able to lift himself. Even though he was doing plenty of push-ups with footy training, it still hadn't given him the upper body strength.

He stood staring at the bar connecting the swings, contemplating his current strength. Walking over, he inspected the swings and bar further; testing his weight against the bar, it seemed quite stable. Looking up, he took a deep breath, bent his knees, and jumped high to grab onto the bar. He gripped the bar securely and switched his hold so that his hands were facing him. Pulling his body up was effortless, so he smashed out thirty chin-ups. The muscles in his back flexed with each rep. His biceps bulged, taking on the load.

Switching his hands to a neutral grip pull-up, he was able to stimulate his shoulders and biceps more. He did another thirty reps and found his lats were burning. He exhaled loudly and dropped to the ground.

Using the playground equipment, he leapt, jumped, and swung his way around. Finally, feeling satisfied and having expended all his energy, he wiped the sweat from his brow, rolled his shoulders, and jogged back to his house. Langdon felt impressed with his efforts, he had never run so far or been able to lift his body weight before.

Sweat had soaked his shirt, so he went straight up the stairs and into his bathroom for a quick shower, and when he finished, he stood looking in the mirror. He stared at his reflection from the waist up and couldn't help but notice the increase in muscle mass. He hadn't bulked up, although his pecs were definitely larger, and his shoulders and arms appeared to have more definition. Then, after spraying deodorant across his body and with his towel wrapped around his hips, he swaggered back into his bedroom to throw on some clothes.

Chapter 8

It was Monday afternoon, and Langdon had dropped his friends, Tom and Beau, home and just arrived home with Hayley. Langdon enjoyed driving his parents' Subaru, it was cruisy, and he could easily connect his phone to listen to his playlist displayed on the screen. It was way better than catching the bus, quicker and with no waiting around. Tom and Beau appreciated the ride as well.

'All right, Hayls, grab something to eat and get ready for your dance class. We need to leave in twenty minutes,' Langdon commanded as they walked inside their house.

'Okay,' Hayley skipped off to the kitchen before her brother so she could grab the last chocolate muffin.

Langdon, now upstairs in his room, could hear Hayley opening a packet. He turned, expecting to see her right behind him. But she wasn't there. Strange things had been happening since he had transitioned during the last full moon. He now heard everything clearer and closer, and he was faster; could run for miles! He even saw things with more clarity and much more intensely.

He flew down the stairs and sauntered into the kitchen, and there she was, eating a chocolate muffin. *Hmm,* he thought, his mouth watered from the delicious smell that his nose had picked up. His eyes glazed over as he thought about the flavour explosion his taste buds were craving. The chocolate chips, the chocolate icing, all melting in his mouth, *ooh.*

'Hello, earth to Langdon,' sang Hayley, slowly munching on her muffin.

Langdon, coming out of his reverie, looked at his sister. 'Oh, sorry Hayls, I was miles away!' He chuckled at his own joke before turning his attention to the sweet treat.

Hayley rolled her eyes and gazed at her muffin. She licked her lips and took another bite, moaning with pleasure.

'Ohh, what's that you're eating?' Langdon ambled over, eyeing the muffin in his sister's hand.

'Get away,' warned Hayley, slipping off her stool at the breakfast bar and moving slowly backward, knowing her brother well enough to be cautious.

But Langdon moved faster than she could predict, and was beside her, one arm around her shoulders to keep her from moving, and swiftly took a large bite of the muffin. He stepped away in victory, savouring the bite he stole. 'Mmm, delicious,' he taunted.

'Hey!' Hayley grumbled, holding her muffin closer, protecting it from the claws of her annoying brother. She quickly devoured the rest before he could steal some more.

Langdon laughed as he walked back into the kitchen in search of food to satisfy his growing hunger.

When it was time to leave for Hayley's dance class, he called out to Hayley that he would wait in the car. He wanted time to pick a fast-tempo song for the trip.

By the time Hayley had climbed into the passenger seat, Langdon was ready to go. A ten-minute drive had them arriving at the popular Dance Revolution, where he easily found a spot in its designated parking area.

Walking into the dance studio, Langdon tried to keep his focus straight ahead, while trying not to ogle at the gorgeous dancers, wearing nothing but skin-coloured tights and a black leotard. He was looking forward to checking out some of the girls in his sister's dance class.

The studio was remarkably busy and pumping with music. Dancers were rushing in and out of rooms, some holding their dance shoes already late for their class. There were multiple classes at any one time, and teachers were quite prompt about a starting class on time.

Hayley led the way around the maze of studios, with Langdon following until they arrived at the studio where Hayley had her hip-hop lesson. The room was bright and airy thanks to the wide, open windows on one end, and the luminous lights shining from three different beams that lit the generously sized room. A huge full-length mirror took up the entire wall at the front of the room. Wooden bars were lined around the walls, and dancers were stretching their long, flexible legs upon them, gracefully folding their torsos over to grab hold of their toes enveloped in black leather shoes, like the ones his sister wore. This class, he could see, had both female and male dancers. Ages varied, his sister was thirteen, and some students looked eighteen. This was the 'open' hip-hop class.

Langdon walked over to join some of the other parents who stayed to watch. A few chairs were lined along the edge of the front of the studio for them. Taking a seat, Langdon drew his attention to the dancers, who were lining up, ready for class to begin. *Well, this is going to be one boring hour*, he thought to himself, trying to get comfortable.

The teacher entered, bringing to the room silence and attention to her presence. Her elongated physique lightly floated into the centre before her students. She wore a similar leotard as her students, except for the long flowing skirt, with her hair tightly wound into a neat bun on top of her head. She stood tall and poised, as if she were waiting for something.

Quiet.

'Good afternoon, students,' she greeted, her eyes roving around the room once they'd settled.

'Good afternoon, Miss Mills,' the dancers sang in unison.

'Okay, places please, we're going to take it from the top. I hope all of you have warmed up.' The last comment seemed like a warning.

The dancers arranged themselves into four neat lines, twenty-one dancers, Langdon counted, and watched them get into position. Some were sitting with a leg poised in the air, while others had their hip popped to the side and arms either by their side or up above their head in a Y position.

The dancers were ready.

As the music started, loud and rhythmic, Langdon jumped. The sound was too loud. He quickly recovered and repositioned himself to deflect from his reaction. The students seemed to know the moves and danced to a choreographed, rapid beat of the song.

Langdon watched as girls jumped, spun, flexed, and leapt around the room. His eyes settled on one girl who looked about his age, he could see the outline of her chest, and her long, taut midsection. But Langdon wasn't interested in her, his eyes had unknowingly wandered to a tall, strong-looking boy beside her.

The handsome male dancer also looked his age, and he could not help but stare at his toned, muscled physique through his black singlet, already showing signs of perspiration. Langdon looked admiringly at the boy's biceps, his eyes travelling down, down his torso, to his legs, the muscles in his thighs tensing through his bike shorts completely visible as the dancer flipped, jumped, and moved his hips enticingly in time to the music. Langdon was mesmerised.

The dancer continued moving, sweat now dripping down from his cropped, nearly black hair. Suddenly, the music stopped, and the dancers froze in their positions. It was then that Langdon locked eyes with the male dancer he had been stupefyingly watching. Deep brown eyes stared back at him. Langdon's breath hitched until a slow, sensual smile caught the corner of the dancer's mouth.

Time stood still; Langdon felt butterflies roaming playfully in his tummy, as he felt totally and irrevocably captivated. His heart pounded faster until the teacher spoke, breaking the spell that was upon him.

'Okay, class, that was better, but still needs improvement.' She clapped her hands three times. 'Girls in the back, Simone, Taylor and Hayley, move to the second row and Tash, Bree and Sonia, go to the back for now. Good work, Finn, lovely formation in the leap to triple pirouette.'

The teacher clapped her hands again, calling her students' attention.

'Again,' she commanded. The music started, this time Langdon was prepared for the assault to his ears.

He watched as the dancers performed the same routine, but this time in a different formation. Langdon tried not to stare at Finn. *Finn.* So, that was his name. Langdon looked around the room, admiring the efforts of the dancers and their funky moves. They were moving fluently and in time with the beat as their hips gyrated seductively.

As he was glancing at different dancers, he thought he could feel Finn looking his way now and then. At that moment, he flicked his eyes in Finn's direction and met the boy's eyes before Finn moved again to focus on his steps. Langdon had goosebumps and felt his arousal as he looked back at Finn, his muscular body flexing and jumping.

The rest of the class went by quickly, and before he knew what was happening, the music had stopped, and the teacher was dismissing her students. Hayley skipped to him, sweating profusely and grinning.

'What'd you think?' Hayley asked her brother.

'Yeah, good Hayls! You were great!' Langdon was trying to look past his sister at Finn.

'You weren't even looking at me! I saw you looking at the front row!' she complained.

'Oh, no, I was looking,' he tried searching his brain for anything to placate his increasingly loud sister. 'I loved that spin you did and the leap, and I even saw you do the splits.'

When Hayley grinned, he added, 'See, I was looking.'

'Oh, okay, cool!' was all she said as she gathered her gear.

Langdon kept glancing over at the male dancer, watching as he bent to throw his gear into his bag. He tried not to stare as the boy advanced in his direction, his gait easy but swift, sensual even. His heart raced, so he tried to busy himself by helping his sister pack her backpack. His mouth had gone dry, and each swallow felt like a monumental task. Langdon focused on Hayley's bag for a moment.

Then, when he glanced up, Finn walked past, and their eyes locked for a brief moment. All air escaped out of Langdon's lungs as the male dancer smiled a smooth, sexy half-smile that made him weak in the knees. He was glad he was still sitting.

The boy kept walking, and Langdon followed him with his eyes until he could not see him anymore. *Oh god!* Langdon had to adjust himself, hoping no one had gotten a glimpse of his *situation*. He covered his crotch discretely with Hayley's towel that she had dropped in his lap, still thinking about Finn.

'Langdon…Langdon!'

'Huh? What?' Langdon drew his eyes back to his sister, feigning innocence.

'You're sitting there, gripping my towel, and I can't put it away!' She had her hands gripped on the edge of the towel and tried to tug it out of her brother's tight hold.

Langdon let go and quickly regained his equilibrium. 'Sorry, come on, let's go.'

He was hoping he might catch another look at Finn. But when they walked outside, he was nowhere to be seen.

Langdon drove home quietly, half-listening to his sister prattling on about the girls in her dance class.

When they arrived home, he trudged up to his room and lay on his bed, going over the events of the afternoon. *What was that all about?* he asked himself. *Why did I keep staring at that guy? Why did my body react that way? Fuck, I don't know why I felt so nervous.* He shook his head, pushing his feelings and thoughts of Finn out of his mind, and worked on his homework instead.

Later that night, when he was going to bed, he thought about the dance class again. His eyes were slipping closed, but his mind was yet again on the mysterious male…

Langdon walked into the dance studio, seeing Finn in the middle of practising his flips and other dance steps. The beat of the music was pumping loudly through Langdon's skin. The boy stopped dancing; he saw Langdon and made that slow sensual smile. Langdon took a step toward him. Finn calmly and sexily walked over; his gait screaming confidence as he strode across the dance floor.

Stepping forward, Langdon closed the gap between them. He looked into Finn's deep brown eyes and lifted his hand to gently caress his jawline. Langdon stared at Finn's full bottom lip. He licked his own lips. With his heart pounding in his ears, he moved closer. His breath turned heavier the closer they got, closer, closer, their lips almost touching. Closer, he was about to kiss Finn. He could almost taste the guy's sweat. Closer, he needed to feel his lips against Finn's, needed to, ached to. Closer, he inhaled in anticipation, his breath catching as …

BEEP, BEEP, BEEP. The blaring chime of Langdon's alarm startled him awake.

'Ugh.' Groaning quietly, Langdon's mind was full of what could've happened in his dream if he hadn't been so rudely awakened. His pulse racing, he rolled onto his back and moved his hips slightly, his body still humming with sexual desire.

The door to the joint bathroom opened and Hayley stuck her head through, 'Langdon, are you getting up?'

Langdon swiftly threw his hand down and rolled to his side to hide any evidence of his arousal. 'Yes, now get out!' he growled.

'Oh, fine, but Mum sent me to ask if you can drive me to ballet this afternoon.'

Langdon was about to automatically say 'no' but then realised he might see the male dancer. 'Oh, okay, whatever,' he answered nonchalantly.

'Good.' Then she promptly closed the door behind her.

Langdon groaned quietly and swore. Oh My God, what the hell was that dream all about?

Climbing out of bed, he quickly dressed for school and raced to the bathroom. Then, he checked his reflection before running some product through his messy hair. He ran his fingers through a few times before settling on a style. Then, facing the mirror, his eyes travelled to his torso, then to his biceps. Langdon puffed his chest, rolled his shoulders, and walked out of the bathroom.

Running down the stairs to the kitchen, he made himself toast for breakfast, adding peanut butter and banana, then he poured himself a tall glass of milk, to which he added three heaped teaspoons of Milo. He rapidly stirred the Milo in and ate his breakfast while checking his phone. His parents were quickly finishing their breakfast to race off to work.

'Hey Langdon, did Hayley tell you about her dance class this afternoon?' asked his mum.

'Yeah, that's okay, I can take her,' assured Langdon.

'You'll still need to get the bus, and I'll be home by four so you can have the car. It's just that I made plans with Emma to go to a gym class, and she's picking me up at four-thirty.'

'Yeah, that's fine Mum,' he glanced up at her as she ran around trying to find her phone, lifting pieces of paper and magazines before finally finding it beside the kettle.

'Bye hon,' she kissed her husband gently on his lips before turning to her children. 'Okay, I'm off, bye sweetie,' she said to Hayley as she lightly kissed her on the head. 'Bye Langdon,' she called out, then she was out the door.

Langdon's dad was already dressed for work in dark-coloured trousers and a collared shirt. 'All right, kids, I'm off now too, see you tonight.' He waved and was in the carport before Langdon could wash his plate.

***

Later that day at school, Langdon made an extra effort to flirt with girls. He had never, ever in his entire life checked out a guy. Until Finn. In an effort to prove to himself that he wasn't gay, he made himself check out girls' legs as they walked past, and their chests as they stood talking to their friends. In history class, he smiled his sexiest smile at Bridget as she walked past, glancing at him to get to her seat. He thought she was pretty and wondered if he was just overthinking his reaction to Finn.

'Hey Langdon,' she breathed as she was just behind him.

He turned slightly and said hi back, annoyed at his body for having no reaction.

In science class, they were shown a video on solar ovens. He was sitting next to Tom and trying to concentrate on the video, but his mind kept wandering to Finn.

Images of Finn's arms as he did his flips, his toned torso visible through the tight black singlet, his chiselled jaw, his brown eyes, and the way they looked at Langdon when he was leaving the class. Langdon wondered if Finn would be at his sister's class this afternoon, *Oh no, not again*, Langdon could feel himself getting aroused again just thinking about Finn.

'Langdon. Langdon,' whispered Tom. Tom nudged his elbow against Langdon's, gaining his attention.

'Huh? What?' He turned to look at his friend.

'Do you wanna come over after school today and go over our science project?'

Rugby practice had been cancelled due to the rain, since the fields were too wet for practice.

'Can't, gotta take Hayley to dance.'

'Again?' Tom asked in disbelief.

'Yeah, Mum's got something on and wants me to take her.'

'Oh shit, that sucks.'

'Yeah, well, can't be helped,' said Langdon, trying his best to make it appear it was a big inconvenience.

The bell rang, and Langdon filed out with Tom. It had been the last class of the day, thank goodness.

They walked over to their bags and, after throwing one strap over a shoulder, he walked over to wait for the bus.

Langdon was leaning against the pole and staring at Olivia. *She should be the one I'm checking out, not Finn.* He stared at her, taking in her shapely figure. His eyes travelled up her tanned legs, up to her full breasts, lingering there before moving his gaze up to her sparkly blue eyes and long, flowing blonde hair. While he found her attractive, his body didn't have the same reaction as it did with Finn.

'You gonna ask Olivia out?' Tom asked as he saw who Langdon was checking out.

'Nah, just looking,' said Langdon casually.

Tom smiled and shook his head.

Beau walked over with his AirPods in. He took one out to greet his friends and then went back to his music.

The bus ride home was loud. Tom and Langdon were quick to get a seat, but Beau had been pushed to the side, and when he finally stepped onto the bus, he walked down the rows, looking left and right for a seat. Finally, a couple of seats up from Tom, he saw a big guy spread out with his bag on the seat next to him. Beau stood in front of him and pointed, raising his eyebrows in question. The guy nodded and shifted his bag to the floor. Beau sat half hanging off the seat and stared straight ahead, turning up the volume on his phone to block out the noise.

Later that afternoon, when Langdon arrived at the dance studio with Hayley, his eyes darted left and right. His heart was beating slightly faster than normal as he scanned the dancers for the familiar sight he was craving.

They walked to her ballet studio which was a different room from the previous day he was there. Langdon took a seat at the front, on the left side of the room, waiting to see if any male dancers walked in.

Langdon waited and waited. He looked down at his phone for a distraction, scrolling and looking at nothing. His attention was caught by a male voice entering the room. Langdon's eyes shot up to see a fair-headed, tall, skinny guy walk in. This guy spoke in a higher decibel, and his gait was swaying slightly at the hips as he walked over to a group stretching their legs on a bar. Langdon ignored them and went back to his phone.

The dance instructor came in, poised, professional and immaculate, her hair presented neatly in a bun on top of her head. She instructed the class in a shrill voice that had all the dancers obeying her every word.

Langdon glanced around the room, and while there were plenty of attractive girls in all shapes and sizes, he sighed inwardly as he realised this was not what he wanted. His mind wandered to Finn. Strong, gorgeous Finn.

Langdon was glad when the class was finally over. Hayley pranced over, chatting amiably with her dancer friends. Her friends checked him out as they approached, and one whispered something to his sister. She giggled and nodded her affirmation at something.

Ignoring them, Langdon stood and walked out with Hayley, her friends in tow, she said her goodbyes to them and turned her attention to Langdon.

Hayley waited until they got in the car, then exclaimed, 'Sammy wants me to ask if you have a girlfriend!'

Langdon looked at his sister sitting in the passenger seat, her long legs stretched out in front of her, whitened slightly by the stockings she wore. She was staring back, a smile tugging the corner of her mouth and waiting for her brother's response.

'No, no girlfriend at this stage,' he replied.

'Oh, good because Sam…'

'But I have my eye on someone,' he cut her off, trying to focus on the road.

'Oh, do I know her? Is she a dancer?'

'No, you don't know her,' he left it at that. No way was he going to tell her who he was really eyeing.

The rest of the week went by slowly, and Langdon waited until the weekend to suggest to his mum that he drive Hayley to her hip-hop class on Monday. She'd asked why, and the best he could come up with was because he wanted the car.

He said he had so many books to carry, and it would be easier, he added, 'You won't have to rush home to get her to her dance lesson.' He hoped she would allow him to take Hayley, it was the only way he could think that he could test his reaction when he saw Finn again. *Oh, but what if Finn's not there? Shit... well, only one way to find out.*

'Oh, okay. Thanks, Langdon, that was nice of you to offer.'

So, it was set; he would take his sister to the dance lesson. Langdon had to prove to himself that he wasn't interested.

Chapter 9

Finally, it was Monday afternoon, and Langdon stomped around the house, impatient to leave when Hayley was taking her time getting ready.

'Come on, Hayley,' Langdon growled. 'You don't want to be late.' He was anxious and wanted to hurry and get to the dance studio.

'Yeah, yeah, I'm coming,' she called from the lounge room where she was putting her dance shoes on.

Langdon waited by the door to the carport until she finally skipped into sight. He had to admit his sister was very pretty, blue eyes were a family trait, and hers were twinkling with excitement because she loved this dance class.

Arriving at the dance studio, Langdon walked in next to his sister once more, discretely glancing around at the various dancers walking to their classes.

Upon entering the hip-hop studio, Langdon looked around the room, and he saw the same beautiful girls from last Monday. He searched as subtly as possible to see the boy he had been so struck by.

Is that…? He had to move into the room more to see properly, *Yes, that looks like Finn stretching his legs and chatting to a small group of girls.*

Langdon's heart fluttered in his chest. He quickly found a seat alongside other parents and busied himself with re-tying his shoelaces as he stole glances towards the back of the studio. He caught glimpses of Finn's dark, cropped hair and his muscular physique as he stretched his long torso over his body.

Finn turned and scanned the room, his eyes finding Langdon staring back at him. He smiled, slow, sexy, his cheek dimpling as if to say hello.

As Langdon watched, unable to tear his eyes away, Finn walked over to Hayley, who was stretching her long legs on the beam, and he started talking to her. Finn kept peeking at Langdon now and again, and Langdon had to look away as his cheeks burned, to his utter dismay. Hayley glanced in his direction and said something back to Finn.

Langdon felt nausea in his stomach as his anxiety spread. He picked up his water bottle and took a big swig.

Just then, the dance teacher entered the room, and he was thankful that her very presence silenced the room and caused the dancers to arrange themselves in their formation.

'Good afternoon, class,' the dance teacher greeted.

'Good afternoon Miss Mills,' the class chorused.

As the music started, Langdon watched the class move along to the rhythm, moving their hips and practising all the other moves he remembered from last Monday.

He watched Finn as he moved, jumped, and flipped. Mesmerised as sweat lingered on the skin of his arms, his forehead, and the top of his lip. Langdon's breathing became shallow as he dragged his eyes over the lines of Finn's toned body. Langdon felt as if he could keep watching him forever.

All too soon, the class was over; the students bowed to their teacher, and they were dismissed. Hayley skipped across the room to him to gulp down a big drink of water. Putting the lid back on, she began telling him about the additional steps she had to learn.

Langdon was only half-listening, his attention caught between her and watching Finn take a long drink from his water bottle, and Langdon's mouth almost fell open as he watched Finn pour a small amount over his face. Langdon's eyes traced the water dripping over Finn's closed eyes and down to his lips, down his throat to his chest and finally absorbing into his singlet. Langdon felt aroused and gripped the seat. He continued watching as the guy dragged a small towel from his backpack to wipe down his face. Finn looked up in Langdon's direction, and Langdon hastily looked away. *Shit, shit, shit.*

When he looked up again, Finn was walking in their direction. Langdon tried to busy himself, suddenly finding the lines on the timber floor very interesting.

'Hayley, is this your brother?' Finn asked as he strode purposefully over to where Langdon and Hayley were standing. *Oh, his voice.* Finn had a sexy voice, not too deep, but sensuous and insistent.

Hayley, who had been distracted, looked up and saw the tall boy. 'Oh, hi Finn!' she giggled, her cheeks going pink. She looked up at Finn as he patiently waited to be introduced. 'Finn, this is my big brother, Langdon,' she held out her arm, indicating her brother.

'Hi, Langdon,' Finn held out a hand to shake Langdon's hand.

Langdon quickly wiped the sweat off his palm and shook Finn's hand, nodding his own 'Hi,' *firm handshake,* he thought. Langdon's hand tingled where he had touched the other boy, and he felt a magnetic pull, his stomach knotting, as a zap of desire ran through his body.

'What are you guys doing now? Want to grab a drink in the café?' Finn looked at Langdon, a smile curling on his lips, then he glanced at Hayley.

Langdon was about to say no; his heart was already hammering in his chest.

'Oh yes! Can we please?' begged Hayley. She looked longingly at her brother, hoping for a 'yes'.

Langdon sighed, 'Sure, why not.'

With that, the three of them walked casually to the café situated at the entrance to the dance hall.

Approaching the counter to order, Hayley asked, 'Can I have a Coke?' she looked up sweetly between Langdon and Finn.

Langdon, still reeling from these unknown feelings he was experiencing, agreed absentmindedly with a short, 'Yup.' He felt he would have said yes to anything right now.

Finn strode to the counter first before looking at Langdon expectantly, 'Coke?' he asked. Seeing Langdon's nod, he gave the order.

Langdon raised his eyebrows, 'Yeah, thanks.' He hadn't expected Finn to pay. *What the?* 'Here...' Langdon handed over a ten-dollar note to Finn, shoving it towards Finn's outstretched hand on the counter with his own money.

'Nah, man, it's fine, my treat,' Finn smiled at him. That glorious, intoxicating smile…and was that, yes, oh, a very pronounced dimple in his left cheek. *Don't keep staring!* he scolded himself.

Langdon tried to smile back and took a step backwards, mumbling, 'Thanks, I'll get a table.'

Hayley, not taking any notice of the boys, was admiring the sweets in the window. By the time she had dragged her eyes away from the divine-looking chocolate cake, her brother had moved off to sit at a table near the window. She quickly followed and sat in the chair opposite to wait for her Coke.

Finn sat next to Langdon, *too close,* placing the Coke cans on the small table as he sat down. *This table is too small,* Langdon was uncertain about their proximity. Still wearing his dancer attire, Finn's legs were exposed from where the material of what looked like bike pants ended above his knee. Langdon tried not to stare at Finn's legs. The material didn't hide the definition of his muscles.

As the three were drinking their Cokes, Langdon averted his vision to stare at people walking in and out of the dance studio.

'You were good today, Finn!' Hayley said as she smiled up at him.

'Oh, thanks Hayley,' he gave her a grin. 'You did better with your pirouettes this week,' he repaid her compliment.

Hayley positively glowed at the praise.

Finn, drawing his attention over to Langdon, asked, 'So, this is the big brother you've told me about?'

'Yup,' she said between sips of her drink. Hayley grinned, swinging her legs under the table.

'So, what school do you go to?' Finn turned his attention to Langdon.

'BMNH—ah, Blue Mountains North High,' answered Langdon, finally making himself look at Finn.

'Oh, that's why I haven't seen you around, I go to Wentworth Falls South High.'

Langdon nodded, looking into Finn's deep brown eyes. He was trying to think of something to say. He didn't want to just sit there in silence! This was feeling awkward. Thankfully, Hayley grabbed his attention.

'Lang, can I play on your phone?' she asked between sips of her Coke.

'Sure,' he said, happy for the distraction, and handed it over.

Hayley grabbed it from his fingers with raised eyebrows. He *never* let her have his phone.

'Are you into any sports or rec activity?' Finn stared back at Langdon, his knee brushing against Langdon's leg.

Langdon jumped, the feeling sweeping through his veins, his leg was touching Finn's! And Finn didn't seem at all concerned. He tried moving around his seat to hide his initial reaction and responded a little later. 'I play rugby league with the school, and karate at the Martial Arts Centre.' Langdon sat straighter and puffed out his chest trying to appear as strong as possible, and an image of the recent sparring he had during a lesson popped into his mind.

Finn nodded, and Langdon had to hide his grin by having a mouthful of his drink. He saw Finn's eyes roaming his chest, his abs, and back to his mouth. Nerves still fluttered around his body, but he wanted to get to know Finn better. 'Have you been dancing for long?' he finally thought to ask

When Langdon spoke, he noticed Finn staring at his mouth. While waiting for Finn to answer, it gave him an excuse to stare back.

Finally, Finn spoke. 'Yeah, I did ballet a few years back to help with posture and alignment. I've done hip-hop for the last two years and also gymnastics, which I've been doing for five years now. That is where I learnt flips.' Finn's mouth curled at the edges, his dimple popping out.

Langdon, drawing his eyes away from Finn's mouth, said, 'Oh, that's cool.' *What would it be like to kiss those lips*, the thought entered his head.

Hayley, who had been sitting quietly playing on Langdon's phone, broke the tension, exclaiming, 'Langdon! It's almost six, Mum will be wondering where we are.'

Langdon quickly glanced at his watch to confirm the time, then looked back at Finn. 'Thanks for the Coke, but, um, we have to get going.' He stood, 'Come on, Hayley, get your things.' Hayley handed his phone back as she gathered her gear.

'Sure, no worries,' said Finn. 'Hey, you um, want to get together later in the week?' Finn asked tentatively.

'Sure,' Langdon replied, excited at the prospect, though unsure why or what they would do. 'Where do you want to go?'

Finn exhaled in relief, 'I finish gym at five on Wednesdays. We could meet up at the Aquatic Centre to cool off?'

'Sure,' agreed Langdon, dreamily staring back at Finn.

'Great, do you have your phone? We should swap numbers.'

Langdon gave his phone to Finn and received Finn's in return. He quickly entered his number and handed it back, their fingers touching again, pausing in the exchange. Langdon felt that spark once more.

'Yeah, okay, see ya,' Langdon turned and hurried away, but he turned to look over his shoulder at Finn, only to see Finn staring right back at him.

On the drive home with Hayley, Langdon was deep in thought when Hayley asked, 'Are you going out with Finn?'

'What?' His thoughts were interrupted. 'Yeah, going to the aquatic centre—why?'

Hayley giggled, 'Because he's gay! I think he likes you.'

Langdon frowned, 'Don't be silly, it's not like that. We're just getting together as mates.' He glanced at his sister, and Hayley was grinning, staring back at him. *I bet she's making this up so that I ask him to his face if he's gay, and then I'd be embarrassed if he says 'no.'*

Chapter 10

Wednesday afternoon came quicker than Langdon could get his feelings about Finn in order. He had played that Monday afternoon over and over in his mind.

"He's gay."

Langdon could not understand why he had kept staring at Finn and wondered why he felt so nervous and captivated. Not to mention his body's reaction. Every time he saw or thought of Finn, he got an erection. *This is silly. I am not attracted to boys!* thought Langdon. *Anyway, he's just a mate. We're only meeting up to hang out. There's nothing else to it. I've kissed girls before; I find girls attractive. I'm straight...* Even though these thoughts consumed his mind, he tried to fight his feelings. There was still an inexplicable attraction to Finn.

'Yo dude!' Tom slapped Langdon on the back as they walked to catch the bus home from school. 'What's going on with you? I just asked if you wanted to come back to mine this afternoon?'

Langdon, leaving his thoughts still rumbling around in his head, looked at his friend. 'Sorry, not with it today. I'm um, doing something, er, something for Mum.'

'What?' Looking back at Langdon, Tom could see the worry in his eyes. However, if Langdon was struggling with something, Tom always had to wait it out. Langdon was not one to spill what was on his mind.

'Er, she wants my help with putting her new side table together,' Langdon lied.

Tom seemed happy with that, and they walked on.

Tom, Beau and Langdon had managed to get seats together in the back of the bus, but it was difficult to talk because of all the noise. The noise seemed too much for Langdon. Everything just seemed louder. He sat there in silence while Tom and Beau chatted about playing *Fortnite*.

Langdon's mind whirled with thoughts of Finn and meeting up with him later that afternoon. Blocking the noise, the best he could, Langdon stared out the window, still lost in thought.

When they arrived home, Langdon's thoughts went to his stomach as it let out a growl. *Starving again, shit! This hunger!* Langdon felt like he could keep eating forever. He walked into the kitchen and filled up on a couple of toasted sandwiches before going up to his room to wait until it was time to meet Finn.

He lay on his bed and stared out the window, watching as other kids from the neighbourhood arrived home from school.

Langdon knew he had about an hour's bike ride to the aquatic centre from his house, so at 3:45 p.m., he was glad his mum pulled into the driveway so he could leave. Hayley was not allowed to stay home alone. Not until she was sixteen. Sometimes, Langdon hated having to hang around to be there for his little sister. He had asked to borrow the car, but his mum had said no because she was heading out to the shops and would take Hayley with her.

Eager to leave, Langdon ran down the stairs. He called out a quick hello to her and let her know he was off. Langdon had already told her about meeting a friend after school.

He pulled his bike out of the carport and started riding. Had his stamina gone up? *Why is peddling so easy today?* He checked to make sure he didn't have it set in low gear. Nope, it was set to normal. He rode fast through the streets and pathways and found himself at the aquatic centre in forty minutes. *Google Maps said this would take over an hour,* he thought. Langdon shrugged it off, thinking that taking the pathways was a shortcut.

Looking at his watch, he saw it was 4:30 p.m. He was early. All he could do was sit on the steps out the front and wait. To keep himself occupied, he checked out who else was around.

There were many people around him, including parents scolding noisy kids, toddlers crying, and a couple by the fence in a warm embrace. A girl at the top of the stairs was in her swimmers, with a towel wrapped around her waist, on her phone texting. The palm trees surrounding the entrance and larger trees on the sidewalk provided welcome relief from the sun as he waited. Langdon wiped the sweat dripping from his brow and checked the time again.

There was still no sign of Finn, but Langdon knew he still had time to kill. To amuse himself, Langdon looked around, noticing that if he concentrated, he could hear the conversation of any couple or group, even the couple talking on the other side of the car park. His hearing had been more sensitive lately, although he hardly gave it a second thought. He had so much more to think about — the curse, the full moon, Finn.

After waiting twenty minutes, Langdon got fidgety. He stood and looked at his phone for something to do. Just then, someone tapped his shoulder. Langdon looked up in surprise and came face to face with Finn.

A big grin was plastered on Finn's face as he said, 'Hey! How's it going?'

'Hey,' replied Langdon, a smile spreading across his lips.

'Come on, let's go in and get a good spot near the pool,' said Finn as he strode off.

Langdon watched as his companion's back was exposed after just removing his shirt—the muscles shifting with each move. Just as his eyes were travelling down, Finn stopped and looked over his shoulder, 'You coming?' he asked, eyebrows raised.

'Yeah.' Langdon hurried to catch up.

They walked into the aquatic centre and set their towels and backpacks on the bench near the pool. As Finn placed his bag on the bench, Langdon noticed a badge pinned to the top left side. It was a rainbow flag. Langdon knew immediately what this represented. *LGBTQ. Ok, now this makes sense,* he thought. *Hayley wasn't making it up to embarrass me.*

'Race ya!' challenged Finn, as he took four big strides and jumped into the pool. He looked over his shoulder, his mouth curling into a sexy, inviting smirk, and then he turned and started swimming freestyle, fast. Finn was a great swimmer, he was athletic all round, Langdon noticed.

Langdon smiled and did the same. Jumping in, he easily caught up and was deliberately swimming stroke for stroke with Finn. They swam ten laps of the fifty-metre pool, racing and egging each other on. Finn, clearly fit and fast, was matching Langdon with each stroke. But Langdon, with his newly found adrenaline was not even pushing himself, although he did not let on to Finn and made an extra effort to seem out of breath, matching Finn when they stopped.

Standing at the shallow end, the water came up just above their midsections. Langdon wiped the water from his face and looked at Finn. They were close. Finn was staring at him, but he quickly ran his hand through his cropped hair and splashed water onto Langdon's face.

'Ugh!' Langdon wiped his face, and before Finn could do anything else, he returned the gesture. The two of them were laughing and dodging the other's attempts to dunk each other underwater. Finn's hands touched Langdon's shoulders firmly as he pushed down, pushing Langdon underwater, Langdon was so surprised by the touch, and the electricity he felt, that he went with it. But Finn let go, so Langdon quickly rose to the top, grinning.

After their fun, they stood slightly apart against the pool wall. Finn made no attempt to touch Langdon or bring up the subject of relationships. He was enjoying himself and the company and wanted to take it slow. Glancing at Langdon now as water dripped down his face, he saw the smoothness of Langdon's attractive face, the masculine jawline, and his full lower lip. Finn had to stop staring; he was getting turned on. He looked away. Finn breathed a couple of long, deep breaths to steady himself and glanced back at Langdon. He still couldn't get a read about how Langdon felt about him.

Langdon had his arms propped up on the pool edge, his back resting up against the wall as he glanced back at Finn. Their eyes met, and his heart beat faster. The intensity he felt, demanding all of his senses confused the hell out of him, and he did not know if he wanted to punch Finn in the face… or kiss him. *Finn's face— chiselled, soft features, yet intense* — Langdon felt sexually attracted to him. *No, no, oh God,* his arousal had him hard again.

Langdon splashed Finn and dove away under the water, way under, right to the bottom. He had swum a couple of meters when he felt a tug on his leg, then a hand on his upper back before Finn swam back up to the top. Langdon came up for air, sucking in all his lungs could manage. He felt exhilarated and was trying to push down any feelings he thought he was having for Finn. Finn… where was Finn?

Looking around, Langdon found him climbing out of the pool and wrapping his towel loosely around his tanned hips. Langdon could feel Finn's eyes on him as he swam to the edge and pushed himself up and out. A small smile played on Finn's lips as he watched the manoeuvre tightening the muscles in Langdon's chest, his biceps flexing, the boardshorts low on his hips.

Finn quickly averted his vision as Langdon walked over to the bench to grab his towel.

'You all right?' asked Langdon.

'Yeah,' replied Finn, looking innocently at Langdon.

'Wanna grab a drink?' Langdon asked, looking around. 'And sit somewhere?' He added. He didn't want the afternoon to end.

'Sure,' replied Finn.

'Coke?'

Finn nodded.

'My treat!' Langdon grinned cheekily and strolled over to the cafe.

*

Finn waited and mulled over how to progress. He was still trying to get a feel for Langdon. He didn't want to make a fool of himself if Langdon was repelled by his sexuality. What confused Finn was Langdon's body language. The staring, the grins, puffing his chest, not minding when their fingers touched and, in the pool, just now, was Langdon turned on? *He's so hot*, Finn was aching to kiss him, to see what his lips felt like against his. Finn glanced over and saw Langdon was returning, holding a large packet of chips and two drinks.

'Let's go over there,' Langdon pointed to a grassy area off to the side and away from other families and kids.

Finn nodded and followed Langdon to the area he suggested. *This is a bit more private*, thought Finn. Perhaps he would just ask Langdon if he was interested in him *that way*. They spread out their towels next to each other and sat on them. Langdon handed Finn his Coke.

'Thanks,' their fingers brushed together as Finn accepted the drink. Langdon felt tingles when they touched. He wanted to grab Finn's hand, feel his long fingers in his.

They both opened their drinks and sculled until Langdon stopped… and burped.

Finn laughed and let out a louder burp.

Langdon laughed and reached over to grab the chips. He opened the bag of Doritos and offered some to Finn. Finn put his hand in and pulled out a few, hoping to put his hand in at the same time as Langdon to get more. He wanted their fingers to brush against each other again; he loved the spark he felt.

For the next few minutes, they sat watching the families and other teenagers in the pool and around the sides

Langdon looked over at Finn, and he felt nervous again. Without a second thought, he leaned over and wiped a crumb off Finn's chin. Rethinking his move, he quickly shot his arm back and planted it on the ground. Embarrassed, heat covered his cheeks. He quickly rubbed his cheek, feeling the heat, and tried to backtrack. 'Sorry, just saw that crumb and, er, um,' Langdon struggled to find the words. He had been aching to touch Finn, but still would not accept that there was any attraction between them. He desperately tried to ignore his body's ache to touch Finn.

Finn laughed, 'Don't worry about it, I wouldn't want to go walking around with crumbs on my chin!' He mockingly flicked his own chin and flashed Langdon a wicked grin.

Langdon quickly recovered and leaned back on his arms. Both boys were sitting in their swim shorts, with no shirts on. He leaned back, legs outstretched, and closed his eyes for a second. Finn was sitting in a similar position, and all of a sudden he put his hand next to Langdon's, touching. Langdon didn't mind, and when Finn moved his hand to overlap their pinkie fingers, he thought it felt nice. For a second, Langdon thought he could pick up nervous energy, but dismissed it.

With their fingers overlapped, Langdon thought it was a subtle move, so he relaxed and went off in a daydream about meeting Eric when Finn brought him back, saying, 'Hey, Langdon?'

'Yeah?' he still had his eyes closed.

'I'm trying to get a feel for… for what this is. Do you…. do you see us as friends? Or something more?' Finn glanced at Langdon, waiting for him to either laugh in his face or tell him he felt something, too.

Langdon's eyes opened, shock reverberating within him. He slowly looked in Finn's direction. He tried to swallow, but his mouth had gone dry. Langdon was feeling some sort of powerful attraction to Finn, but he couldn't bring himself to admit anything out loud. His mind was saying no, but his body was saying yes.

Finn was looking back at him, his eyes fearful, yet he remained calm and looked sure of himself.

Langdon's mind took over, he just wanted to shut this down. 'Look, I'm straight and I thought we were mates.'

Finn looked visibly hurt, but he said, 'That's okay dude, no harm done.'

They were both quiet for a moment, and then Finn suddenly jumped up, mumbling, 'Back in a minute,' and dashed off towards the back of the amenities.

Langdon's stomach tightened as if he had been punched. He didn't like seeing the hurt look in Finn's eyes. He could actually feel the despair radiating off the other boy. It made Langdon's heart ache. *What have I done?* he asked himself; *I didn't mean it!*

Langdon jumped to his feet and followed to where Finn had just turned behind the amenities block. What he saw shocked him.

'Fuck! I'm such an idiot,' Finn was exclaiming as he punched his fist against the wall and turned just in time to see Langdon standing there watching him. Finn's face crumpled in anguish, and he quickly composed himself as he looked into Langdon's eyes.

Their eyes locked.

'No,' Langdon spoke firmly. 'I'm the idiot.' He slowly walked over to Finn with a deliberate gait, until he backed Finn up against the wall and gently, but firmly, grabbed his arms and pinned them to the side. Heart beating fast, Langdon continued staring into Finn's eyes as he leaned in and pressed his lips against Finn's. So gentle and lingering. Waiting to see what Finn's reaction would be. Once, twice, their lips brushed. Still pinning Finn against the wall, Langdon now had his hips close and touching Finn, with both of their chests expanding and contracting quickly.

Finn attempted to push Langdon back. He whispered, 'Are you sure?'

'Yes,' breathed Langdon, his body becoming hot.

Finn grabbed Langdon's face and kissed him hard. Langdon had been aching to kiss Finn like this since seeing him at the dance studio. Unlike their hesitant first kisses, this one deepened, tongues meeting eagerly. Their tongues met. Pressing closer, Finn explored Langdon's mouth, and Langdon enjoyed the taste and feel of Finn's tongue against his. They kissed passionately, hungrily, holding each other close.

Langdon moaned, *Oh, this feels so good.*

Before he could get too lost, he pulled back, breathing hard and fast, as he stared into Finn's eyes and grinned.

They were both panting harshly.

He let go of Finn's arms and tried to regain his composure before he would combust.

Finn, though just as affected, was the first to speak. 'Friends?' he asked, raising his left eyebrow. A smile tugged the corner of his mouth.

Langdon shook his head, smiling, and let out a small sigh, 'Yeah, well, I guess, more than friends.' He looked back at Finn with his eyebrows raised.

Langdon was still trying to understand what he was feeling here and wanted to get home to think, but at the same time, he didn't want to leave Finn.

Finn took a step forward and drew a line across Langdon's chest and said, 'Just don't go breaking my heart.' He stared into Langdon's beautiful ocean-blue eyes, and his words were heartfelt and somewhat pleading.

Langdon felt irrevocably connected to Finn. He grabbed Finn's hand and kissed it. Then he shook his head. 'Never, let's see where this goes.'

Langdon was still hard and shifted his board shorts to not draw attention, although Finn caught the discreet manoeuvre and grinned, and his dimple showed. Langdon glanced down and saw Finn in the same predicament. They smiled at one another and went back to sit on their towels.

The conversation now came easily. Langdon explained how he had never been with a boy and apologised for what he said earlier. Then he admitted having an attraction to him After admitting his attraction, he wanted to find out about Finn's past.

'Have you always known? You know…'

Finn chuckled. 'Yeah, kinda. When I was younger, I tried to get interested in girls. In year eight, I asked one out and kissed her just to try it, but it did nothing for me. Couldn't take my eyes off the football team!' he chuckled again.

Langdon emitted a small chuckle as well. *He would have been checking me out if we went to the same school!*

'Langdon, can I ask — well, tell me if this is too forward, but were you checking me out during my dance class?'

'That obvious, huh?' Langdon smirked and raised his eyebrows.

Finn chuckled and bumped his elbow against Langdon's arm. 'I couldn't get a read on you! Usually, I can tell if a guy is straight or gay. But you, shit, you had me guessing.'

'If I'm being honest, I still don't think of myself as gay.' When he saw the look on Finn's face, he quickly added, 'Sorry, don't get me wrong, I am attracted to you, it's just that you're the first boy I've liked.'

Finn was still frowning, so Langdon said, 'Shit, I'm not good at this.'

Finn reached over and had a few of their fingers touching. 'It's okay, take your time.'

'Well, I can't get you out of my head.'

'Wow,' Finn breathed, 'your eyes are gorgeous. They're such a piercing blue that I can't stop staring into them.'

Langdon blushed and looked away for a second. He'd been staring into Finn's eyes, but couldn't articulate what he liked.

'Sorry, I can't get you out of my head either,' Finn admitted.

'So, have you had past boyfriends?' Langdon finally got the courage to ask.

Finn told him he'd been in relationships with a few guys, with only one being kind of serious.

They sat side by side, their hands only just touching. They could both feel the sexual chemistry, the curious magnetic pull. They were drawn to each other.

All too soon, it was time for them to head home. They were saying goodbye on the steps when Langdon invited Finn over Friday afternoon. 'Come over around four, I get home from school by three-thirty. And my parents won't be home until six. I'll give you my address.' He held out his hand, 'Phone?'

Finn handed over his phone with Langdon's contact page open.

Langdon quickly typed in his address and handed it back, smiling, brushing his fingers purposefully against Finn's again.

'Okay, see you then.' Finn smiled and quickly, but discreetly brushed his fingers over Langdon's before turning and walking over to his vehicle.

Langdon rode home in a daze, playing the afternoon over and over in his mind. *This* he was keeping to himself.

Chapter 11

Thursday seemed to drag on for Langdon. One positive outcome was that he had the car because his parents were working late, and he had wanted to stay after school to visit the library and use their computer and possibly some books to research werewolves. He'd gotten out of karate, saying he had to do research for an assignment, and his mother was pleased he was showing interest in his schoolwork, saying that missing one lesson would be okay.

This is probably all bullshit, thought Langdon. *I probably won't turn into anything during the next full moon. But....*

Langdon was pulled out of his thoughts by his foot being kicked. They were in math class; it was the last class of the day and the teacher was rambling on about superannuation and calculating tax brackets for different wages.

'What's going on with you!' Tom whispered, his voice edged with insistence.

'Thinking about you know what,' Langdon responded quietly.

'Yeah, sorry I can't come to the library with you.'

'No worries, Beau's coming.'

'Great,' Tom raised his eyebrows. 'This is a turnaround!' Tom whispered back.

'Well, since our visit back to that castle…' Langdon paused and glanced at the teacher before continuing. 'Um, I guess he's okay.'

The bell rang, and as the students were dismissed, Langdon said goodbye to Tom and raced to his backpack. The library was practically on the other side of the school, a fast three-minute walk had Langdon arriving excited about what they might find. Beau was standing out the front waiting for him, one leg crossed over the other, and his bag lay next to him on the ground.

'Hey Beau,' Langdon greeted. He tried being more friendly toward Beau since he offered to help with research, considering he used to be notoriously sarcastic to him.

'Hey,' replied Beau. He smiled, tossed his backpack onto the port rack and followed Langdon inside to the back of the library where the computers were.

'So, we're looking for information to see if there is such a thing as werewolves and if there is anything on the "werewolf curse" and also if there is a cure.' Langdon breathed out heavily, the task weighing on his mind.

'Right, okay,' agreed Beau. He had already logged on to his computer and was searching.

Langdon logged on and began as well.

After a few minutes, Langdon stated, 'It says here that werewolves are mythological animals, and then it talks about legends and how if you are bitten or scratched by a werewolf, it is a curse, and you will turn into a wolf when there's a full moon.' His face fell. This was not the information he wanted to see.

The frown he wore made Beau mirror him with a frown as well. Beau, in his searches, both in books and on the internet had found much of the same information. 'Hey, let's look up cures; there must be something,' encouraged Beau.

He immediately modified his search engine to words relating to werewolf cures. Scanning his eyes thoroughly over each site, he finally thought he had something. 'Langdon! Check this out,' Beau pointed excitedly at his screen.

Langdon turned to Beau's screen, and right before his eyes was information about a plant. 'Anethum graveolens: it says here, it is a plant found all over the world. It has healing properties such as antimicrobial, anti-inflammatory and wound healing.' Langdon read. Both Langdon and Beau were staring at the picture.

'I'll write that one down,' said Beau, getting out his notepad. 'Also, I found another one called wolfsbane, but it only grows in Europe, Asia, and North America. Not much help to us here in Australia. Oh, never mind, it says it's poisonous anyway, with fatal consequences. Gee, I'm glad that one isn't here then.' Beau had his eyebrows raised, looking closely at the screen.

Langdon typed, *healing herbs in the Blue Mountains—werewolf cure*, he added the last bit and crossed his fingers. Site after site about Aboriginal culture or private practitioners showed up, and he ignored the ones about the Netflix series related to werewolves. So many links were related to popular teen movies or a series about werewolves.

'Hey Beau, check this out, it says there's a hierarchy. There's the Alpha—the one in charge, the Beta—the one who comes under the Alpha and then the Omega who has no pack.'

'Yeah, I've heard that, but check this out. A study by Dr L. David Mech, a leading expert on wolves, says that the concept of the Alpha/Beta/Omega wolves comes from flawed, outdated science. He said that the Alpha is just the parents and the kids are the offspring. You know, there probably aren't even that many wolves in reality. Eric has an extensive property and has never seen one, other than the one that bit him. I think there's a lot of made-up stuff on the internet.'

Langdon continued his search for a cure and clicked on the site of Aboriginal culture for a look. Clicking his mouse on the side tabs, he found healing waters and healing plants; he read page after page. But he was disappointed to not find the information he was seeking. 'Ugh, this is fucking useless!' He let out a low groan but kept his eyes on the screen, unwilling to give up.

Beau, having no further luck, looked over at Langdon.

Langdon ran his fingers through his messy hair in frustration, scrunching his hand into a fist as he grabbed the ends, then released his hand to flop onto his lap. A glance in Beau's direction told him Beau was deep in thought. Langdon looked back at his screen, feeling hopeless.

Beau nudged him. 'Hey, I have an idea.'

Langdon looked over expectantly, raising his eyebrows in question.

'Didn't you say that Eric had old diaries from his uncle? There might be something in one of those.'

'Nah,' said Langdon. 'Eric said he'd read all of those and found nothing, only some ramblings about wolves.'

'Yeah, but it's an old castle, and what if there's some hidden compartments or something?' Beau suggested.

'Doubt it. I'm sure Eric would know about it if there were.' Langdon glanced away, thinking about the possibility.

'Are you going to go out there for the next full moon, like he offered?' asked Beau.

Langdon thought about it and replied, 'I don't think so. I mean, I doubt it will even affect me. I still don't know if I believe in all this,' he confided in Beau.

Langdon's friends could tell that he was clearly struggling emotionally after meeting Eric and hearing about the curse. He knew he'd been distant lately, but the wolf curse wasn't the only thing on his mind, and he wasn't ready to talk about that yet.

'Langdon,' Beau paused. 'Let me know if there's anything I can do to help. You can stay at mine anytime, and I can cover for you.'

Langdon, looking back at Beau, finally saw why Tom was friends with him. Beau might be a skinny nerd, interested in computer games, but he looked out for his mates. Now Langdon felt like they were mates too. He smiled at Beau and nodded his thanks.

After a few more minutes of searches that provided no new information, Langdon huffed and said, 'Let's get out of here.'

The boys turned the computers off and packed up their books.

Walking back outside, Langdon turned to Beau, 'Thanks for your help with that,' he said sincerely.

'No worries,' Beau smiled at him.

Langdon had offered Beau a ride home, so they walked off together and chatted more about Eric and what the next full moon might bring. After Langdon dropped Beau home, he drove himself home and was feeling somewhat better. He pulled his parents' car into the carport and went inside. His parents were home, sitting in the lounge room watching the news when he walked in.

'Hi love,' called his mum. 'Dinner will be in twenty minutes if you want to go have a shower.'

'Okay, thanks.'

Langdon went upstairs to his bedroom and pulled out his phone. He had been thinking about Finn. They had swapped numbers at the aquatic centre, and Langdon was keen to see if there were any messages. He didn't want to check when he was with Beau, although he felt his phone buzz while they were at the library. Looking at his phone, he read -

Hi, CU2MR.

Langdon smiled and texted back. ☺ *can't wait.*

Chapter 12

On Friday afternoon, Langdon could not wait for the bus ride to be over. Tom and Beau had already gotten off at their bus stop, and Langdon's was two stops away from theirs. The kids on the bus were annoyingly relentless with noise. Langdon had to put his AirPods in for a distraction, but his normal volume setting was now much too loud for his sensitive ears.

After getting off the bus at their stop, Langdon and Hayley walked the remaining five minutes to their house.

'What are your plans this afternoon, Hayls?' Langdon asked, looking towards his sister. She came up to Langdon's shoulder, thin and athletic like him from years of dance.

'Bit of homework, and then I'm going to read my book.' She looked up at Langdon with a questioning frown.

'Well, I'm having a mate over, so make yourself scarce.' He said, trying to sound casual.

'Who? Is it Tom?'

'No.'

'Beau?'

'No, it's.... Finn. You know from dancing?'

'Oh cool, I like Finn!'

'Yeah, well, stay out of our way all right,' he added.

'All right,' she agreed as they walked to their front door. 'What time do Mum and Dad get home?'

'Probably around six tonight, Mum's got exam marking, remember?'

'Oh yeah, that's right.'

They walked inside and went straight to the kitchen after dumping their bags in the entryway. After grabbing a bite, Langdon went up to his bedroom to look out his window. He checked the time, seeing it was 3:45 p.m. Beginning to feel anxiety in the pit of his stomach, Langdon began pacing.

Suddenly thinking about how he looked, he wandered into the bathroom and glanced in the mirror. Then, after seeing a soft shadow of fair hair on his face, he moved his jaw from side to side, thinking he was nearly due for a shave. But it gave him a rugged look that he admired. He ran his hand through his messy hair, but there was no taming it. Then, he rolled his shoulders to ease the growing tension and walked back into his bedroom to look out the window again.

Still no sign of him. How am I supposed to greet Finn? I don't want to attack him like I did at the aquatic centre. Will he make the first move? ....

A knock at the front door pulled Langdon from his thoughts. He raced down, making sure Hayley was in her room as he walked by.

Langdon opened the door and saw Finn standing on his doorstep. He smiled. Finn smiled back. Finn was wearing a blue Rip Curl shirt that he filled out well, paired with black shorts. *God, he's gorgeous, I just want to… ugh, stop it!* Langdon mentally scolded himself.

'Hey,' Langdon greeted shyly, a smile curling the corner of his lips.

'Hey,' Finn greeted confidently back, smiling, as he stared into Langdon's ocean-blue eyes. They didn't appear as bold or piercing as he'd seen before, and Langdon seemed nervous but calmer.

'Come on in,' Langdon moved to the side and allowed Finn to walk past him.

'Thanks,' Finn smiled and met his eyes.

'Can I get you anything? Water? Juice? Coke?' *Me?*

'Um, no I'm good, thanks,' Finn's eyes wandered around the entryway, noticing the family photos.

'You sure? I'm having a Coke…'

'Oh, okay, yeah, that'd be nice, thanks.'

Finn followed Langdon into the kitchen and looked around at how spacious it was. The bench tops were mostly black mixed with a deep blue laminate, and the doors were made from lightly stained timber, and it was a generous size. Langdon opened the refrigerator door and grabbed two Cokes, handing one to Finn.

'Come on,' said Langdon, 'let's go into the loungeroom.'

Finn followed Langdon into a massive lounge room. He looked around, seeing a deep blue three-seater leather couch and two recliners, one on each side. There was a large blue and tan rug covering most of what looked like a timber floor and a massive TV sitting on a low cabinet. DVDs were piled high on each of the timber box-style shelves. There was also a timber coffee table in the middle of the room. Finn looked back at Langdon, unsure of what to do. He was feeling nervous as well.

Langdon sat on the three-seater couch and placed his Coke on the coffee table. He looked expectantly at Finn, so Finn sat next to him, close, but not touching.

'Gee, glad it's Friday,' Langdon quipped, staring at the floor, suddenly finding the patterns in the rug remarkably interesting. He cleared his throat, nerves winding from the pit of his stomach up to his abdomen like butterflies.

Langdon could feel Finn's eyes on him, and it made him nervous. Then, with his eyes still glued to the rug, he felt Finn's hand move closer so that their pinkies were now touching. Langdon wasn't sure what to do. His breaths were coming shorter and sharper, and he felt Finn's energy next to him. It appeared Finn was waiting for something because Finn had told him he'd been with other guys.

Finn moved his hand on top of his and started caressing with his thumb. His touch sent shivers down Langdon's spine. He felt a pleasant warmth, as if a blanket had been placed over his shoulders. Langdon felt like he needed to be closer, so he purposefully relaxed his leg to the side so that now their knees were also touching.

Langdon's breathing quickened, he liked the feel of Finn's callused thumb. The gentle gesture was making his hand tingle, echoing through his body.

'You okay?' Finn asked in a soft voice.

'Yup,' Langdon's voice hitched. 'I'm good,' he murmured, trying to maintain his composure.

Finn knew he had to take this slow, so he made small talk about school and talked about his interests in hip-hop and gymnastics.

Langdon relaxed a bit more and responded with talk of sparring and the different techniques he learned at karate.

Langdon began to feel more comfortable and noticed they had a few things in common. Finn also liked working out at the gym to develop his body strength for bar work at gymnastics.

'I usually do twelve exercises, three sets of each, and a couple of them are supersets.' Finn answered Langdon's question about his programme at the gym. 'What about you?'

'Yeah, similar supersets, although lately I've been doing split training,' replied Langdon.

Langdon looked over at Finn, noticing his brown eyes staring at his legs. He continued watching Finn as Finn's eyes travelled up and met Langdon's eyes, locking them in intense desire. Finn leaned over, closing the small space between them, Langdon could feel Finn's breath as his lips brushed his own. His body still, Langdon leaned in further to deepen the kiss, his hand moving to rest on Finn's thigh. Finn moaned softly at the touch and shifted closer.

Meanwhile, Hayley, feeling like having a snack, left her bedroom and ran down the stairs, hoping to see Finn. She walked into the kitchen and rummaged around in the pantry, deciding on a packet of chocolate Tiny Teddies. Opening the packet, she headed to the lounge room where she expected her brother and Finn to be playing on the Xbox.

As soon as he heard his sister in the kitchen, Langdon pulled away from Finn. He moved to put space between them. Apologetically, he said, 'I don't want my sister to know about us yet.'

'That's okay,' Finn assured him, his eyebrows lifted slightly.

Hayley strode in casually to the loungeroom eyeing her brother and Finn sitting on the couch. They looked like they had been deep in conversation. She walked closer, staring at Finn. 'Hi Finn,' she smiled as she walked over to sit on the recliner.

'Hi Hayley, how's things?' Finn asked, composing himself well by casually placing his foot onto his knee and turning slightly in her direction.

'Good,' she replied, staring back, munching on her snack.

No one said anything then. The room went quiet. Langdon willed his sister to look at him and away from Finn, annoyed that she did not stay away. After what seemed like ten minutes, but was probably only two, Langdon was becoming increasingly frustrated.

Hayley glanced at her brother to find him glaring, his eyes drilling holes into her. Langdon scrunched his nose and tilted his head in the direction he wanted her to go. Getting the message loud and clear, she jumped up, saying she had an English assignment to work on, and quickly left.

Finn laughed quietly and looked at Langdon.

Langdon looked back at him and shook his head. 'Sisters!'

'That's okay,' Finn smiled at him.

Staring into Langdon's eyes, Finn whispered, 'I like you, okay… a lot. I know this is new for you, and we can go at any pace you're comfortable with.'

Langdon swallowed. 'I like you too,' he said, 'but can we keep this between us?'

'Absolutely,' Finn agreed.

They both leaned in, still staring into each other's eyes. Langdon placed his hand behind Finn's head to pull him closer. Finn, already breathing heavily with desire, leaned the rest of the way to lock lips with Langdon. Passion overcame them both, their kiss deepened, and Langdon demanded more as he thrust his tongue inside. He dragged his other hand down Finn's chest, down his toned stomach to rest it high on Finn's thigh, close, too close to his manhood, yet his fingers ached to feel more. Still locked in the intensity of the kiss, Finn's breathing caught in his throat. He moved his hand from Langdon's jaw to put his hand on top of Langdon's, stopping it from going further.

'Stop,' Finn pulled his mouth to kiss near Langdon's ear, then he whispered, 'unless you want me to take this further, right here, right now.'

In response, Langdon's breathing turned heavier, his heart beating fast. He wanted to take Finn back to his room…

The carport door went up, and they both stopped upon hearing the sound, Langdon's eyes widened but seeing Finn's questioning look he softened his features with a half-smile. 'Sorry, my mum just arrived home, ah…'

"It's okay," Finn also smiled, and they both leaned in, their foreheads touching as they tried to even their breathing.

Finn gently grabbed hold of Langdon's hands and moved back to stare into his eyes. He smiled, still a little out of breath. 'I should probably get going. When can I see you again?'

'We should get together over the weekend, I have a game on tomorrow afternoon. Why don't we meet somewhere for dinner? Somewhere private,' Langdon suggested.

'I live with my dad, and he goes out Saturday nights, so come by after six, he won't mind if we just grab a pizza and sit on the patio. Dad will just grab a few slices and stay in the lounge room watching TV anyway until about eight when he goes out.'

'Okay, sounds good.' Still holding Finn's hand, Langdon asked, 'Where do you live?'

'Thirty-four Cuttersfield Street, near Sparters Lake,'

Langdon grabbed his phone and quickly typed in the address. 'I know that area. That's about twenty minutes from here.'

'Yeah.' Finn watched as Langdon's fingers typed in the address.

Finn stood and pulled Langdon up, still holding his hand. They strolled out the front, and Langdon could see Finn's car parked on the side of the road - a recent model, silver dual-cab HiLux.

'Nice ride,' Langdon stared appreciatively at Finn's car.

'Thanks, I got it earlier this year.' It suddenly occurred to him that Langdon might not have access to a vehicle for their get-together tomorrow night. 'Want me to pick you up?'

'Nah, that's okay, I'll borrow my parents' car or ride my bike…'

He saw the look on Finn's face, eyebrows raised as if to say. *"ride your bike… are you joking?"*

'Yeah, it's not that far, jeez. I'm used to riding to get places.' Seeing that Finn still looked worried, he added, 'Mum will let me borrow the car, it'll be fine.'

'All right, but if you get stuck, text me,' he added, finally satisfied with Langdon's words.

'Fine, I will, but I'm sure I'll have a ride.'

'Okay, see ya,' Finn said as he squeezed Langdon's hand one more time before letting go and turning to walk to his car.

Langdon watched, a smile playing on his lips as he watched Finn walk away. Finn looked back over his shoulder and saw Langdon still standing there, staring and smiling. A smile caught the edge of Finn's lips as he turned back, climbed into his Ute and drove away.

When his mum walked in through the carport door, she had her arms full of shopping bags. She sighed as she trudged into the kitchen to dump them on the bench. Lifting her handbag from her shoulder, she placed it alongside all the other bags. Langdon walked into the kitchen noticing and peeked inside one.

'Hey Mum,' Langdon greeted her. 'What'd you buy?'

She sighed deeply and plonked herself on the stool, 'Hi, love. Oh, we were out of a few things, and I thought it might be nice to make a stir-fry tonight.'

'Yum sounds good, I'm starving.'

'Well, don't eat too much now,' she said, jumping up and slapping his hand to stop him from opening the chocolate biscuits she'd bought. 'Eat some fruit if you must have something now.'

'Ow, fine.' Langdon turned to the fridge to grab an apple.

As she was unpacking her groceries, she paused, 'Hey hon, whose car was that in front of our house?'

Langdon tried to act casual, 'That was just a friend visiting.' He quickly left the kitchen to avoid any more questions.

Chapter 13

On Saturday afternoon, the school rugby league team was at halftime with their match against Whitehaven School. Ugh, how Langdon hated Whitehaven! It was their rival school, and BM North High had lost several games because of Whitehaven's top player, Derek Priestly. Filling out as a burly, tall, dark-haired star player, he was ruthless on and off the field. Langdon had been roughly tackled many times in the past, and so these past couple of weeks the coach, Mr Dean had been training them intensely with several sprint techniques, gym workouts at the school, and training sessions on the field that left them feeling wrecked.

Their coach huddled the team in a tight circle, 'Williams, I want you on centre right-wing.' As Tom nodded, the coach's brown eyes drilled into Langdon's. 'Core! You need to rein it in. I'm putting you in a half-back position, no more half killing the other team,' he growled as he stared menacingly at Langdon.

Langdon just could not stop staring at his bushy eyebrows and had to hide a smirk with a swipe of his hand under his nose, merely nodding his agreement.

'Jennings and Thompson, wing-back, the rest of you go hard, we're 8-12, we can still win this!' They needed this to get into the semi-finals.

The timer, a loud whirring siren, sounded announcing the end of halftime. Langdon flinched at the harsh sound and had to refrain from covering his ears.

The boys ran back out onto the field and into their positions. Langdon now had to take it easy because, in the first five minutes of the first half, he had knocked two players out cold in a tackle and three others to a bad fall when his strong athletic body crashed into them, making them fall to the ground hard and fast. He had to tone down his speed as well, otherwise, he would score every few minutes. He already had blood—not his own — staining his jersey.

The next half of the game saw Langdon slow his speed and agility. However, he still moved quickly and weaved his way past the opposition. He reached the ten-metre line, and Derek's large frame was blocking his path. Langdon ran straight at him, faked a turn at the last second, and pivoted his body to dive past and land over the line, scoring the goal.

The crowd cheered.

Derek growled at him, 'Lucky break, Core, better watch your back.' Langdon just grinned back mockingly.

He continued to play hard, just enough to win the match without drawing too much unwanted attention. Although the coach was incredibly pleased with his last three tries, unpredictably winning the match! The team had raised Langdon up, supporting his weight high in the air, everyone around him cheering and whooping. He was dropped back on solid ground, which made him stumble to regain his footing, but he was then congratulated by the coach, and the entire team grinned, thrilled from the turnaround in the score.

Langdon sauntered over towards his family, his every stride exuding confidence. Grinning, he saw his elation reflected in his parents' smiles. They had been watching the match and were impressed with their son's speed and determination on the field.

'Well done, son!' His father cheered, slapping him on the back.

'Great work out there,' his mum said, throwing her arms around him. He was a head taller than her, and her slight frame was lost in his strong build.

Langdon quickly untangled himself from her, embarrassed but pleased at her praise. 'Mum! Stop it.'

Hayley was standing beside their mum, arms folded, bored and waiting to leave. She flicked her long hair over her shoulder as she watched sweaty, rugged players walk past laughing and speaking loudly. 'Can we go now?' she asked, pleading eyes directed at her mum.

Leah put her arm around Hayley and nodded. Then she looked back at Langdon and Mitchell, motioning everyone to leave. They collected their bags and walked over to the car, Mitchell patting his son on the back again in a proud gesture.

After they arrived home, Langdon ran straight for the shower and made sure to apply deodorant, taking a quick sniff before throwing on his jeans and t-shirt. He ran back downstairs and thanked his mum for the car as he grabbed the keys to see Finn. Langdon had told his parents he was going over to a mate's place for a pizza and promised to be home by ten.

Arriving at Finn's shortly after six, he knocked tentatively at the front door. Langdon ran his hand through his hair in nervous anticipation.

The door opened to a broad yet sculpted, tall man. He resembled Finn, with the same dark features, but looked older. The man greeted him by saying, 'Hello, you must be Landon?'

'Hi, no,' Langdon then corrected him, 'It's Langdon,' he said, emphasising the letter 'g'.

'Oh, Langdon,' said Finn's dad, smiling roguishly.

Langdon just stood there, staring up at him, wondering what to say. But just then, Finn's dad introduced himself, 'I'm Daniel. Come on in, Finn is on the phone ordering dinner.' He stepped aside to allow Langdon to walk inside.

Langdon walked in, and the lounge room was the first thing he saw, noticing it was not quite as large as his own. There was a large LCD TV sitting on a cabinet and a comfortably worn couch with a blue, black, and gold swirl pattern. He followed Finn's dad into the kitchen, where Finn was just hanging up the phone.

'Pizza will be here in twenty minutes.' Finn looked at Langdon, seeing him looking nervous as hell next to his towering father, and smiled, knowing he had to rescue his *friend? Boyfriend?* 'Hey Langdon, come out to the patio, it's nice this time of afternoon,' Finn gestured for him to follow him outside.

'Hi.' Langdon followed Finn past the kitchen, glancing around, he thought it was small but roomy enough for two people and out the sliding door to a spacious, tiled outdoor patio. It had a cover on top and lots of plants of all shapes and sizes around the edges. There was a relaxing feeling drawing Langdon in. He caught the scent of dominant, earthy smells as well as floral and spicy fragrances. The unenclosed patio let in the sun, however, now that it was early evening., downlights offered a soft glow, illuminating a round plastic table in the centre. They were finally alone after Finn's dad left them to go back to the TV.

'So, how are you doing? My dad didn't make an idiot of himself, did he?' Seeing Langdon's face looking too torn to admit anything, he added, 'He likes to joke around.' Finn walked closer, bridging the two-step distance, near enough to lean in and kiss him. But instead, he brushed Langdon's hand and gave a gentle tug to come and sit at the table.

Langdon, feeling slightly better, had felt tingly all over, but followed Finn to sit at the table, not quite opposite each other so that when he stretched his long legs out, they brushed against Finn's equally long legs. Finally, he spoke, 'I'm okay, yeah, I didn't know what to make of your dad.'

'Oh, he's harmless,' Finn assured.

They flowed into easy conversation, Langdon telling Finn all about his game and how they won. Finn told him about the mishaps he'd endured at gymnastics and clarified when he saw Langdon's concerned look, explaining that he worked at the gymnastics centre on Saturdays with little kids.

'Hey,' Langdon paused, wondering how to word his question. 'What did you tell your father about me coming over?' He looked into Finn's brown eyes, wondering how much his dad knew about his son's sexuality.

'Oh, I just said I had a mate coming over for pizza and if something good was on Netflix, we'd watch that.'

Langdon frowned. *Oh, I thought his dad must have known.*

Finn continued, 'Look, I haven't told my dad much about any of my relationships. But he knows I'm gay. He met my previous partner, but didn't know what happened.' He smiled at Langdon in reassurance. Reaching across, he held Langdon's hand, focusing on his fingers as he gently rubbed up and down.

Langdon's cheeks heated, feeling himself getting aroused by Finn's ministrations, his touch causing blood to rush down south. He cleared his throat and shifted restlessly in his seat. Staring at Finn's mouth, and his lips, he unknowingly licked his own bottom lip.

'That's a turn-on when you do that,' Finn nodded at his mouth.

Heat travelled through Langdon like a freight train, hearing Finn speak like that. 'Really?' Was the only response he could think of. He glanced down at Finn's fingers, caressing his thumb, mesmerised.

Hearing a loud knock on the front door, Finn pulled his hand away as his father stuck his head out the sliding door to tell them the pizza had arrived. Langdon followed Finn inside and watched as Finn grabbed a pizza box, leaving his dad with the other, and came back out to the patio.

Getting comfortable, Langdon and Finn hungrily ate until all the pizza was gone, washing it down with cold drinks they had also grabbed as they walked out.

Finn

Sitting back, his hunger satisfied, Finn reached into a nearby shelf and pulled out a pack of cards. He raised his eyebrows at Langdon, who smiled and nodded.

Finn could see that Langdon was nervous, and past experiences showed that a game of cards took the pressure off. Right now, that is what they both needed. Seeing Langdon shift in his seat, clearly aroused, Finn had to avert his eyes. He didn't want to scare Langdon by being too forceful. He knew how to take it slow.

For the next hour, they played card games, not really talking, just content with each other's company. They played on until Finn's dad called out to tell them he was heading out for a bit.

When they heard the car leave, the air became heated with the promise of what was to come. Finn glanced at Langdon shyly and saw Langdon staring back at him. Finn could see the heat in his eyes, confirming he felt more at ease. Finn slowly rose to his feet and grabbed Langdon's hand. Neither of the boys breathed a word as Finn pulled him inside and through to the lounge room, which was dark, the only light coming from the TV's soft glow. The sound was on low and provided a lull of white noise.

Finn pulled Langdon onto the couch, sitting so close that their thighs were touching. He was still holding Langdon's hand. They sat facing each other, their hearts pounding in anticipation. Not wanting to rush in, Finn waited, gauging Langdon's responses.

Langdon stared at Finn's lips. They were so close that their breaths were mingling. Slowly, gently, he ran his free hand along Finn's smooth jawline. He wanted to pull him in, drink in his scent and drown in all that he offered. Inhaling deeply, he picked up the scent of vanilla mixed with something earthy, igniting his senses.

Finn let go of Langdon's hand to caress his cheek, desire sweeping through him. He leaned forward and waited for Langdon to close the distance.

Langdon could feel Finn's breath on his mouth, and unwilling to wait a second more, he snaked his hand behind Finn's head and pulled him closer, their lips finally meeting, melting into a deep, intense kiss.

Finn released a low moan at the contact and moved his hand to feel Langdon's muscular chest after easing his fingers under his shirt. His hand stayed there, touching, exploring the broad expanse of muscles, feeling the bumps of his hardened nipples, the dip of his pecs. Langdon moaned; this was really turning him on. Finn gradually moved his fingers down, reaching Langdon's stomach, and placed them there, gently caressing his fingers along Langdon's toned, smooth abs. Finn could tell that Langdon was enjoying his touch. He moved his fingers lower, exploring more, his fingers slid along the waistband of Langdon's shorts, and he paused. 'Too fast?' Finn breathed.

'Don't stop,' Langdon gasped.

With Finn's mouth, his hands, and the way he was touching his body, Langdon could not think, his emotions were all over the place. His body was reacting in a way it hadn't before, and Finn could tell he was enjoying every touch.

Langdon leaned into Finn, puffing his chest, as Finn moved his hand back up to the front of his chest, pushing him down onto the couch. Both boys' hearts were beating fast, their breathing heavy and unrelenting. Finn progressed his teasing, his fingers skilfully making their way back to the waistband, then placing his hand on the front of Langdon's shorts and with only mild hesitation, he caressed the bulge lightly before gripping it, causing Langdon to inhale sharply.

'Yes,' breathed Langdon, pulling Finn closer as they kept going…

Later, they lay facing each other on the couch, with Finn's arm resting on Langdon's bare skin. As they leisurely recovered their breathing, Langdon nuzzled his face into Finn's neck and sighed. They held each other close until Langdon had to go.

'Do you have any free afternoons this week?' Finn was already looking forward to their next date.

'Too risky for me to come to your dance class. Tuesday, I have footy training until five, so what about Wednesday?'

'Oh, can't. After my gymnastics lesson, I've been rostered on to work with the kids. What about Thursday after school?'

'Sorry, I have karate from five 'till six, and I need to get two assignments done by then. What about Friday night?'

'Friday it is then.' Finn leaned over and kissed Langdon gently on the lips. 'You can come by here again if you like. Dad gets home about five o'clock, but won't care that you're here. Might have to keep it G rated though,' he smiled cheekily, his dimple showing.

They said goodbye, and Langdon was smiling dreamily all the way home.

Chapter 14

All week, Langdon and Finn texted each other. Langdon thought about Finn and how his body had responded to his touch. It made him quiver just thinking about it. He longed to see Finn, touch him, kiss him. He had given hardly any thought to what Eric had told him about the curse. He had pushed that to the back of his mind, and his focus was now on Finn.

He hated lying to his friends about where he was on Saturday night. Tom had asked him over to catch up with him and Beau. They had planned a gaming night, pigging out on pizza and chips, and Tom was going to sneak in some bourbon to go with their Coke. Langdon had said he was busy and had to stay home.

Tom was surprised that Langdon had made an excuse–that wasn't like him at all. Tom knew Langdon was keeping something from him, but he also knew his friend well enough to know that Langdon would tell him when he was ready. *Maybe he's just worried about the next full moon,* Tom had thought.

Tom hadn't spoken much to Langdon in the last few days, except about school. The air was thick with emotion and sweat. He approached Langdon and threw a punch.

He missed.

Grunting in frustration, he adjusted his stance and kicked his foot towards Langdon's stomach. The impact should have knocked him to the ground. But Langdon braced his abs and took a step backward, receiving a minor whoosh of Tom's roundhouse kick.

Tom and Langdon were sparring at karate.

Langdon punched Tom, almost connecting with his jaw, before moving swiftly, pulling his upper body back and to the left to surprise Tom with an uppercut.

Tom dodged, jumping backward.

Tom was sweating, he wiped his brow and glanced at the clock, seeing there were still ten minutes left of their karate class.

Langdon had barely worked up a sweat. He had needed to back down with his powerful blows because it was a non-contact sport. That benefited Tom more so than Langdon because Langdon had quicker reflexes now. He could also hear the swoosh of each punch and his fast roundhouse kicks. Langdon returned a striking punch of his own. Tom moved out of the way just in time. Langdon had premeditated the speed to allow for Tom to duck.

Breaking Langdon and Tom's concentration, the whistle blew loudly. The Sensei was calling them in for stretches.

'So, what did you get up to Saturday night, seeing as you were too busy to come over?' asked Tom, curious to see if Langdon would finally spill what had been going on.

Langdon, trying to act casual, said, 'Oh, Mum and Dad went out, so I had to be home for Hayley.'

Tom looked sceptically at Langdon. *Really? That never stopped him from sneaking out before.* Tom decided to not push it, he had noticed Langdon acting weird at school and put it down to the visit with Eric. It was not the place or time to ask further questions, especially about the next full moon.

'Come over this Saturday night if you're not doing anything. Beau's coming over, and we're planning a gaming night again.'

'Yeah, sure, I'm in for that,' agreed Langdon. He knew he had been shutting his friends out this week, deciding it was time he spent some time with them. He would see Finn the next night, anyway.

***

Friday

School dragged out, the minutes seeming more like hours. Langdon couldn't focus at all on his last lesson. In his religion class, even though the assignment work was set, he was mostly finished, so he used the lesson to play Tetris.

No one did any work on a Friday afternoon anyway. The guy to his left was also playing Tetris, and the girl next to him was watching *Suits* on Netflix.

Langdon glanced at the time on his laptop, counting down the minutes. He was relieved when the bell finally rang. All the kids packed up and practically raced down to their bags. Everyone had somewhere to be.

Langdon had somewhere to be.

He was seeing Finn.

He was aching to see Finn.

*

Arriving at Finn's house soon after 6:00 p.m., he nervously waited for the door to be answered. Langdon wondered how he should greet Finn. Their goodbye a week ago replayed in his mind, thinking Finn had held his hand, then left.

Normally, *he* was the one to instigate a kiss if he were dating a girl–but a boy? *Who takes charge? Finn? Because he had more experience? Or Me?*

Because he had a confident and domineering personality. Mulling this over in his head, he couldn't believe he was overthinking it and silently reprimanded himself. Taking a deep breath, Langdon shuffled his feet impatiently and stared at the door, willing it to open.

A second later, it did. As it opened, he locked eyes with Finn, and a smile automatically curled on his lips. Finn grinned and leaned forward to grab Langdon's hand and close the distance to brush his lips against his. They lingered close and connected again to kiss a bit harder.

Finn pulled away first, smiling, and ushered him inside, saying, 'Come in.'

The way he said it made Langdon's heart skip a beat. He was instantly aroused. Langdon followed Finn inside, and Finn's dad was nowhere to be seen. Finn saw him glancing around and said, 'Dad's in his room.'

Finn linked his fingers through Langdon's and guided him to the lounge room. There was no way Finn was going to take Langdon back to his room when his dad was only in the next room. The walls were paper thin. Finn sat with Langdon on the couch and asked about his week. 'How was karate this week, your grading is getting close, isn't it?'

'Yeah, it's about six weeks away and the sensei, Mr Anderson, has been pushing us harder to learn our blue belt pattern.'

'Do you think you'll go all the way to a black belt?'

Langdon laughed, 'I hope to, but that's a couple of years away. I'll need twelve months of active training as a blue belt before I can go for my brown belt. Then I'll have eighteen months of active training on that level.' He saw the confused look on Finn's face, and added, 'Oh, there's a minimum amount of time you spend on each level.'

'Wow, there're different amounts of time for each belt colour?'

'Yup,' replied Langdon, grinning.

Finn looked impressed, so Langdon told him more about what was required for him to pass his blue belt. Finn told him he'd like to be there to watch. Langdon smiled, happy that Finn was interested in him and the activities that he did.

They continued talking quietly, catching up and soon, being so close to one another, Finn placed his hand on Langdon's thigh and began caressing. Langdon wanted to kiss Finn again. He enjoyed kissing those soft, full lips and hearing the tiny sounds Finn would make.

Langdon could hear Finn's dad in his room, and it sounded like he was turning a page of his book now and then, so Langdon knew they wouldn't be caught. He leaned forward, placed his hand behind Finn's head, and kissed him gently on the lips.

Finn parted his lips, allowing Langdon to gently caress his tongue against his. Tasting him, breathing his warm vanilla scent, he pressed himself closer, immersing himself. Heat grew between them, and their kissing became more needy. Langdon moaned into Finn's mouth, and Finn could feel Langdon's arousal. Finn shifted his hand away from Langdon's thigh, and breathing heavily, placed his hands on each side of Langdon's face. Finn pulled away to look Langdon in the eyes, seeing that they were full of desire.

'Langdon,' Finn spoke softly, maintaining eye contact, 'I want to do more with you, but not with my dad in the next room. Do you mind if we just watch something? Otherwise, I don't think I can keep my hands to myself.'

'Yeah, yeah, sure.'

They both smiled and sat holding hands, calming down a bit as Finn grabbed the TV remote to find a movie to watch.

It took a little while for Langdon to recover; he was so aroused. He wanted to be closer to Finn, touch him, hear him moan. *Ohh,* Langdon had to get his mind on something else, *6x6=36, 5x5=25.* He continued doing times tables in his head until his arousal subsided.

Finn's dad came out soon after and made dinner for them. Langdon enjoyed holding Finn's hand, his fingers gently caressing Finn's the whole time they watched the movie. Even though they sat with a small space separating them in Finn's dad's presence, he was enjoying the gentle, secret touches.

Langdon was home by 10:00 p.m. and when he went to bed, he couldn't sleep. He could still feel the sensation of Finn's lips. He eventually fell into a restless sleep, dreaming of biting Finn and turning him into a wolf.

He woke up sweating profusely and tried regulating his breathing to get back to sleep. Secrets. He had so many secrets right now. He couldn't talk to his parents; he couldn't talk to Tom. It was getting to be too much for him.

Chapter 15

Saturday afternoon, Langdon was getting ready to head over to Tom's. He felt as though he hadn't seen Tom or Beau much lately.

As he was drying off after his shower, his mind wandered to Finn. *His lips*, Langdon had a quick shave, *his fingers,* gently sliding the blade across his rugged jawline, *the teasing*—'Argh! Cut myself!'

Langdon had been lost in thoughts about the previous night when he had the 'G' rated visit with Finn. He liked Finn greeting him with a soft kiss when he arrived just before he entered the house, then a brush of the fingers here, an accidental rub along his thigh there, the night had been excruciating. It was hard keeping his hands to himself.

At one point, he had to sit on his left hand to avoid stroking Finn's thigh. When Finn's dad joined them, they had to sit slightly apart, and Finn's dad had sat in the other two-seater and constantly made remarks about the movie they were watching. Not that Langdon could pay attention anyway. It was an enjoyable night overall. Finn's dad, Daniel, had cooked them a steak for their burger and was friendly enough.

Langdon ripped the corner of the toilet paper to use as a blood clotting aid, however, when he looked back in the mirror, the nick on his jawline was gone. It had been a deep nick that normally would have bled for ages. Langdon shook it off, thinking it must not have been much of a cut after all.

*

Arriving at Tom's, he quickly settled into old banter. Tom was claiming most of his double bed, so Langdon had nestled himself on the edge, with his back leaning against the wall for support.

'So, have you thought about the next full moon? It'll be on a Tuesday, the twelfth of November,' Tom asked.

'Nope. Not even sure anything will happen,' Langdon wriggled around to get comfortable.

'Maybe you should think about where you could be when you transition.'

'It may not even happen again,' he saw the look Tom was giving him. He sighed, 'Look, just because Eric changes into a fucking wolf doesn't mean that I will. He could just be a fucking freak. Inherited it from that uncle or some shit.'

'In denial much?' Tom raised his eyebrows as he stared back at his friend.

Langdon shot him a dirty look. His hands curled into fists by his side, flexing.

'Jeez, don't get your jocks in a twist. I'm only suggesting you should have a plan in place. Look, you can stay here or just tell your parents you are.'

'Maybe.' Langdon didn't want to think about it, let alone talk about it. He wanted to change the subject. 'Hey isn't Beau coming over?'

'Yeah, he said he'll be here by about six o'clock.' Tom relented from his questioning and looked at his watch.

Langdon heard his quiet footsteps before Beau entered the room, greeting them. 'Hey guys.'

'Hi,' greeted Tom.

'Hey,' Langdon looked up and nodded his greeting.

'What are we doing?' asked Beau.

'Waiting for the pizza and trying to find something we haven't seen yet,' Tom answered as he scrolled through the options on Netflix.

'Give me that,' Langdon said as he reached over and snatched the remote from him. 'Here we go, how about…' he scrolled through the list, 'yup, here it is, *Jigsaw*!'

'Yeah!' Langdon cheered.

'Noooo,' cried Beau. 'That movie is too gory. What about *Endgame*?' He glanced at Tom, then back at Langdon.

Langdon groaned loudly, expressing his answer.

'Oh, too long,' groaned Tom. 'Fine, put on Jigsaw, Beau, you can look away at the gory parts,' he smiled.

'Oh, you guys suck,' complained Beau, peeved that he had been overruled.

Tom pulled the bourbon from under his bed and received nods from Langdon and Beau as they passed their cups over.

'Now we're talkin',' Langdon crooned. He waited while Tom filled his large cup with a quarter of bourbon, and then he went back and poured his can of Coke into the alcohol.

Beau did the same.

The boys didn't always drink, and definitely not when any of them were driving. Beau only had to walk next door, and Langdon had ridden his bike over. If he ever drank too much, he would just crash at Tom's and go home the next morning.

They watched the movie and enjoyed throwing things at Beau when the music changed to a scary part. Beau had jumped about ten times throughout the movie, and the other two found it hilarious. Beau was not happy, but knew he'd get payback when they pulled out the Xbox. He'd kick their arses with his strategic moves.

After the movie, Tom set up Halo for them to play. They were ten minutes into the game and chilling out eating chips when Langdon's spartan was shot dead by Beau's.

'Take that!' Beau quipped.

'Hey!' Langdon cried out when his Spartan died. When it restored, he carried on playing.

They played for the next two hours, and all that could be heard was the clicking of the controls, crunching of chips, and the odd groan when one of their characters went down.

Langdon smiled; it was just like old times. He settled back to enjoy his drink. He enjoyed the rest of the night with Tom and Beau and forgot his worries about the next full moon. He'd gone back for a second drink and was confused about why he wasn't well on his way to being drunk. He felt sober - well, mostly sober.

Chapter 16

Wednesday 6th November

It had been a week and a half since Langdon and Finn had seen each other because of Finn's dad's work. Daniel worked in the mining industry, and occasionally he had to fly out to different sites. Therefore, Finn had to stay with his mum. She lived further out of town which made it impossible for Finn to come into Wentworth Falls as his car stayed at his dad's. The bus to school was Finn's only option. He was arriving back on Wednesday because he had to work at the gymnastics centre. Finn had said the earliest he'd be able to see Langdon was Friday night. During the time Finn was away, they had been texting every day and arranged to meet on Friday night at Finn's place.

Langdon pulled out his phone to look back at the texts.

Hey, Finn texted.

Hey, wrote Langdon as he smiled at the text.

Miss you, Finn had messaged.

Miss you too wrote Langdon. *Wish you were here*.

Me too. It's boring out here, messaged Finn.

Langdon sighed, wanting time to go faster so he could see Finn already.

Even though Finn loved seeing his mum, she lived in a town called Orange, which was a two-hour drive away. It was much larger than Wentworth Falls. As Finn grew older, he didn't like it because all his friends were in Wentworth Falls. Langdon was in Wentworth Falls.

That had been two days after he had left.

After that, the texts became more and more personal.

Thinkin' about you, Finn had messaged.

Oh yeah? Langdon was curious.

Yeah, and the things I'd like to do to you.

Langdon's breathing hitched, reading the text again. He was practically aching for Finn's touch now.

The week seemed to drag on without Finn around. Langdon busied himself with school, karate training, then rugby training, willing time to fly so he could see Finn again.

The following week, all his emotions had intensified. His sister had made a crack about him PMSing. *What!* He didn't even understand what PMS was. He kind of knew his sister had started her periods and every month at a certain point, she would cry at the drop of a hat or yell and scream about everything. Langdon contemplated his outbursts; *well, I have been losing my temper this week more than usual.* He just needed to see Finn, that's all it was. He needed to know that Finn's feelings about him hadn't changed in the past two weeks.

Langdon had arrived home from school yelling at his sister for leaving her skates in the walkway where he almost tripped over them. He felt fired up.

His inner frustration and anger had built and were now more intense. This led to Wednesday afternoon, and Langdon had energy to burn and needed to expel the pent-up emotion.

He jumped on his bike and rode. He didn't know where he just needed to move. Before he knew where he was headed, he realised he was near Finn's gymnastics centre.

Glancing at his watch, he saw: 4:45 p.m. *Maybe I could wait to see Finn after work? Would Finn be happy to see me? Yes*, he decided.

He rode quickly and took every pathway and shortcut he could find and, with his extra speed, he arrived with ten minutes to spare before Finn's session would be over.

Skidding his bike into the car park of the mini-mart across the road, he dismounted to lean it against the wall so that he could blend in. He leaned against the rough brick wall, one leg propped up behind him, staring in the direction of the gymnastics centre. Knowing that Finn had to stay for the duration of his rostered shift of work, he also knew that he would come outside for a short breather between the sessions. Langdon's plan was to wave and cross the street to see him.

After some time, he heard laughter and talking as a group of teenagers, both male and female, walked out of the centre. Spotting Finn easily in his black compression shirt and athletic shorts, Langdon smiled. But just as soon as he did, he felt his face fall. Jealousy gripped him as he watched Finn swagger over and put his arm around a tall brunette. She was skinny, with her dark hair wrapped neatly into a bun on top of her head. Her breasts swelled out of her skin-tight leotard, catching the eye of more than one of the guys in the group.

Just a friend, Langdon sternly told himself, reigning in his sudden anger. Although his hands formed into fists by his side as he watched.

His hand is practically hanging over her chest! The girl laughed at something Finn said, and she turned her head to whisper something in his ear. A low growl sounded in Langdon's throat. He felt possessiveness wash over him.

Langdon strolled menacingly across the street, each step adding fuel to his fire.

Finn didn't see Langdon until he was directly in front of him, gaining the attention of all the students standing on the footpath. 'Can I see you for a minute,' Langdon spat, his face hard as stone.

Confused, Finn followed him around the side of the building and jumped when Langdon punched the brick wall, causing a small crack in one of the bricks. 'What the hell is wrong with you!' Finn demanded, with his hands firmly placed on his hips and frowning back at Langdon.

'I saw you hanging off that chick like you owned her!' accused Langdon angrily.

'What! That's ridiculous,' Finn expressed his frustration by throwing his hands up in the air, and Langdon saw the hurt in his eyes.

Finn's hurt feelings hit Langdon head-on.

Langdon, now lost for words seeing the suffering in Finn's eyes, looked at the ground, his anger dissipating as quickly as it had fired up. He sighed and lowered his eyes.

A few seconds passed, then he looked up again into Finn's eyes, 'Look, I'm sorry,' he said quietly, 'but I just wanted to see you and…' he trailed off into barely a whisper. 'I couldn't wait for Friday.' Langdon's cheeks bloomed pink by the second, 'I missed you.' Langdon's voice had become quiet with a slight quiver.

Finn shook his head and chuckled. He grabbed Langdon's hands firmly and looked him directly in the eye and said, 'I'm with you, no one else.'

Langdon nodded and wanted to kiss him. He felt so much calmer and grounded with Finn near him, and with Finn touching his hands, it sent soft tingles through his body.

Finn sighed, 'Look, I have to go, I'm due to start work. But I will see you Friday,' he gave Langdon a stern look.

Langdon watched Finn walk back into the centre and decided to go home. He didn't know what had come over him. He rode home faster than humanely possible, going straight to his room and flopping onto his bed, angry with himself for looking like a possessive idiot.

*****

Finally, it was Friday. Langdon arrived at Finn's, feeling sheepish. Finn greeted him at the door, and because his dad was in the shower, he pulled Langdon close and pecked him on the lips, biting his lower lip before pulling away.

Langdon smiled, 'I'm sorry about Wednesday. I don't know what I was thinking.'

'It's forgotten,' Finn's mouth twitched into a smile.

They walked into the lounge room and sat side by side on the couch, desire filling the air until his father strolled in. Seconds before his appearance, the boys sprung apart, leaving a generous space between them.

Finn had just grabbed the remote when his dad spoke. 'So, what are we watching tonight, boys?'

'Still looking,' Finn said, scrolling through Netflix. Moments later, he chose an action movie. The boys started watching while his dad cooked up sausages on the BBQ grill.

Fifteen minutes later, Finn's dad called out, 'Come and get it!'

Pausing the movie, the boys went into the kitchen, piled up their bread buns and returned to the loungeroom to continue watching.

In the kitchen, Daniel's mobile phone rang.

'Yes?' he answered, his voice rough and deep.

'Oh, that's fine, what about Steve and John?'

Daniel paced the space between the kitchen and loungeroom with the phone pressed to his ear.

'Oh. Yup, no worries. Sure, next week then. Right-o. Bye.' He hung up his phone.

Finn's dad looked at the boys 'Well, looks like I'm staying in tonight boys, but I'll leave you to your movie, I'll be on the patio reading.' He walked to the kitchen, grabbed his food, and headed out the sliding door.

Langdon could hear Finn's dad drag out a chair and sit, and while Finn probably heard that too, Langdon's hearing also picked up the turn of the pages.

Finn

After Finn's dad walked out, Finn and Langdon looked at each other. Finn's eyes travelled to Langdon's bottom lip. Finn wanted to lean over and brush his own against Langdon's. Although he was too aware of his father, only ten feet away. That kind of killed the mood. He tried to think of the movie and stopped any further thoughts of what he would like to do. How he would like to touch, caress, and hear Langdon's sighs, his gasps, *stop!* Finn reprimanded himself. Tonight would be about enjoying his partner's company… at least he could be discreet and gain his fix by sitting close, close enough to hear him breathing. He glanced at Langdon's chest, his muscular pecs hidden beneath his shirt, and diverted his eyes back to the screen and tried to focus.

Since meeting Langdon, Finn didn't question his attraction. He found the guy hot and felt attracted to him. He craved Langdon. Touching him, kissing him.

During the movie, Finn gave gentle caresses along Langdon's hand, his arm, and his mid-thigh. First, they were gentle strokes, growing slightly firmer in places. Finn always found himself aroused around Langdon.

Langdon

Langdon felt his nerve endings responding. He was slowly getting turned on, his breathing becoming quicker. He leaned across and bit Finn's lip…

But the sound of footsteps pulled Langdon right back to his side of the couch.

Finn's dad walked into the lounge room to see the boys sitting next to each other, 'Boys, you want a hot chocolate? I'd offer you something stronger, but you shouldn't be drinking at your young whipper-snipper age.' He chuckled at his amusing play on words.

'Sure Dad, thanks.'

'Yeah, thanks,' echoed Langdon, still hazy from the threat of almost being caught.

Ten minutes later, they were drinking the best hot chocolate Langdon had ever tasted. 'Mmmm, what's in this?' asked Langdon, turning his head to look at Finn.

'Oh, Dad likes to add Nutella to the cocoa,' Finn said in between sips.

With his hands occupied holding the steaming mug, Langdon relaxed on the couch and tried to enjoy the movie.

Towards the end of the movie, Finn's dad strolled back in and as he walked past them, he said, 'I'm off to bed, boys, might read for a bit, so I'll see you next time, Langdon. Goodnight, Finlay.'

The boys responded with their own goodnights as Finn's dad continued down the hall and disappeared into his room.

'Finlay?' Langdon asked, eyebrows raised in amusement, a smile tugged at his lips as he turned to face Finn.

Finn rolled his eyes. 'Yes, yes, my name is Finlay. Mum's Irish, and apparently it means, … and don't laugh,' Finn warned, his brown eyes narrowing.

Langdon feigned innocence with his hands up in surrender, he had to hear this!

'Fair-haired courageous one,' Finn frowned and pulled on his short, dark hair.

Langdon hid a smirk. 'I like it,' he said. He lowered his voice to a sexy whisper, 'You're my Finlay.' His gaze became intense as he stared into Finn's deep brown eyes.

Finn looked at Langdon and smiled, slow and sexy. 'We won't see my dad again; he'll be asleep in minutes. And nothing will wake him,' he added sexily.

The heat Langdon saw in Finn's eyes almost caused him to come undone right then and there. He tried to swallow, but his throat had gone dry. He could feel the desire coming off Finn. His own inner desire burned like fire as well.

Langdon couldn't hold back; he leaned forward, placing his hands on the sides of Finn's face, and pulled him close. Finn's breathing deepened; Langdon could feel the heat of his breath across his skin. He crept closer to meet Finn, who leaned the rest of the way and bit Langdon's lip, hard. Langdon moaned, he liked it when Finn did that and it made his arousal climb higher.

He needed to touch Finn. Firmly holding Finn's jawline, he kissed Finn passionately, their kiss deepening. Both were panting harshly, and their hands were all over each other; under each other's shirts, down below–they explored.

Langdon moaned loudly; the sound caught in Finn's mouth. Finn groaned, enjoying the feel of Langdon's hands on his body. Langdon's heart was pounding in his chest, this was what he had been craving, what he needed. The release he found with Finn ripped through him until his body relaxed and he held Finn close.

*

It was after ten that night when Langdon arrived home, and he went straight to bed, feeling spent.

Chapter 17

The following Friday, Finn arrived at Langdon's right on time. 4:00 p.m. Langdon's parents were not arriving home until after six as they were going grocery shopping after they both finished work. Langdon had thought they might have more privacy with his parents out compared to Finn's place.

Hayley was upstairs in her room—as coerced by Langdon. She did not want to have her phone taken off her—and that was the deal. That and she would be on the receiving end of a punch on the arm if she bothered him and Finn. Hayley knew her brother would not punch her, it was only a threat to establish boundaries. This is how she knew to take him seriously whenever he talked like that to her.

When Finn arrived, Langdon greeted him by grabbing his hand, pulling him into the house, and leading him into the lounge room. Finn could feel the desire coming off Langdon and grinned at him. Langdon kissed him gently on the lips as a hello, lingering and kissing him again, enjoying the feel of his lips against Finn's. He was still holding Finn's hand and pulled back to look into his brown eyes.

'Hey,' he finally said, smiling.

'Hey Langdon,' Finn smiled, sensing that Langdon wanted to do more. 'How was your week?'

'Yeah, all right, just glad it's the weekend now. I really wanted to see you this week.'

'Same.' Finn told Langdon about the extra hours he was getting at the gymnastics centre and how he needed the money for his car's first service next week.

Langdon was interested because he wanted to buy his own car soon but needed a part-time job first. He talked to Finn about the sort of car he'd like to buy. They talked about cars for the next twenty minutes, Finn giving him tips about buying privately or which dealer to use.

As the conversation gradually tapered off, they gazed at each other. Finn ran his hand up Langdon's arm and gave him a slow, sexy smile. Langdon was mesmerised and pulled Finn over to the couch.

All week they had been texting each other, wanting to see each other sooner, however, after-school activities took precedence. The distance and lack of physical connection built a need in Langdon. Finn had texted him, saying he wanted to kiss him and not just his lips. Langdon had counted down the minutes until he could see Finn, touch Finn, and be in the same room as Finn.

The mood was becoming intense. They were sitting side by side on the couch, thighs close enough to touch. Finn was so close that Langdon could feel his breath on his neck. Langdon turned to face Finn, meeting his eyes.

Langdon leaned in and brushed his lip over Finn's bottom lip before biting it, making Finn groan quietly. Finn, aroused by Langdon, threw his leg over Langdon's, separating his strong muscular legs. The move increasing Finn's dominance turned Langdon on, and his shorts suddenly felt tighter.

'You sure your parents won't be home for a while?' breathed Finn.

'Nope, not until six at least,' Langdon grinned wickedly.

Finn kissed Langdon hard, parting Langdon's lips with his tongue, and Langdon made a noise of pleasure at the caress against his own.

He moved his hands to hold both sides of Finn's face and felt the roughness of his jawline.

Finn could feel Langdon's desire with every move; he was a little rough, which only intensified the heat between them.

Langdon moved one hand behind Finn's head, threading his fingers into his hair and pulling firmly. Finn moaned, low and sexy. Langdon didn't even hear the footsteps…

'Oh shit! Sorry.' Tom stood at the entrance to the lounge room, looking utterly astounded. He quickly turned and hurried back the way he'd come in…the back door. That was why Langdon didn't hear the sliding door. Tom mumbled, 'I'll come back later,' and turned and rushed out the door.

Langdon froze. 'Fuck!' he cried. 'Fuck, fuck, fuck.' He jumped up and ran after Tom.

Finn sat, stunned and unsure what to do.

Langdon had to chase Tom down the street. Tom was on his bike, but Langdon caught up before Tom made it to the corner.

'Wait! Tom, listen to me!'

Tom stopped, threw his leg over his bike steadily, and propped it against the fence to look at Langdon—he looked distraught.

'Look, it's okay, Langdon, I didn't know you were gay,' said Tom.

'I'm not gay!' Langdon frowned. 'This just happened.' He threw his arms up in frustration. 'Don't put a label on it!'

'I just saw you kissing another dude.' Tom tried to understand the image of Langdon with another male popping into his head.

Langdon started pacing. 'I'm not gay,' he repeated. 'I don't know what it is, I just felt drawn to him, I can't explain it.'

'How long has this been going on?' Tom asked.

'About a month,' Langdon stopped his pacing and looked at Tom.

'Where did you meet him?' asked Tom, trying to understand what was going on with his friend.

'When I took Hayley to dance; he's in her class.'

Tom sighed heavily. 'Look, it's okay. I don't care if you're into guys or girls.' He stayed quiet for a minute. His eyes drifted to the road but widened as though something had occurred to him. 'But,' he paused, 'I've seen you with girls; you dated Brooke for three months earlier this year.'

'I know. I was into her. It just didn't work out,' sighed Langdon.

'So, what's his name?'

'Finn.' Langdon then realised something. 'Oh shit!' he threw the palm of his hand to slap his forehead, 'I left him sitting on the couch. I've gotta go, I'll talk to you later.' He turned and started running.

By the time Langdon raced back, and into the house, Finn was gone.

Langdon grabbed his phone, fingers furiously tapping a message.

Finn, I'm sorry for running off.

He waited, holding his breath for those three little dots to appear. No response.

Langdon frowned and pulled at his hair in frustration. He tried again, **Finn, please talk to me.**

When he saw no response, even an hour later. Langdon tried one last time.

Finn, I'm sorry, please forgive me.

*

The entire weekend, Langdon either closed himself away in his room, AirPods in music blaring, well, on a low volume, but it still sounded loud, or he had to go out for a run. He ran and ran, but nothing could fill the void in the pit of his stomach. He missed Finn.

*****

On Monday, Langdon texted him again, hoping that this time, he would answer.

Finn, please talk to me

In the afternoon, he sent another message: ***Finn, please.***

He kept checking his phone, hoping that the guy would respond so that they could talk. But he never did.

Later that night, he messaged Finn again, *Finn, I miss you and I'm sorry.*

Chapter 18

On Tuesday morning, Langdon texted Finn repeatedly, barely focussing on lessons at school. He was withdrawn and snapped at anyone who asked him what was wrong. His friends gave up, allowing him time to himself. Langdon had a tendency to be rude and arrogant at the best of times, but this sombre mood was unlike him. As the day wore on, his mood darkened.

His rugby training in the afternoon allowed him to vent his frustration and misery. He was ruthless. Speed, strength, and aggression consumed him to the point where his coach sent him off the field to cool down.

Later that afternoon, he went for a run. Blared his music and wanted to punch something. Nothing relieved his growing frustrations.

He wanted an early night, but couldn't shake the intense aggression and energy pulsing through his body. He could not sit still. His breathing started to become ragged. It was getting late, and the transition was catching him unaware.

Langdon was not prepared. He had given no thought to the full moon. He was having the same symptoms and feelings in his body he had experienced one month ago–when he'd gone out for a run and went through the agony of his body transitioning into a wolf. By the time Langdon acknowledged and admitted to himself that something was happening, he grabbed his phone and called Eric.

Eric answered quickly, and his hello sounded like a growl.

'Eric, I don't…Please help, I-I don't know what to do!'

'Langdon?'

'Yes,' Langdon cried in frustration.

'Shit. Where are you?' The sense of urgency with which he voiced the question alarmed Langdon.

'I'm at home. In my bedroom,' Langdon's eyes darted around the room. Everything was intensified. He could hear his mother downstairs washing up some dishes. The sound of Hayley speaking softly to her friend on her phone was so clear—something about liking a boy in her class…

'Has the transition started?' Eric's voice called his attention back to the phone.

'What do you mean?' Langdon couldn't think straight.

'Well, are you feeling aggressive? Lots of energy?'

'Yes, and yes,' blurted Langdon, his breathing becoming heavier.

'You need to get out now, Langdon. Get yourself away from people or you could hurt somebody,' Eric's voice sounded both urgent and pleading.

'Okay,' Langdon's panic rose.

Hanging up, he threw his phone on his bed.

But a notification drew his eyes back to the device.

He had just received a text message… from Finn!

Langdon scrambled for his phone and fumbled with it in his hands, dropping it on the floor. 'Shit,' he quickly picked it up with shaking fingers.

Hi Langdon, sorry, was grounded when I got home and Dad took my phone, only just got it back…
Want to see U, R U free now?

Langdon's heart raced, each breath came in ragged puffs of air. *Finn,* a growl vibrated through his body and out of his throat. Langdon felt frustrated and angry. He wanted to see Finn. He tried to text, even though the phone felt foreign in his hands. Dropping it on the floor, he growled, 'Shit,' then he quickly picked it up and tried again.

Finn, mss   Wnt 2 c u but cat 2nite

Langdon's texting was atrocious, he couldn't focus on the letters, and he was becoming increasingly feral. He dropped the phone again and looked desperately around his room. His eyes were drawn to the window, and he stumbled over to it.

Just as he was opening the window, his shoulder dislocated from the beginnings of the change, and he fell to the floor and released a gurgled cry. The pain caused him to curl up, bringing his knees to his chest, groaning in pain.

'Are you alright in there?' asked his mum. She had been walking up the stairs to see Hayley and heard a muffled sound that worried her.

'Yeah, I'm good,' Langdon managed to grit out through his teeth, surprisingly coherent, using every ounce of strength to compose himself. He prayed his mum would not come in. He heard footsteps fade away, but could not even let out a sigh of relief. The pain of further changes in his body was too much.

Langdon looked down at his hands. His nails were stretching out into claws, and his back legs were breaking and changing shape. He ripped off his shirt, his body feeling like it was on fire–a raging furnace. His skin felt tighter, his bones ached, and something cracked. Langdon gasped loudly, a painful whine escaping his throat. *Not now! Not here!* he thought frantically. Looking around his room, his eyes kept darting to the half-open window. *The window!* Langdon scrambled over on all fours and looked outside.

He had to risk it. He had to jump. The house was two stories high, and Langdon's room was upstairs. Pushing the window open wider, Langdon jumped. Letting out a muted 'Oomph!' He landed on all fours and rolled.

Recovering quickly, he bolted for the park across the street, still on all fours, still partly human. *Shit! Why are there kids in the park this late?!* They were older, two boys sitting on the kiddie's swings smoking a cigarette.

Langdon veered away from the park as part-human and part-animal. Before they could see him, he veered towards the creek, a moving flash of part-human, part-animal.

Upon reaching his destination, Langdon groaned loudly, allowing his body to surrender to the change. He was curled on the creek bank, half in the water, half out. He felt every bone break into formation, his jaw elongating painfully. He screamed as the transition took over his body.

As his cries slowly quieted, Langdon stood fully transitioned. Now a wolf, he howled at the moon. The act was entirely on instinct, he couldn't help it. All of his senses were alert and magnified. He sniffed, *human*. The wolf salivated and snarled as he heard human voices drawing steadily closer.

'Hey! Did you hear that?' One voice asked.

'Yeah! Let's go check it out, it came from over in the creek,' the second voice sounded excited.

'Get your phone out, let's record it,' the deeper voice suggested.

'Yeah, cool,' the other answered excitedly.

'What do you reckon it is?'

'Some kind of animal? It looked huge.'

Running! The wolf could hear the humans running towards him. His humanness had picked up the words of the humans approaching and understood–*danger*.

He knew he had to run, he couldn't risk humans seeing him in this form. The wolf's sympathetic nervous system acted like a gas pedal in a car, triggering his fight-or-flight response. The wolf ran up the side of the creek, dodging tree roots protruding from the bank, and ran as fast as he could away from the danger and towards the road.

Car lights blinded his vision. Breaks screeched. A loud beep sounded nearby. Yet he kept running further and further away from houses and roads. Across pathways, *fewer houses now, less danger.*

He kept running, kilometres went by. Staying clear of the road as much as possible, he stuck to the National Park, hidden by the trees.

He sniffed the air—*eucalyptus, damp moss, a minty pine, more damp moss*, it felt familiar to him. He was finally at the Blue Mountains National Park.

He continued running through the dense foliage and trees. The wolf stopped and sniffed again:–*food*, he could smell food. The wolf circled in on its prey, testing its weaknesses, its eyesight twenty times sharper than his human form. He slowed to a quiet pace to confront his prey. In one swift move, he attacked from behind, the tiger quoll's body pierced by the wolf's elongated canines. Happy with its hunt, the wolf ate. Finishing up his meal, he barked in joy, and then let out a howl of jubilance.

A deep, long howl was heard off in the distance, answering his own. Listening raptly, he recognised something familiar. He howled back in response to the scent he picked up. The light brown wolf sprinted, following the scent, another loud bark determining its direction. He kept running until minutes later he stopped, facing another wolf.

The dark wolf growled in dominance, his ears pulled back and held close to its head. He growled - *My territory;* he thought. The confident dark wolf carried its tail high as a visible sign of authority, a clear sign of rank.

He approached the light brown wolf. The dark wolf stood taller than the light-haired wolf. They were now face to face, the dark wolf pulling rank. His stance and the way he positioned his body displayed his dominance. The light brown wolf immediately lowered into submission, rolling over and showing his belly—the most vulnerable part of his body. He whined, communicating that he came bearing no threat.

The dark wolf acknowledged the show of submission and allowed him to stand. The wolves had been picking up each other's scents from the moment the light-brown wolf had entered the dark wolf's territory. The wolves looked each other in the eye, silently communicating a greeting. A silent conversation occurred where the wolves understood each other perfectly.

Langdon.

Yes.

You made it out okay.

Yes, some danger—kids.

Did you bite one?

No, I ran.

Good. Let's hunt now.

The two wolves ran deeper into the mountain, hunting and chasing prey. They ran together, the dark wolf slightly in the lead, their speed gaining them kilometres through rough terrain. No matter their speed, they could easily weave through the dense trees. The light brown wolf cooperated with the other wolf, they worked together for each animal they hunted. They tested their prey, sensing weaknesses through visual cues, hearing, and scent.

They ran long distances, and when the prey was being circled, the light-haired wolf would sit back to watch as the dark-haired wolf took down the prey aggressively and quickly.

When the wolves grew tired and had satisfied their hunger, the dark wolf led his companion back through the mountains. The light-haired wolf kept up, and when they neared familiar territory, his scent picked up more familiar smells — the floral aromas, and earthy smells near the castle.

***

Langdon squinted; the sun was shining brightly in his eyes. The ground was hard and wet from the morning dew. He ran his hand over his face and moved his tongue around in his mouth, *Eww!* He used his fingers to pull out bits of hair. There was blood around his mouth and on his hands.

He had a feeling of déjà vu, remembering how he had woken up similarly to the last full moon. Propping himself up on his elbows, he looked at his surroundings. He saw himself surrounded by plants, foliage, and strongly scented eucalyptus trees. He could hear a rustling sound in a nearby shrub. A lizard. Then he noticed Eric lying about ten metres away. Naked. Facing away from him.

Langdon looked down at himself, *Oh crap, I'm naked.* As he quickly covered his modesty with his hands, Eric began to stir. Langdon saw him sit up, running a hand over his face and pulling something out of his mouth. Then he looked around and saw Langdon.

'Oh, hey,' Eric greeted Langdon, a sleepy tone in his voice.

"Hi," Langdon said, blushing slightly, averting his eyes.

'Come on, let's walk to the castle and get ourselves some clothes,' Eric avoided staring back at Langdon.

The two gradually rose, covering themselves as much as they could, averted their eyes from one another and walked the two kilometres to the castle.

They stopped once along the way to relieve themselves behind a tree. When they continued walking, Langdon broke the awkward silence to explain how he had quickly left his house and tried to get as far away as he could. He told Eric about the kids he could smell, and he had sensed danger, so ran and ended up there.

'When I was in wolf form, I remember communicating with you,' said Langdon.

'Yes, that's new to me as well,' admitted Eric, wondering more about their communication.

'It's like I could read your thoughts.'

'I know,' Eric sounded surprised.

They chatted more about their night and were soon at the castle. Their feet were sore and aching from walking barefoot through the forest. Both had numerous minor cuts on their feet, but the wounds soon grew smaller and had healed by the time they crossed the threshold.

Once inside, Eric quickly threw Langdon some track pants and a t-shirt as he slipped into another pair with his back turned.

Finally decent, He walked into the kitchen, calling Langdon in to have some breakfast. Langdon needed to wash the dirt, blood, and grime off his hands and around his mouth. Using the kitchen sink, he squirted a generous amount of hand soap and scrubbed roughly until he felt cleaner.

'Here,' Eric tossed him a towel to wipe his hands and face.

'Thanks' Langdon rubbed his face haphazardly, then wiped his ears and dried his hands.

He placed the towel on the kitchen bench and groaned, leaning onto his elbows. 'Oh, my God. I'm wrecked!' Langdon ran a hand over his face, squeezing his eyes shut, then slowly rose and glanced at Eric. 'Does this seriously happen every month?' It still seemed surreal.

'Unfortunately, yes.' Eric still sounded groggy, like he was waking up. 'Ugh, I need a coffee.'

Eric trudged across the slate floor to the bench where he kept the coffee machine and began working.

Oh shit, thought Langdon, 'What time is it?'

Eric looked at the clock on the wall, 'Just after six.'

'I've got school!' exclaimed Langdon, panicking.

'It's okay, I can drive you home in a minute, I just thought you'd be hungry. We'll have a quick breakfast, and I promise to get you home in time.'

Langdon nodded, silently calculating the time it would take to drive from the castle to his house, get showered and dressed, *and* then be in time to catch the bus at 7:40 a.m.

Eric noticed the concern on Langdon's face and asked if he wanted to call anyone.

'No, it's fine. It's just that I have to catch the bus to school at twenty to eight.'

Eric thought for a minute, then said, 'What if I drive you to school? I'll drive you home to get ready, and then you won't have to catch the bus?'

'Yeah, but I take my little sister with me, she'll be waiting for me.'

'I'll drive both of you. It's no trouble, really.' Eric's calming tone relaxed Langdon's tense features, and he smiled his thanks.

So, with a plan in motion, they sat and ate toast with Vegemite and a cup of coffee which they both desperately needed.

When it was time to leave, Eric locked up the castle.

True to his word, Eric drove as quickly and safely as he could to Langdon's house and waited in the HiLux while Langdon went inside.

Langdon hurried into the kitchen and checked the clock on the way, seeing it was only just after seven-thirty. After grabbing a large glass of water–he was thirsty! Langdon raced up the stairs and was confronted by his sister. She was all dressed for school, tying her hair back and grinning at him like she had a secret.

'Ohh, you're in trouble,' she sang.

'Why?' Langdon asked, not at all amused by her smug attitude.

'Because you never came home last night, and Mum rang Tom to see where you were, and he said you were there but couldn't come to the phone. She's mad that you never let her know. *And* on a school night,' her eyes become wider to emphasise "school night".

'Where's Mum now?'

'She had to leave early for work. We're gonna miss the bus, Langdon!' Hayley looked up at him, her blue eyes showed concern.

'It's okay, I have a friend waiting in the driveway, he's going to drive us, just give me ten minutes to have a quick shower and get dressed.'

'Yeah, you better. You stink,' she squished up her nose at his sweaty odour. 'And what are you wearing!' she exclaimed, staring at his baggy, oversized grey track pants and a black t-shirt that looked two sizes too big.

'Never you mind,' he grumbled as he strode purposefully into the bathroom.

Langdon quickly showered and dressed and met Hayley downstairs. They were about to walk out when she came to a halt, 'Wait. Who's this guy driving us?'

'A friend. Now come on,' he was getting impatient.

Langdon locked the front door of the house, jogged to the passenger side and climbed in, and Hayley cautiously climbed up and into the backseat.

Eric turned around to look at Hayley, 'You look just like your brother.' He smiled, 'Same bright blue eyes! And blonde hair, although you're prettier,' Eric chuckled, emphasising he was just being playful to put her at ease. Then he smiled at her. 'Hi, I'm Eric.'

'Hi,' replied Hayley as she stared back at him and checked him over suspiciously.

'Your brother had to help me with something this morning, so I offered to drive you both to school,' he explained as he backed out of the driveway and onto the road.

Hayley seemed to buy the excuse, as she asked no more questions.

Eric dropped them in the school drop-off zone and continued on his way. Since the conversation in the car had been minimal, he had played his favourite tracks on the car stereo. The siblings had thanked him before rushing into the school, worried that they were late.

Langdon ran to his contact class and found Tom waiting, looking both concerned and angry.

'Where the hell were you?' Tom demanded, his normally calm blue eyes had darkened a shade.

'Please,' sighed Langdon, 'don't start.' He felt tired and was not in the mood for an argument.

'Well?' Tom asked, glaring at Langdon.

They were sitting in the back row, keeping their voices low as their teacher read out the morning notices.

'Look, *it* happened, okay? I didn't think that it would, and I wasn't prepared.'

'Where did you go?' Tom whispered, anger dissolving as he grew concerned about Langdon's latest full moon behaviour.

'I jumped out my bedroom window and raced to the creek, and after that, it's a bit of a blur. But,' Langdon paused, 'I remember hearing some kids as I was *changing,* and I freaked out, so once the change was over, I just ran.'

Tom was staring back at him, eyes wide, taking everything in, 'What happened then?'

'It was really strange… I think I met Eric in his,' he lowered his voice to barely a whisper and said, 'Wolf form, and we could talk to each other.'

'Holy shit!' exclaimed Tom, a little too loudly. A few heads turned around, but confronted with Langdon's glare, quickly turned back to the front.

'So, I heard my mum rang looking for me?'

'Yeah, that was batshit crazy! She was *not* happy. I told her you were in the bathroom. She told me to send you home when you came out.'

'Oh shit,' Langdon went pale. *I'm going to get it when my parents get home this afternoon,* he groaned and let his head fall onto his desk.

Chapter 19

That afternoon, after arriving home from school, Langdon made his afternoon tea quickly and scoffed it down before heading up to his room. He'd reluctantly left his phone at home on the charger as it was completely dead. There was nowhere at school to recharge it. Now, he was desperate to see any messages from Finn.

Striding over to his bedside table, he picked up his phone and saw that he had five messages and three missed calls. 'Oh, shit.'

Langdon, are you there? Finn had texted Tuesday afternoon.

R U OK? A second text from him.

Missed call at 9:15 p.m. from Mum.

Second, missed call at 9:19 p.m. from Mum.

Message from Tom at 9:20 p.m. **Langdon! Your mum rang—I covered 4 u**

The message at 9:35 p.m. from Tom read, *Where r u? Ring me!*

The third message was from Finn—***Langdon, what's going on?***

The last notification was a missed call from Finn at 10 p.m.

Langdon sunk onto his bed in exhaustion. He quickly messaged Finn back.

Finn, sorry about yesterday, you there?

A few seconds passed before he watched the dots appear, indicating that Finn was typing.

And finally, Finn responded, ***Langdon! R U OK?***

Langdon messaged back, *yeah, sorry*

Finn replied, **want to come over?**

Langdon sighed, - **can't, mum's on warpath, I might be grounded.**

Shit

IKR

Friday arvo meet me. Aquatic centre, Finn messaged.

I will

The next message from Finn made Langdon smile.

miss u

Miss u too. Langdon quickly responded.

Langdon was determined to see Finn. Not giving a thought to his punishment that he knew was coming—one way or another, he would get himself to the Aquatic Centre. He wanted to explain and set things right with Finn. But he was just glad that Finn didn't seem mad, and that would tide him over until he could meet him face to face.

Finn finished with "**xx**" which Langdon sent back as well with a smile.

Just as he set aside his phone, he heard the carport door go up. *Mum's home, time to face the music.* Langdon ran down the stairs and waited in the kitchen. His heart hammered in his chest because he knew his parents would be pissed at his actions. Not calling and staying out on a weeknight was totally against the rules. He had not done that in the past two years.

Two years ago, in grade nine, he had been off the rails. He kept getting into fights at school. Someone only had to look at him wrong, and he would be in their face—Bam!

One time, Langdon had smashed his fist into the locker beside a boy's head because he had made a snide remark in class about him failing science that term.

Back then, he used to sneak out the back door numerous times to hang out at the Aquatic Centre after dark or go over to a mate's house—not coming home until the following afternoon. That incident was the final straw, and his parents enrolled him in karate to teach him respect and obedience, and as an outlet for his aggression.

Langdon was pulled from his thoughts when his mum walked in and saw him sitting at the breakfast bar. Surprised at first, her expression turned furious at her son. 'Langdon, since when do you go to Tom's on a school night and not come home?' she asked, her tone escalating with each word.

'I'm sorry Mum, I needed to work on an assignment with him.'

'And you couldn't use the phone?' his mum's voice was rising. She was now standing with her hands on her hips. She flicked her long fringe out of her eyes as she narrowed her eyes accusingly at her son.

'No, we lost track of time. He had to show me diagrams for science.' Langdon tried to reason with her. He knew that if he wasn't convincing enough, he'd have hell to pay.

Just then, the door to the carport slammed. Langdon's dad was home.

'Yes, well, you didn't tell us you were going and didn't even bother to phone! Don't you know we were worried sick?!'

Heavy footsteps strode down the hallway. Langdon's heart hammered while he waited and watched his father's expression. He couldn't help but fidget.

When his dad stepped around the corner, his eyes were narrowed and his mouth set in a thin line

Punishment would come from his father. It didn't matter how mad his mum was–well, it did, but his dad could de-escalate her fuming disposition. Langdon knew he needed to appeal to his dad to get out of this alive. Because if he were to be grounded? He felt like he would die from not seeing Finn.

'What's going on in here? I could hear you both from the carport!' his voice bellowed as he approached the kitchen.

'Your son is finally home,' Leah retorted, looking at her husband with her arms folded.

Mitchell strode further in, placed his laptop case on the kitchen bench, then dropped his keys on the bench and narrowed his eyes at his son. 'I thought we were past this sort of behaviour?'

'We are,' Langdon responded in a desperate tone. He looked between both his parents to see them silently communicating. His mum looked more annoyed than his dad.

'Yes, well, you gave your mother quite a scare. She heard you making all sorts of racket in your room and then you were gone. Why didn't you tell us you were going to Tom's?'

'Er, because it was a last-minute thing, I needed to check his notes for science.'

'So, you snuck out?' His father was looking angrier by the minute.

Shit. 'Well, yeah, I didn't think it would be a big deal.' Langdon shrugged, but his eyes were wide open, staring back at his dad.

'You didn't think. That's the problem, Langdon, you only ever think about yourself.'

Langdon opened his mouth to object when his father held up his hand to stop him, 'You're grounded.'

'What!' Langdon cried. 'That's not fair.' His hands had balled into fists as he squeezed his nails into the palms of his hands. Anger rose from the pit of his stomach, whirling through his blood. He wanted to yell and scream at his parents that they had no right to keep him locked up.

'No, it is fair. You broke our rule. No phone and no going out until Sunday,' his father reprimanded firmly.

'No! You can't take my phone,' Langdon protectively placed his hand over his back pocket which was holding his only way of contacting Finn.

'No arguments, or you'll be grounded for a month. Now hand it over.' Mitchell held out his hand. The glare he was sporting resigned Langdon to his fate.

Langdon reluctantly and slowly started pulling his phone from his pocket, thinking, *how am I going to contact Finn?*

'NOW!' Mitchell yelled, his patience wearing thin at his son's behaviour.

Langdon handed his phone over to his father and stared defiantly back into his father's eyes.

His dad pocketed the phone and glared back.

'Can I go now?' Langdon was practically shaking with rage, but needed to restrain himself from any form of aggression, as he knew his father would only make life harder for him.

'Fine,' his father relented. 'But I want you to use this time to think about your actions, young man.'

Langdon walked away, his gait speaking volumes about his irritation.

When he strode to the staircase, he raced up the stairs to his bedroom and furiously slammed the door shut. Pacing the five-step distance from one end of his room to the other, he wanted to punch the wall. But he knew that would leave permanent damage because of his strength now.

Breathing heavily, he lengthened each breath to calm himself, and after a few minutes, he plonked himself heavily onto his bed.

Laying on his back with one arm propped behind his head, Langdon stared out the window, fuming at his father's punishment. He couldn't see much from his position, only the tops of the trees that were swaying uncontrollably in the afternoon's strong wind. It seemed to mirror how he felt.

He was lying on his bed, quietly fuming, his hands curling into a tight fist and uncurling when his sister tentatively opened the adjoining door to his room.

'Hey,' Hayley attempted a smile with her eyebrows raised. She was attentively gauging his reaction to her entering his room.

'Hi,' Langdon mumbled without looking at her.

'Heard Dad yelling at you downstairs,' she said sympathetically.

'Yup. I'm grounded.'

'That sucks.' Hayley had always looked up to her brother, he had looked out for her since she was born. He never let anyone pick on her at school (that was his job, he used to say mockingly to her). With four years between them, they'd always been close. Although recently she felt he had changed and was going through something. She knew he had secrets. Well, who didn't? But she couldn't help but feel sorry for him lying there on his bed.

She was about to turn around and go back to her room when she said, 'You can borrow my phone if you need to.' Then she left him alone.

Langdon lay stretched out on his bed, thinking of a plan for Friday to meet Finn. He couldn't risk getting in more trouble. Knowing that his parents didn't arrive home until after five o'clock, hence the reason he and his sister caught the bus, gave him an idea.

He wondered how much time he could risk spending with Finn. He needed to see Finn; he was aching to hold him again.

Langdon couldn't stand being away from him, from his touch. He missed their bond.

Later that evening, his family was sitting down to dinner, watching the news visible from the dining room. Langdon was piling another mouthful of spaghetti Bolognese into his mouth when he heard the newsreader say, 'A wolf was seen by two teenagers on Tuesday night in Jane Creek, Wentworth Falls. Amazingly, they were unharmed. Here is the footage they managed to capture.'

Langdon froze, his eyes meeting the TV screen for the first time that night. His whole family was watching the video which showed a full-sized, light-haired wolf crouching on the creek bank. The reverberating howl that was released from the wolf's open jaw and its actions were caught on camera—every movement the wolf made, including leaping up and out of the creek and into the distance.

Langdon felt panicked. He couldn't swallow, couldn't breathe. His fork slipped from his hand, landing with a loud clank as it hit his plate. *This is a nightmare!* He started choking, his face turning red. His mum quickly jumped up and slapped him hard on the back. Everyone was looking at him. They knew! His biggest secret was out! *What the hell am I going to do now? How can I explain what happened to me?* He stared at his parents' faces, concern expressed heavily on their indented foreheads as their eyes searched his face.

Langdon finally swallowed–hard. He tried to think logically for a second. His parents had shown no sign that they knew it was him in the footage.

No, wait, they couldn't know. How could they? *You idiot, breathe! They're looking at you because you're choking.* Langdon regained his composure, swallowed again, and slowed his breathing.

'You all right there, son?' Gently, his dad slapped his hand in the centre of his son's back. Langdon hadn't even noticed him getting off his chair.

'Yup,' Langdon squeaked. Still recovering from the obstruction. He cleared his throat and tried to act as normal as possible. Turning his attention back to the TV, he heard the news reporter say that Animal Control would be out in the area for the next few weeks. Traps would be set, and other measures taken to keep people safe. A number flashed onto the screen–a hotline for any information or sightings.

'Well, that's unusual for this area,' mused Mitchell.

'Yes,' agreed Leah. Looking between Hayley and Langdon, she said, 'You two better keep an eye out, especially you, Langdon. You often go out in that area for a run. If you see a wolf, stay as far away from it as you can.' Concern showed on her face as she stared back at him.

'Yes, Mum, sure.' Langdon almost laughed at the irony.
Everyone went back to eating, and the news reporter moved on to the weather report.

I wonder if Eric saw this, thought Langdon. *I wish I had my phone to text him. I'll borrow Hayley's. NO—she'll read it. Shit!*

He'd have to wait until he saw Tom the following day. *UGH, this is so frustrating,* Langdon settled on finishing his dinner, resigned to the fact that he really could do nothing else at the moment.

Chapter 20

'It's almost seven-forty. Hurry up, Hayley!' yelled Langdon. His voice travelled up the stairs to his sister, who was still in the bathroom getting ready for school.

Hayley poked her head over the railing, calling out, 'I'm coming!' before disappearing again.

Langdon heard the tap turn on, then off, a spray of perfume, and a couple of thuds. Then Hayley ran down the stairs and flew out the door that Langdon was keeping open for her.

Quickly locking the door, he threw his bag over his right shoulder and jogged down the road, not concerned that Hayley was lagging ten feet behind.

Langdon and Hayley jogged until they reached the crossing, seeing that the bus was already there. *Shit,* thought Langdon, *I'll never get down the back to reach Tom at this rate.*

They crossed the road, arriving to see twenty other kids lined up raggedly, pushing their way to climb onto the bus.

Smaller kids went to the pavement and had to hang back to gain a spot. It wasn't just kids from BMNH, but other schools as well. Langdon pushed his way forward, squeezing himself in between two girls to get near the front. *Oh God*, Langdon clenched his fists. If he had to stand at the front of the bus, he'd probably yank a seat off its hinges in frustration.

Gradually, the line moved forward, so he quickly scanned the crowd for his sister. He spotted her a couple of metres away, behind the taller kids. Langdon called out her name.

He waited for her to look up at him, but the kids were all talking loudly, swapping stories from their weekend. Hayley didn't hear him. The line was moving forward again, and he was almost at the door.

'Hayley!' he yelled her name, projecting his voice. This time, she heard and pushed her way through to stand at his side.

'I couldn't find you. You just took off and left me,' she whined.

'Sorry Hayls, come here,' he grabbed her by the shoulders and pushed her in front of him, his hand still resting firmly on her shoulder.

Hayley glanced over her shoulder up at her brother, he was focused straight ahead and appeared agitated. She understood he didn't want them missing the bus and also didn't want to be the last ones on, or they'd miss out on a seat. She was hoping that her friend Jasmine was saving her a seat. Jasmine usually did, and Hayley could count on her.

Hayley raised her leg to take the first step up, but had to pause because the line was moving at a snail's pace. Then, as the line moved, she finally walked a short way in before hearing her name, seeing Jasmine waving to her. Hayley gratefully climbed into her seat, plopping her bag in front of her legs. The two girls preferred the front rows, it wasn't as noisy as the back. Plus, they had the perfect view of the boys they liked.

Langdon saw Hayley climb in next to her friend and walked further along, squeezing past anyone on his way to reach the back. Then he breathed a sigh of relief when he spotted Tom and Beau waiting for him. And oh, thank goodness, Tom had placed his bag beside him to save the seat for him. Beau was sitting across the aisle with some kid he didn't know.

Langdon sat down heavily and glanced at Tom, noticing that he was looking expectantly at him. His eyebrows were raised, and his eyes were clouded with frustration. 'So? What's been going on?'

Langdon sighed heavily and adjusted his position to be able to lower his voice, 'Do you want the long version or the short version?'

Tom stared back, clearly agitated. Tom was in no mood, and Langdon could sense his irritation.

Langdon relented, explaining everything from his unsuspecting 'change' which Tom had already heard bits and pieces of at school and said he knew *that* was coming due to the piece on the news and finally Langdon finished by saying he was grounded, including his phone being taken off him. Tom had seen the news. The whole of Wentworth Falls, to Springfield and even the surrounding districts had seen *that* piece of news.

'What are you going to do?'

'About what?' questioned Langdon. He had so many issues right now, and he didn't know which one Tom was referring to.

Tom threw his hands up in frustration, 'Your next change? Animal control? And, well, you know, your, um, your…boyfriend?' Tom asked, his voice trailing off quietly.

'Well, in that order. I need to speak to Eric.' *Better to speak to Eric in person,* thought Langdon. 'Actually, I'd like to meet up with him this weekend in person, see if he can meet me at the castle, but I'm grounded until Sunday, so it would have to be then. And,' he paused. A slow smile lifted the corner of his lips. 'Finn,' he said, emphasising his name, enjoying the feel of his name on his lips. 'I'm meeting up with him on Friday afternoon. I'll have until five o'clock to make it home, so my parents won't find out. Please keep that to yourself.'

Tom nodded.

*

Beau looked over at Tom and Langdon. They were huddled close, having a private conversation. The bus was so noisy that he couldn't hear them speak. Music was blaring from the back seat, nothing new there, and kids around him were listening to music on their AirPods or having their own conversations, so he had just sat quietly playing *Fortnight* on his phone.

As the bus jostled along, he looked over again at his friends. They looked highly engrossed in whatever it was they were talking about. *I bet it's about the wolf curse.* He was feeling ostracised. He'd ask Tom later about what was going on. He'd seen the news and wondered if it was Langdon. No. He knew it was Langdon. *Geez, Langdon was in such denial, he had given no thought to it happening. He had to have a different view of his curse by now, surely;* he thought to himself.

The bus finally pulled up at their school, and they all rushed out, everyone cramming together. Someone pushed Beau, and he lurched forward, grabbing the seat to save his fall. Then, all of a sudden, no one was behind him. Beau turned around. He was nearly off the bus and saw Langdon holding a tall, burly senior boy by the scruff of his shirt, saying something menacing into his ear. The boy had his face all scrunched up in anger until fear crossed his features, and he held his hands up in surrender. Beau turned and kept walking slowly, making his way off the bus. He walked, avoiding the popular kids, and looked for a place to stand to wait for his friends. He waited a few meters away from the bus stand. Crowds of students in different uniforms were huddled in groups, some waiting for the next bus to their school. Beau looked past all the kids as he stood waiting.

Langdon and Tom jumped off the bus and walked directly over to him.

'Hi Beau,' greeted Tom.

'Hey Beau,' Langdon nodded. 'How's it going?'

'Okay,' said Beau, looking thoughtfully at Langdon.' *Did he really stand up for me?* He decided to let it go and not make a big deal of it, seeing that both Tom and Langdon appeared apprehensive about something. He wanted in. He stood facing them, waiting. Waiting for someone to say something about their conversation on the bus.

'So, guys,' Langdon said, looking at his two friends. 'Who's up for a visit out to the castle on Sunday?'

'I'm in,' said Beau, glad they were finally getting somewhere, perhaps now he might find out more.

'Sure,' agreed Tom. He looked to Langdon and then to Beau, nodding in his direction. Beau could tell they were silently communicating about something.

Langdon gave a half nod and then turned to Beau, 'So, Beau, did you happen to see the news last night?'

'Uh, yes,' said Beau tentatively. He shifted his weight uncomfortably, moving his backpack to his other shoulder.

'So, you would have seen the part about the wolf?'

Beau nodded.

'Yours truly,' Langdon grimaced, aiming his thumbs at his chest. He was obviously feeling outed like he was the only one dumb enough to not know it was going to happen. His facial expression quickly dropped into a sullen demeanour as he continued speaking. 'My parents have grounded me and taken my phone for being out all night. They thought I was at Tom's, so he covered for me,' he glanced appreciatively in Tom's direction before continuing. 'So now, I need to speak to Eric to see if he saw the news and what he thinks we should do moving forward.'

Beau listened and was happy his friends had confided in him. Beau handed his phone to Langdon, 'Here, call Eric.'

Langdon raised his eyebrows and accepted the phone graciously, 'Thanks, man.' He patted Beau on the shoulder and walked a couple of paces away to make the call. He didn't remember the number, so he pulled his wallet out of his pocket to retrieve the business card Eric had given him. Tom and Beau stood watching his movements as he was speaking to Eric, waiting patiently.

'All good,' said Langdon when he strolled back over. 'He said he'll head out early Sunday morning and pick us up at ten o'clock at the entrance to the park. Let's meet at the park entrance by nine-thirty. If we all leave our houses by nine, that should give us plenty of time to get out there.' Langdon handed Beau's phone back, grateful that he had friends he could count on. He half-smiled at Beau as a thanks.

'Did Eric say anything about the news?' asked Tom.

'Yeah, he said he saw it, but not to worry. We'll talk about it some more when we're all at the castle.'

The three boys walked off to class together.

Chapter 21

Finally, Friday afternoon arrived, and after school, Langdon went straight from school to the aquatic centre. It was much closer than getting the bus home and having to ride his bike. He'd told Hayley he needed to stay back at the library, and she'd bought his lie. He'd made sure she had hopped on the bus safely, with the house key, then he jogged to the Aquatic Centre, arriving at 3:20 p.m. Finn was already there, waiting. Langdon jogged up the pathway and spotted him sitting on the steps to the entrance.

He slowed his pace and approached quietly, admiring Finn's ridiculously good-looking features. The way his short-cropped dark hair spiked up, and his deep brown eyes peered down at his phone, his brow furrowed in concentration. Finn was wearing long black boardshorts that ended at his knees and a dark blue shirt that clung to his biceps.

'Hey,' greeted Langdon, slightly breathless from seeing Finn.

Finn's eyes lit up at the sound of Langdon's voice, 'Hey yourself,' he greeted, getting up to stand directly in front of Langdon, not caring if anyone was watching. And before Langdon knew what was happening, Finn leaned in and gently brushed his lips against his. He then surprised Langdon again by grabbing his hand, holding three of his fingers, and lightly tugging for them to continue walking into the centre.

Langdon was pleasantly surprised. They had not kissed in public before, and he quickly glanced around to see if anyone was watching. As they walked, he gently squeezed Finn's hand to confirm he was happy to see him. Although he wasn't a fan of public displays of affection. At this moment though, he wasn't going to pull away. Not after their last encounter where he left Finn to run after Tom.

'So, if you're grounded, how can you be here?' asked Finn.

Langdon gave him a wink and said, 'What they don't know won't hurt them.'

'Really?' asked Finn, raising his eyebrows. 'How long did they ground you for?'

'Until Sunday,' complained Langdon. 'But I needed to see you, I just need to leave around four o'clock to make it home before them. I know that doesn't give us long, but at least we have some time together.'

'Oh, that's sneaky.' Finn laughed, holding Langdon's hand tighter. 'We better make the most of it then,' Finn added as he smiled cheekily, his dimple prominently displaying itself. 'So, what happened Tuesday afternoon? Did you catch up with your friend? It's just…we haven't really talked since then.' Finn lowered his eyes to the ground.

Langdon looked at Finn as they were walking. He stopped and held Finn's hands in his as he said, 'I'm so sorry I ran out on you that day, I was just surprised that my friend saw us. I'm sorry, it was nothing against you,' he paused. 'I just needed to explain it to him. I told him how I feel about you.'

Finn smiled and nodded. 'You did, hey?' He smiled. 'So, he was okay with you being with me?'

'Yeah, he honestly doesn't care. It just took him by surprise, that's all.'

'Mmm, okay. Come on, let's make the most of the time we have this afternoon.' He tugged Langdon's hand as they walked further inside.

They walked straight to the kiosk and bought a packet of chips and a drink each. Then, they headed for the back grassed section beside the pool. They spread out Finn's towel before sitting side by side, their hands entwined again.

Finn gently swept his thumb over Langdon's hand, the small but significant gesture sending chills through his body.

They were sitting in a quiet area, away from the crowd. Finn released Langdon's hand to open his packet of chips, so Langdon did the same. They ate hungrily and popped the drink cans open to take a big swig. The fizzy drink caused them to burp, making them laugh. They spoke about their day as they ate and looked around at the organised chaos.

After-school swim lessons were taking place, so half the pool was sectioned off. The noise was loud — swim instructors yelling stroke corrections, kids screaming, and Langdon could even hear the heavy breathing from the effort of the swimmers. The parents' attention was focused intently on their children, while other children were swimming or being reprimanded for mucking around. Finn and Langdon had wisely chosen to set up as far away as they could manage.

They talked about their after-school activities, catching each other up on their week. The weather was heating up and sitting this close to Finn, who was touching and caressing, made his senses go into overdrive. Langdon thought that if he didn't burn the intense energy stirring in his body, he would combust.

'Come on, let's go for a swim,' Langdon tugged at Finn's hand before jumping up, pulling his t-shirt over his head, revealing a toned stomach. Then, glancing down, realised his sports shorts were tighter in the front. Hoping it wasn't obvious, he took off in a jog, then slowed, taking large strides to dive into the pool. He began swimming freestyle and was at the other end of the pool before Finn jumped in.

Finn

Finn had to hide his smirk as he waited for Langdon at the shallow end. He'd seen the pleasure his light caresses to Langdon's skin had caused. He'd noticed Langdon's breathing change, he'd listened as it became faster and saw his chest rising and falling in his sideward glances. He knew Langdon was restraining himself. Finn knew because he felt exactly the same way. He enjoyed Langdon's company, and his feelings were growing stronger each time they were together. They seemed to draw out the best in one another, and Finn had only seen kindness, gentleness, - okay, sometimes not so gentle moves. But that was a turn-on, and he knew Langdon would never hurt him. Langdon was never rough with him, and Finn felt lucky and grateful for that. Finn had been in one relationship where a male partner was not so gentle and sometimes moody, it had not ended well. He felt he had a connection with Langdon; more than just physically, they had connected emotionally.

Finn stood firmly with his back against the pool end, with both arms resting over the edge. One of his knees was bent so his foot was against the side, watching Langdon swim.

Langdon

Langdon swam two more laps before swimming up next to Finn. He rested against his side, elbow resting on the edge, watching Finn. He looked into Finn's deep brown eyes. He loved getting lost in there, their earthy tone grounded him and sparked the electric connection he felt. He lowered his eyes to Finn's lips, his gaze falling onto Finn's full bottom lip.

Damn it! Langdon looked away, shaking his head to clear his mind, towards the people around the pool and the parents at the other side of the shallow end eagerly watching their child's swim lesson. If he hadn't looked away, he wouldn't have been able to help himself. He would have kissed Finn right there in front of everyone.

Finn

Finn loved it when Langdon's attention was on him. He liked the way Langdon stared into his eyes; he felt their connection and the desire sparking to life. He looked around to see that they were secluded at the far end of the pool.

'Hey, did you see on the news there was a wolf in the area where you live?' asked Finn, directing his full attention to Langdon. He had watched the news and thought it was remarkably close to his boyfriend's place.

Langdon

Langdon stopped breathing, his anxiety grew like a wildfire in his stomach. 'Uh, yeah, I saw that.' He tried his best to sound casual while pretending to adjust the tie on his shorts so that he wasn't making eye contact.

'What do you make of it?' Finn pressed.

Langdon, breathing finally back under control, looked up at Finn. 'Nothing really. I don't know why it was in my area, but it's gone now, and it didn't hurt anyone.'

Finn could hear the change in Langdon's voice, the defensiveness like he were protecting the wolf. 'Well, I think it's cool. I think wolves are misunderstood, and I hope he's now somewhere safe.'

Langdon looked at Finn and smiled. He didn't want to talk about the wolf, as he could never tell Finn his secret. To change the subject, he filled Finn in on what happened Tuesday night–the story he gave his parents and about how mad they were. He finished by telling Finn that as well as being grounded, his dad had taken his phone off him.

'Gee, that sucks, he took your phone? Why weren't you able to text me on Tuesday, though?'

'I'd left my phone at home on the charger.'

'Yeah, but later, one of your texts didn't sound right? Were you drunk?'

'No, I was tired, and I was typing quickly, so my typing was a bit shit.'

'Oh, that's okay, I was worried about you, you know, when you didn't respond.'

'Yeah, sorry about that.'

'Bugger, I was hoping you'd come over Friday night,' Finn's eyes showed his disappointment.

Langdon found it unbearable to see Finn disappointed and leant in to kiss him gently before pulling back and reaching for his hand. Holding it under the water, he gently caressed it with both his hands, running his rough fingers over the palm of Finn's hand, and down each finger, 'I'm sorry, but I promise to make it up to you.'

Finn's mouth tugged into a half-smile before thinking and said, 'Hmmm, all right, I bet I can think of some way for you to make it up to me.' His smile transformed into a cheeky grin.

'Ohhh,' breathed Langdon, moving closer, his other hand moving to discretely rub the front of Finn's shorts.

Finn's breath caught in his throat, he swallowed hard, 'Ohh.' He closed his eyes, beginning to pant under Langdon's ministrations.

Langdon could feel every bit of Finn enjoying what he was doing. Finn's eyes popped open, suddenly recalling where they were. He quickly put his hand firmly against Langdon's, stopping his actions. 'Not here,' he breathed, looking around.

'No one can see,' whispered Langdon, close to Finn's ear.

'Not the point,' said Finn determinedly.

Langdon smiled and removed his hand, going back to just holding Finn's hand underwater. They stood close, whispering until Langdon said it was time for him to go.

'Come here, then.' Finn gently placed his hands on Langdon's jawline, pulled him in, and planted a big kiss on Langdon's lips. He pressed closer, pushing his tongue to open Langdon's mouth and caressed his tongue sensually before pulling away, leaving Langdon slightly breathless, wanting more.

Finn smiled, giving Langdon's hand a gentle tug before turning and pushing his body up and out of the pool. Langdon followed, and they walked over to get Finn's towel. Langdon waited patiently, not minding he was without a towel. There was no way he could have brought one to school. His schoolbag was heavy and full enough.

'Do you want to get together Sunday?' asked Finn as he dried the water off his toned back.

'I'm busy in the morning and won't be free until late afternoon.'

Finn's eyebrows raised in question, 'Doing what?'

'Getting together with my mate Tom–ah, the one you didn't get a chance to meet because I stupidly left you on my couch to run after him.' Langdon's features soured, his nose bunched up, and his deep blue eyes half-closed at the memory.

'That's okay. Can't have you all to myself, can I,' teased Finn. 'Hey, here,' Finn passed his towel to Langdon. 'Dry off.'

'Thanks,' Langdon grabbed his towel and ran it over his hair that had continued dripping down his chest and back. 'I'll see what time I get home, and I'll text you.' Then he quickly dried himself and handed it back.

'Deal,' agreed Finn. 'So, am I ever going to meet your friends?'

'Sure, one day.'

Finn nodded, holding onto Langdon's hand again.

Glancing at his watch, Langdon said, 'Shit, I gotta go, it'll take me an hour to run home, and I can't be late, or I'll be grounded longer.'

'No worries. Hey, why don't I give you a lift?' He saw Langdon considering and added, 'Come on,' and dragged him by the hand to his silver HiLux parked on the sidewalk.

In just ten minutes, Langdon made it home, had time to dry off completely, and was sitting in front of the TV before his parents returned.

Chapter 22

Langdon was grateful for Sunday to roll around, eager to get to the castle to see Eric. He needed to talk more about what Eric thought about him being on the news and also ask him if the offer was still on the table for him to stay out there during the full moon. He was grateful that Eric had been so nice about it when they spoke on the phone Thursday morning.

They'd arranged to meet at the park entrance on Sunday morning. Langdon would no longer be grounded, his punishment lifted, and iPhone returned to him, however, not without a lecture on respect and rules from his father. Langdon had just nodded and went along with everything his father had said, he could not risk further restrictions.

Arriving at the park before his friends, Langdon stood by his bike and checked his phone, scrolling through Instagram and checking out the latest gossip. Langdon heard them minutes before he saw Tom and Beau arrive together.

They were early. Eric said he would pick them up at ten o'clock, so they had twenty minutes to spare. The three of them stood casually beside their bikes to wait and catch up with each other.

Beau

Tom had been talking to Langdon about their karate blue belt pattern. Langdon was moving his arms in a set formation combining controlled kicks, a roundhouse, and then a set of punches to emphasise the correct formation, his biceps flexing with each jab.

Beau looked at Langdon, he envied his tall athletic body and hated that he always had the attention of the girls. Langdon had always flirted so easily, and he never became nervous like he was around girls.

Beau thought back to Friday, in English class, when he had seen Stacey, beautiful, graceful Stacey. Oh, he'd had a crush on her since the start of the year when they were put in the same class.

Beau had watched as she had walked towards Langdon's desk, her sports shorts, sitting high on her petite frame, showing too much thigh and the shorts hugging her bottom tightly. As she had approached Langdon, she had flicked her long, light brown hair over her shoulder and stopped beside his desk. She'd glanced down at Langdon, but he had looked straight past her, then back at his book. Stacey had leaned over his desk and asked to borrow a pen, Beau was sure Langdon would have been able to see her cleavage if he had looked, but he just reached into his pencil case and handed her what she asked for.

Beau wished she had asked him for a pen. A pen, a ruler, his virginity — he wasn't fussy. Anything to get her attention on him and not Langdon. Beau thought about asking Langdon about her.

Beau waited for them to finish before asking, 'Hey Langdon, are you interested in Stacey?'

Langdon

Langdon turned to face Beau, his eyebrows scrunched together as he asked, 'Why?'

Tom had to pretend to wipe something off his mouth to hide his smirk as he waited for Langdon's response.

'Oh, just because I saw her ask you for a pen in English, I think she likes you.'

'Nah,' Langdon dismissed the idea quickly.

'So, you don't want to ask her out then?' asked Beau.

'No, I don't. Actually, I'm already seeing someone,' Langdon added, looking Beau directly in the eyes for the question he knew was coming.

'Oh,' said Beau, a bit surprised. 'Who? Do I know her?'

Langdon took a deep breath and was glad to be standing next to his bike so he could fiddle with the handlebars. 'No, and it's *he*.' Langdon stared seriously back at Beau.

Beau's expression didn't change.

Langdon could see the unease in Beau's eyes and could tell he didn't want to say the wrong thing.

'Is this a joke?' Beau narrowed his eyes.

Langdon shook his head.

'So, you're seeing a guy?' Beau asked tentatively. He waited for Langdon to burst out laughing and say, Nah, got ya. But he didn't.

Langdon nodded, chewing the inside of his mouth. He hated the look he got when he told Tom, and now Beau looked shocked, and he waited to see if Beau would be repulsed.

'Pick up your jaw off the ground, Beau,' Tom chuckled.

Beau scowled at Tom. Then he asked Langdon, 'Are you coming out?'

Langdon shook his head, 'I'm not gay. Look, I met Finn, and we hit it off and started going out. I don't want anyone putting a label on it.' He paused and looked at the ground, kicking the dirt with the toe of his shoe, and then he continued, 'You can't help who you're attracted to. It is what it is. We've been seeing each other for a couple of months now. I really like him.'

That took a lot for Langdon to say to Beau. He had felt nervous but not ashamed. He was proud of his relationship. He thought there were so many labels these days: gay, straight, bi, trans, queer— Langdon hated that last term for describing someone's sexuality. The way he saw it, relationships only came down to the way the other person made you feel, how you made them feel, the way you spoke to each other. The heart wants what the heart wants. Sometimes, it's not black and white, it is what it is. Finn and his touch made him feel alive, connected, and special, it all resonated within him. Without needing to justify his existence, he was able to just be himself. Finn was fond of him, just for who he was.

As Beau thought about it for a minute, Langdon wasn't sure if he was okay with his sexuality. He would tell Beau to get the hell out if he said anything remotely negative about his relationship. He would defend it, and Finn to the ends of the earth.

Langdon stared back at Beau, the moment felt charged with a defining moment of their friendship. Beau's next words broke the thick air.

'So, you don't mind if I ask Stacey out then?'

Langdon and Tom looked at one another and burst out laughing. They had never seen Beau ask a girl out before. He had always been so obsessed with computer games. Langdon was also relieved that the topic of conversation was taken off of him.

'No, I don't mind,' said Langdon, recovering from Beau's question.

'Great,' Beau smiled.

'Hey Beau, I'd rather you keep this to yourself. Um, I haven't told anyone yet.'

'Sure, I won't tell anyone.' Beau glanced at Tom to see his reaction, but he was just conveniently admiring his shoe, digging at something in the dirt.

'My parents and sister don't know yet,' Langdon went on. 'But for now, I just want to see where this goes, no pressure. For now, we just like being together.'

Beau nodded in understanding.

They'd been so engrossed in their conversation that Langdon hadn't paid any attention to the vehicle approaching.

He looked up to see Eric's HiLux drive slowly into the small car park. It looked dirty, with dried mud sprayed along the panels. With the engine still running, Eric rolled the passenger window down and called out, 'Hey boys, jump in!'

Langdon jumped into the front seat beside Eric, while Beau and Tom climbed into the back seat, all greeting a hello. Buckling his seatbelt, Langdon glanced at Eric.

Eric

Eric smiled in greeting and after they were buckled up, he put the vehicle in reverse and then drove onto the dirt track leading to his castle.

Langdon stared out the window as he drove. Hundreds of trees passed by as Langdon idly watched the different shaped leaves, the greenery flashing by with each kilometre they drove.

The vibration reverberating through the vehicle's suspension lulled Tom and Beau to quiet in the backseat. They sat with their eyes transfixed on the passing vision of the lush forest, the green, yellow, scarlet, and orange bared on foliage and plant life bleeding into a blur under their gaze. The heat of the morning sun was strong, already awake hours before to warm the land and trees. The rising temperature had warmed the passengers enough for Eric to lower the air conditioning throughout the vehicle for their comfort.

Eric made small talk on the twenty-minute drive to the castle. He chatted about the weather, his drive from Sydney, and asked about their bike ride to the park. Eric was glad that Langdon had made contact. He was concerned the boy would cause injury or, worse, death to anyone unlucky enough to cross his path in wolf form. He had been aware on the day they first visited him at the castle that even though he had given warnings and tales of his own misguidance in coming to terms with the curse, Langdon was in denial.

Eric knew that at first, Langdon did not believe the curse was real, nor did he want to take Eric up on the offer of accommodation throughout a full moon. This had riled Eric up, but he had maintained a balanced mood, a balanced equilibrium to enable his senses to read Langdon and his friends. He had picked up on the fear, curiosity, regret, and some excitement, only the excitement was mostly from one of the other boys.

He knew it would take time, time that Eric could not rush, for Langdon to give in to the curse and learn to live his life safely. For with the curse came an increased level of speed, better hearing, more strength, and stealth. Unfortunately, it also came with an increase in emotions and testosterone, and their desire to mate intensified. They can also intensely smell chemosignals, which allows werewolves to know what someone else is feeling. These are read through unconscious messages sent through body odours for them to interpret emotional states. Eric had learned a lot since submitting to the curse and everything that came with it. Now he needed to teach Langdon.

The result of intensified emotions was that Eric found he needed to find a release. His body would become so pent up with energy and sexual tension and the need for release which he could only moderately find with a long run. But ultimately, his desire intensified the need to be with his partner. Physically and emotionally, Eric had noticed his increase in sexual need in his relationship with Summer.

Although, there was always the week before a full moon when his emotions were extremely heightened, he would rise quickly to anger and had to learn to control his actions. A punch in the wall after a fight affected him so much that he never wanted to see that fear in Summer's eyes again.

God, he'd been so angry, the anger had flowed through his veins like venom. He had never hurt Summer, however, at times just before the full moon he would yell and growl about everything and needed to lace up his joggers and head outside for a run to get his emotions balanced. A run would always clear his head, a mix of songs playing in his ears by *Imagine Dragons* being his favourites. He was also particularly attached to the techno version of "Eye of the Tiger".

His higher testosterone meant a higher sex drive. *Geez, he was constantly aroused—mostly around Summer.* This had increased much to Summer's pleasure, as he had become more attentive, more in tune, reading her desire, scenting her pheromones, and understanding how to increase her desire.

Thinking about Summer now, he could recall her beautiful green eyes that had a fleck of gold when he looked closely, and her long thick light brown hair, always out unless she was tying it back for work. She had a petite frame, Eric thought she was perfect and told her so often. Eric stroked his thumb along the steering wheel as he thought of her. He had to focus more on the driving track to ease the arousal that arose with his thoughts of his girlfriend.

'Oh, seeing that castle in the light of day is so different from the night,' Langdon said to whoever was listening. 'I notice different things each time I come out here,' he mumbled.

Eric glanced over, 'Yeah, it used to freak me out at night-time when I first started coming out here.'

Langdon looked at Eric, surprise and question in his eyes.

'Well, you've been here at night. It has an eerie feeling. I've always thought it was haunted.' Eric laughed, pushing away his thoughts from some strange nights he had spent out there. He'd definitely heard a person's voice on a couple of occasions, but no one else was there, and he couldn't clearly hear what they were saying. There had also been some bumps in the night, some scrapes, and he had just convinced himself that it was just his imagination every time.

'Yeah, that night we were out here, I felt something up in one of the rooms.' He paused, then stammered, 'Oh, um, I mean, we thought someone might have been home. It looked like a light on upstairs, so I went up to see, but it was only the moonlight shining in the window.'

'Mmm, this castle is old, who knows what went on here years ago,' mused Eric.

Eric pulled his HiLux slowly onto the property, down the hill, and parked in front of the castle. Everyone climbed out and walked to the front of the vehicle. The boys waited for Eric to take the lead. Eric wasted no time walking them towards the castle and inside, taking the sheets off the couches and telling them to make themselves comfortable.

'I only come out here once a month, so I keep the furniture covered to keep dust and moths off. Usually, I arrive a day before the full moon to clean the place up a bit, open the windows and allow fresh air to vent into the rooms. Although occasionally I only arrive in the afternoon of the full moon and don't have time to do much.' Eric was considering how much he had told them on their first visit out here a month ago, but he knew that at the time, the boys were nervous and wouldn't remember some of the conversation.

'Oh, so that's why sheets were covering the couches the first time we came here,' Tom stated in understanding.

'Yeah, that was a bit of a rushed one. I made it out late and only had time to throw the food I'd bought into the fridge and bread on the kitchen table. I didn't have time to go around opening all the windows.'

'What made you smash through a window that night we were here?' asked Beau.

'It's hard to explain. I guess I sensed a trespasser on the property, and I could smell humans inside my house. A scent I did not recognise, and it was an instinct to attack. I'm sorry to say that you were in the wrong place at the wrong time, and I could have killed one of you.' Eric looked at Langdon, with remorse and sorrow filling his deep brown eyes. He lowered his head slightly.

It was as though Langdon picked up the emotion in Eric's body language because he quickly said, 'Yeah, but you didn't and it's our fault anyway, we shouldn't have come here,' he looked around at his friends for support.

'Yeah, it was a last resort, our camping trip had gone to crap, and it was raining so much. We were lost and thought we were lucky seeing this castle, as it was the only shelter for us,' explained Tom.

'Oh well, what's done is done,' said Eric sombrely.

They were all just standing in the lounge room, so Eric motioned for them to sit, and he walked into the kitchen to grab some cans of Coke from the fridge, remembering from their last visit what the boys liked.

Walking back into the lounge room, he saw Langdon and Tom sitting on the two-seater, and the other boy had sat in the recliner. He passed the drinks around, hearing a murmur of thanks in response, before sitting himself comfortably in the remaining recliner nearest Langdon.

Eric could tell that Langdon and his friends were a package deal, they stuck together, and Eric thought it was ideal that Langdon had their support.

Soon, the boys looked at ease, and Eric decided it was an appropriate time to ask Langdon about Tuesday night, the last full moon that had been upon them, and how it was on the news. 'So, made the news, hey Langdon?' Eric joked, trying to lighten the mood.

'Yeah,' Langdon suddenly looked sombre. 'What do we do now?'

'Well, there's nothing we can do about what happened. Although moving forward, I feel it's in all of our best interests that you come here to the castle for every full moon.'

He looked over to see the hesitation in Langdon's eyes.

'Langdon, before you say no, it's not safe for you to be transitioning and running around town as a wolf, putting others at risk of your bite. As a wolf, it is instinct to hunt and to get to safety, and if you end up in a place where you don't feel safe, you will take it out on anyone around you. Not to mention Animal Control will be on the lookout for the next few weeks, probably right through to our next full moon.' Eric studied Langdon seriously, waiting for his reply.

Langdon let out a breath, his shoulders sagging as he realised what he had to do. 'Yeah, I guess,' he agreed. 'I was an idiot before. I thought maybe it wouldn't happen to me again, but now I get it, and I know it will be safer for me here with you.'

Tom

Tom noticed the exchange and thought that it looked as though Langdon was compliant with Eric. He wasn't argumentative or sarcastic, he just seemed to agree with Eric. Tom knew it made sense, but seeing Langdon with Eric, he saw a change in dynamics. He thought back to when Eric was apologising for biting Langdon and how he'd lowered his head and Langdon tried to console Eric. *Langdon didn't use to be like that.* It would make sense though because he had looked up werewolves, and *Eric bit Langdon, so that would make him the alpha and Langdon the beta.*

Eric

Eric nodded in approval. 'Good, I'm happy to hear that. So, for the next full moon, I suggest we meet at the park. Hang on, I'll just check my phone to see when it is.' He scrolled and tapped on his phone, 'Thursday, twelfth of December.' He looked up to meet Langdon's eyes. 'Okay, since it's on a Thursday, bring everything you need, and the following day we will call back to your house for you to get ready for school and also pick up your sister.'

'Oh, Eric, I'm on exam block next week, so I only need to go in for my exams. I won't need to go on that day. Hayley will still have to go to school, but Mum is on her long service leave then and, because it's the end of the year, she may let Hayley have the day off. They're not doing much in her grade, anyway.'

'Oh, okay, right, um,' Eric thought for a second. 'Well, I can still pick you up around three o'clock. I'll try to get to you as soon as I can, however this month it'll be later than usual, I have a meeting with a client at lunchtime, that I can't reschedule. Do you want to ride your bike, and I'll pick you up at the park entrance? Or I can pick you up from your house, it's not that much further.' He looked at Langdon, waiting patiently for a response.

'Yeah, um,' he thought about what the best solution for his next transition would be. 'Maybe you could pick me up? If that's not too much trouble. But not at my house, could you meet me beside the park on Wheeler Street?'

'Yeah, that's not a problem. I'll try to be there by three, I'll text when I'm nearly there, okay?'

'Sure, that'd be great.'

Langdon looked at Tom, 'I'll have to tell my parents that I'm staying at yours that night.'

Tom nodded. He knew how serious this was, and he needed to be there for Langdon.

Eric turned his attention to Langdon, 'Langdon, because it will be late afternoon, we will both be on edge and chomping at the bit to be outside. So I'll get us here, and we can go for a walk in the forest for the transition, that way we won't break anything. Also, now that we have acclimated while both of us were in wolf form, we will get on fine.'

'Does this mean we are a pack or something? I read a few things about wolves online.'

Eric's mouth twitched into a smile, 'I don't know anything about packs, Langdon. I only know what I've seen in movies. But I think a lot of that is made up, and we just need to take things as they come. I will look out for you, though.'

Langdon nodded, 'Thanks,' he responded, keeping his eyes on the rug, as though he was deep in thought.

Tom and Beau glanced at each other as if silently saying, *Can you believe this?* Eric noticed all the minor exchanges of glances between the three boys.

The boys quietly drank their Cokes and looked around at the interior of the castle. You could see the stone bricks from the inside, but they weren't showing damage like they were on the outside. The couches were a few years old but looked newish because they were covered with sheets so often. There was a painting on the wall of a lake surrounded by a lush forest, a deer half hiding behind a tree and tiny white flowers spread across the ground like snow. It was a peaceful scene.

Langdon asked Eric a few more questions and got to know him more, finding out what he did for work, and Eric told them about his girlfriend Summer. Tom and Beau joined in now and then, finding Eric friendly and accommodating. He kept offering biscuits and sandwiches and more drinks.

'No, we're fine, thanks,' said Tom in reply to yet another one of Eric's offers.

'Any other questions?' Eric looked at each of his guests in turn.

Beau surprised all of them by asking, 'Eric, do you think there could be any hidden compartments or secret cupboards or doors in this castle?'

'No,' replied Eric, looking curiously at Beau. 'Why do you ask that?'

'Oh, because I've been reading up on old castles and back in the day, they used to hide secret papers and stuff in places. Some had secret cupboards or a bookshelf that opened when you pulled a certain book.'

Eric chuckled. 'Well, not that I've seen, although this castle has been here for over 100 years. A few generations have lived here, so it wouldn't surprise me if there were, but I've never found any.'

'Do you think one day we could all have a look and search for any secret holding places?'

'Sure, we can do that. What do you think we might find?' asked Eric. This piqued his interest, and he was fond of Beau with his analytical nature.

'A diary or something that could lead us to a cure,' Beau said, making eye contact with Eric.

Eric smiled at Beau; *he is definitely the analytical one*. 'You never know.' He winked at Beau. 'We'll have to arrange a time for you to come back and have a good look, but unfortunately, I need to get back to Sydney. I have a job I'm working on.'

'Sure, no worries,' Beau, excited at the prospect of being able to find a cure, was eager to make plans.

Eric looked at his watch. It was after 1:00 p.m. Time had gone by fast while they had been so busy discussing everything and getting to know each other better. 'How about I drive you boys back to the park?'

'Yeah, thanks.' Langdon stood and walked into the kitchen to throw his empty Coke can in the bin, his friends following to do the same. They then followed Eric out to the HiLux for the drive back.

*

Langdon

It was late afternoon by the time Langdon arrived home. He had ridden his bike fast and knew he would arrive home before Tom and

Beau. Now, his thoughts went to Finn. He pulled out his phone to text him.

Hey, what u doin?

A few minutes went by before he saw his reply.

Not much, **you?** Finn texted.

Home now, can I see u? Langdon texted.

Sure, want to come here, Dad's out.

Being alone with Finn is a chance Langdon would never miss—they had so little time to themselves.

Be there in 20, Langdon quickly typed and hit send, before looking for his mum to ask if he could borrow the car.

'Mum,' Langdon called as he walked towards the kitchen.

When he didn't receive a reply, he called out louder.

'I'm out here,' called his mother.

Langdon knew that 'out here' meant at the clothesline. He walked quickly, making large strides in his rush. He stopped at the line to help her take the remaining socks and jocks off before asking, 'Mum, can I please borrow the car for a couple of hours?'

'You just got home. Where are you off to now?' asked his mother, turning to look up at her son, who was at least a head and shoulder taller than her. He looked at her with pleading eyes, smiling as innocently as he could and pleading with his hands placed together.

'I told a mate I'd call by, I, uh, I have some science notes for him.' Lie. Langdon held his breath, waiting. He needed to stay on good terms with his parents to allow him the privileges he desperately needed. The subject of science had always been his downfall, so that was his best excuse. He'd added the last bit to persuade his mother to agree. His mother had always encouraged studying and said school came first.

'Okay, fine, but be home by dinner.'

'Great! Thanks, Mum.' He leaned over and kissed her softly, yet swiftly, on the cheek. Sometimes he did that when he knew his mother was in two minds about letting him do something, and showing his appreciation with any sort of affection seemed to butter her up. She had always encouraged affection; however as Langdon had grown up, he had pushed her away, not a fan of cuddles. But occasionally, he wanted to show her he loved her, and that she was a great mum.

Langdon turned and jogged back inside to grab the keys off the kitchen bench. 'See ya,' he called as he went out the carport door and settled into the car. Putting the key in the ignition, he started the car and reversed slowly and was soon on the road to Finn's house. He was buzzing with excitement and anticipation of seeing him.

Arriving at Finn's, he knocked three times and waited. Shuffling uneasily from each foot, he stared down at his thongs, wiggling his toes as he waited. He could hear Finn's footsteps and waited in anticipation to see the guy who had totally and irrevocably stolen his heart.

The door finally opened, and seeing Finn overwhelmed Langdon with desire and need. He stepped forward and greeted Finn with a firm brush of his lips against his, drawing back to look into his deep brown eyes, drinking in his features.

'Well, hello to you too,' breathed Finn.

Langdon grinned. 'Hi.'

They had needed to restrain themselves at the pool the previous day, and Langdon wanted to feel Finn's skin against his, and Finn's lips on his own—he thought back to the way Finn gently bit his lower lip, the sensation sending pleasant chills through his body.

Finn could see the desire shining out of Langdon's eyes and grabbed his hand to pull him inside. They stood together, entwining their fingers as they looked at one another. Their gazes spoke volumes of sexual desire. Langdon stroked the soft skin of Finn's hand, enjoying the gentle touches. But he was also ready for more.

'Where's your bedroom?' breathed Langdon softly.

Without a word, Finn, still holding Langdon's hand, turned and walked down the hall into a medium-sized room with a king-single sized bed in the centre. The walls were an off-white colour and had posters of different bands and a couple of dancers that Langdon assumed Finn admired.

Not a word was spoken before Finn turned to him, leaned in and kissed Langdon—properly—like he had wanted to at the aquatic centre. His mouth pressed firmly against Langdon's, he guided Langdon backwards before deepening the kiss to a more sensual caress of his tongue.

Too occupied with his hands full of his boyfriend, Langdon's back subtly grazed against the wall until he got the hint and allowed himself to be pressed firmly against it.

Langdon grabbed Finn's hips to pull him closer, now both feeling the other's arousal. A deep groan escaped Langdon's mouth, in turn causing Finn to moan in pleasure. Finn ran his hand through Langdon's unruly blonde hair as he drew his lips along Langdon's mouth, running his tongue over his bottom lip, and the top, before gently moving his kisses across his jaw, down to his neck.

Langdon's breathing only turned heavier as Finn ran his hands down his chest and lifted his t-shirt to trace his hands against his bare skin, to feel the firm muscles that seemed to flex at his touch. Finn moved his hands in gentle movements across Langdon's chest.

He continued his caresses, his fingers riding the bump of Langdon's hard nipples, then he moved his hands lower, his mouth accompanying them lower and lower until he was kneeling on the floor with his lips at Langdon's toned stomach.

The sight of Finn on his knees nearly made Langdon combust. He swallowed thickly, heart hammering in his chest, and his mouth went dry. Anticipation of what might come had his body tingling all over.

Finn gripped the waistband of Langdon's shorts and placed one hand on Langdon's growing bulge. Langdon's breath hitched, letting out little moans of ecstasy, and he closed his eyes, relishing the touch.

Finn looked up from his position at Langdon as he moved to lower Langdon's shorts.

'Okay?' Finn asked, wanting to know if Langdon wanted to stop.

'Yes,' sighed Langdon.

Finn had them off in one swift move. What he did next had Langdon groaning loudly in pleasure. With one hand gripping Langdon's thigh, Finn's other hand nudged the door shut.

Chapter 23

The next two weeks went by with the regular routine of school, footy training, and karate for Langdon while Finn was busy with academics, gymnastics, and dance. During the school week, it had been difficult to navigate their way to each other. Instead of quick visits, they had to devote their attention to school assignments and after-school activities.

They did not, however, miss out entirely on each other's attention. Texting every night, and long talks on the phone kept them close; even phone sex became a hot contender to satisfy Langdon's increased desire.

It had come about one night when it had been three days of not seeing one another. Finn and Langdon then took turns initiating smooth, sexy talk, especially on the nights they had more time and hadn't seen each other.

It was a Wednesday night after Finn arrived home from gymnastics; it was after 9 p.m. because he had to work as well. Langdon had taken their conversation from school to more personal subjects—asking questions to find out more about Finn's history and relationships. Finn was relaxed and comfortable enough to share more about his past two relationships and when he first found he was attracted to males.

Finn had told him he had tried to go along with the regular crowd of dating girls in grades eight and nine, but didn't feel the same passion as when he first hooked up with another male gymnast. He had made the decision then that he wouldn't deny his attraction to guys.

He'd also been a victim of gay slander but didn't let it get to him because he liked affection but didn't go overboard with public displays of affection and believed that no matter your sexuality, no one has the right to judge. 'You can never please everyone,' Finn had told him firmly. 'So instead do your best to look after yourself, treat yourself and your partner with respect and don't take anything less than you deserve. I'll always do right by you, Langdon,' he had promised.

'And I'll do the same.' Langdon had never felt so connected to another person who he believed he may be falling in love with. He didn't want to say those three little words over the phone though, no, he would wait until he could say them looking deep into Finn's eyes.

Langdon, Tom, and Beau had discussed their plans about heading out to the castle to do some thorough investigating. They wanted to search the walls, floorboards, and any hidden compartments for letters or papers relating to a possible cure for this curse that had been put upon their friend.

Langdon had also been texting Eric, and arrangements had been made for them to meet up on Saturday morning. Eric had been very accommodating about them investigating his castle. His texts had been quite jovial, and he'd ended the last text saying he was looking forward to it.

Chapter 24

Eric

Eric was easily able to get away early to meet the boys at 9 a.m. as Summer was working. Her catering event had been for a wedding, and she needed to be there bright and early to open and start preparing breakfast and would be contained most of the day with that contract.

Eric was glad that the boys wanted to come back out to the castle since he had to go out there, anyway. In fact, this was the most he had been to the castle in a single month. He knew he had to help Langdon with his transitioning because he didn't have anyone to help him. He felt protective of him and liked that the boy now felt comfortable enough to contact him. They had become friends, unlikely friends, but friends, nonetheless.

Between work commitments and his girlfriend, Eric could usually only get out to the castle on a full moon. On this occasion, when he was meeting Langdon and his friends, he had fortunately tied the visit with his work schedule and Summer's.

Some weekends, he had needed to go out to the castle for maintenance to either fix the outside structure or parts of the interior. The outside was overwrought with mould or chunks of block, either partly or completely removed, as though someone had hacked at it with an axe–which is possibly due to the age of the castle.

Eric had been told it had been built back in the early 1900s. He had put in many hours on the inside as well; the heavy grey stone blocks also formed the interior and did not - thankfully, need any work. However, the kitchen needed new benchtops and cupboard doors. After inheriting the castle, he donated the old, faded, and torn couch that reeked of piss and purchased a new velvet blue couch with recliners to provide him comfort for the time he spent out there.

Eric knew he could never tell anyone his secret. It was not the sort of thing anyone would believe, anyway. He would just have to endure the curse once a month and try to live his life accordingly. Now, he also felt responsible for Langdon. It was his doing after all that succumbed Langdon to the curse. He wanted to mentor Langdon with everything he knew and all he had learned about werewolves.

True to his word, Eric was waiting in the car park at the entrance of the driving track leading to the castle when the three boys arrived on their bikes.

The drive out was bumpy and scenic once again, just as the boys remembered. Beau used the time to ask Eric questions about the castle. Unfortunately, the boys weren't told anything they didn't already know. They knew it had been in Eric's family for over a hundred years and handed down through the generations, most recently from Eric's uncle, who had also succumbed to the curse.

This information was found only in the diary Eric had found in the collection of books left to him. Eric never found who it was that bit him, as he never came across another wolf while he was in human or wolf form. He had spent his time after becoming a werewolf within the premises. His property stretched for many kilometres, it was a private estate, so privacy was never an issue.

Once inside the castle, they sat in the lounge room enjoying the refreshments offered by Eric. The boys were taking quiet sips from their Coke cans while Eric sat with a coffee, gently blowing the steam off the top.

Beau, sitting in the recliner this time, glanced around the lounge room. He kept looking towards the fireplace and looking lost in thought.

Seeing that the boys had nearly finished their drinks, and they'd eaten the biscuits he had put on the table, Eric set down his mug. 'All right, boys, where do you want to search first?' He looked at each of them, eagerly waiting to see what they would do. Eric was getting a kick out of this. He could scent the excitement and some nervousness from the boys. The castle felt alive with energy, an enormous improvement from the dreary time he normally spent out here alone.

Beau moved first, slowly rising from his recliner. He walked over to the fireplace, squatted down onto his knees, and peered inside. Reaching his arm in, he felt around the interior and back section to feel for any clues to openings.

Eric watched on in amusement as Beau reached as far up as he could then moved right down to the base, then ran his fingers along each side of the brick blocks, feeling for a groove that might shift.

Beau groaned loudly when he retreated with his hand covered black from all the soot and ash. He turned with his arm extended so he didn't get any black soot on his clothes.

Tom and Langdon laughed. 'No luck, hey Beau,' chuckled Langdon.

Beau just shook his head, his green eyes lowered in disappointment.

Eric jumped up laughing, 'Come on Beau, you can clean up in the laundry.' He led the way down the hall and out the back to a wash area. Beau turned the water on and scrubbed his arm clean, thankful to be able to remove the ash so that he didn't suffer any superficial burns.

'Thanks,' said Beau, shaking the droplets of water from his arm and wiping it dry on his denim shorts.

'Come on,' called Eric as he walked back into the lounge room.

'Why don't we all split up and search different parts of the castle?' suggested Tom.

Langdon and Eric nodded, and Beau announced, 'I'm going to the sitting room to check around the bookcase.' He strode away with renewed enthusiasm.

'Right-o,' nodded Langdon. 'Hey Tom, check upstairs with me?' Langdon was not keen on entering the same bedroom he had the night of the storm. Not by himself, anyway.

Eric went about working on his laptop and smiled as the boys went in different directions to search his castle. He shook his head. He didn't think they would find anything. Not that he had searched for any secret passageways or openings. Although throughout the time he had spent there and checked the walls for any damage, he had not come across anything suspicious or resembling a possible hidden compartment.

Langdon

'Do you reckon we'll find anything?' asked Tom as they entered the first bedroom on the left, after walking up the stairs. It appeared to be the main bedroom, with a queen-sized bed, a side table, and a tall cupboard that Langdon supposed held some of Eric's clothes.

'Dunno,' Langdon replied absently as his eyes wandered around the room.

They searched under the bed and behind it, both boys grunting as they pulled the heavy timber frame back from the wall to have a better look. They ran their hands along the blocks of brick, checking for any latches or grooves that moved a block in or out. However, nothing unusual showed up in that bedroom, or the next one they checked.

They were finishing off in the last bedroom when Tom piped up. 'This is useless, we aren't going to find anything. Eric comes out here all the time, you'd think he would have come across something if there was anything to find.'

'Yeah, I think you're right,' agreed Langdon.

They gradually made their way back to the landing, pausing now and then to check the slate floor for any part that may lift, but none did.

'So, that's cool that Eric is not phased about what was on the news, hey?' Tom looked at Langdon, who was in a crouched position to scratch the join of two slate floor pieces.

'Yeah,' agreed Langdon absentmindedly. *Is this a deeper dip? Could one of these tiles lift? Maybe if I pull it up a bit.* Langdon tried digging his fingers lower, but the grout was not allowing any penetration. Langdon stood back up to look at Tom. 'I guess he has a point, there's nothing to worry about if we are out here, it's so secluded.'

'So, you're definitely coming out here next full moon then?' Tom asked.

'Yup.'

'How do you feel about that?' Tom asked hesitantly as he bent to investigate some joins along the wall.

'Eh,' Langdon grunted, sighing as he continued, 'I guess it's for the best, at least I won't be able to hurt anyone.'

'Are you going to tell Finn?'

'No way!' Langdon looked both shocked and scared when he looked over at Tom.

'Do you think he's noticed anything different about you?' Tom paused his scratching at a line in the brick to look over at Langdon.

'What do you mean?'

'Well, you're faster and notice things before the rest of us now.'

'No, I try to tone all that down when I'm with him.'

Tom nodded. He had known Langdon for over two years now, and in the beginning, Langdon was very cocky and self-absorbed. He swaggered around school like he owned it. Sometimes with a girl hanging off him and other times, he hung with the football guys. Tom had also sat with the footy guys but had gotten to know Langdon better when he joined karate. They were often paired up because their fitness levels were similar. He had noticed Langdon had settled down a lot more this year, with hardly any bullying. Now he was even being nice to Beau. Tom thought he'd never see the day.

Tom

Tom wondered how he had never picked up that Langdon was into guys. He'd always seemed to check the girls out. Tom had only known Langdon to have one girlfriend who lasted a few months at a time, but he didn't think it had gotten too serious. It didn't worry Tom; if Langdon was into guys - maybe he was bi? Langdon never acted weird around him, like he might have been into him, so that was a relief.

The two boys continued searching all areas of the wall for any signs of secret compartments. Their silence magnified how quiet it was inside the castle. The sound of birds chirping outside was a welcome break, with all of their different calls. Some were cries of the magpie, and others were softer and melodic. It lulled them both into a thorough method of searching quietly.

'Tell me about Finn,' said Tom suddenly, looking over to where Langdon was squatted, looking at some joins in the wall.

Langdon's breathing hitched for a second. 'Okay, well, um, he's pretty cool, he's into gymnastics and he's in Hayley's hip-hop class.'

'You really like him, don't you?' asked Tom.

'Yeah, I do.' Langdon's expression softened as he glanced across at Tom.

'If you were dating a girl,' Tom paused, 'I'd be asking if you'd had sex yet.' Tom continued his search along the wall, pausing to look at Langdon.

Langdon's features melted into a slow smile. His blue eyes twinkled as he looked at Tom and said, 'I don't kiss and tell.'

Tom smiled and shook his head, 'That's all right, I don't want to know too much detail, anyway.' He paused, 'I saw enough that day I called into your place.' He grinned, as he knew he was riling Langdon up for his own amusement.

Langdon was used to Tom and knew he wouldn't say anything outright mean, so he smiled and said, 'Hmm, yes, that was a bit unexpected.'

Tom saw Langdon's cheeks turn pink and chuckled. 'What, me being there? Or what you two were getting up to?'

'You being there,' Langdon squinted his eyes and scrunched his nose in mock dismay.

Tom and Langdon both laughed and trailed off as they heard someone running up the stairs.

'Did you guys find anything?' Beau asked as he reached the top and saw Tom and Langdon crouched on the floor.

'No, nothing.' Tom stretched his legs, cracking his joints as he slowly straightened up.

'Yeah, we checked the bedrooms, the walls, the floor and found nothing,' added Langdon.

'Oh, that sucks,' Beau looked disappointed.

Langdon pushed off the wall and said to his friends, 'Oh well, let's head back down.'

'Wait!' cried Beau.

Tom and Langdon had already started heading back down the stairs, but turned to look at Beau.

'Did you guys check that small toilet area back there?' he pointed past the bedroom.

'No, but you can if you want,' said Langdon. 'We'll wait.'

Beau walked back toward the short, narrow passageway to the toilet and into the small space. There was no door, but a right-angle turn for privacy. What was once made from a shaft hole in the masonry, covered by a wooden bench, was now converted into a modern-style toilet. As he entered, he examined the wall from top to bottom, checking all the stone blocks for any odd markings. He then squatted to look behind the toilet and ran his hand around the edges.

There was nothing on the left side, so he shifted his position to the right and tried again. As he ran his fingers along the block, his fingers caught the edge of a protrusion at the base. He looked closer and pivoted his fingers to test for movement. To his surprise, the small block moved. He needed to use both hands and angle his body into an uncomfortable leaning position. With a bit of force, he pulled the block out. It was small and about fifteen centimetres deep.

'Hey guys,' Beau called out excitedly.

Tom and Langdon walked down the hall to find Beau on his knees with a stone block in his hand and a gap in the wall.

'Oh shit, what'd you find, Beau?' exclaimed Langdon.

'I can see something back here, hang on,' Beau grunted before leaning forward. He reached in as far as he could, and his fingers grasped an old, thin piece of paper that was rolled up. He carefully pulled it out and showed it to his friends.

He stood up carefully, still holding the paper. The other two watched as he unravelled it and then huddled together to read what it said.

Ethan,

I hope this letter finds you well. I miss you terribly and cannot wait to return. My family is well. I needed to hide the mark you placed on my neck when claiming me. I have come across other wolf shifters in both human form and wolf form; they can tell I am yours. You were right about claiming me. I wore a scarf so my mother would not notice. I am keeping our secret, love. I shall be back before the next full moon. I didn't realise how difficult being away from you would be. Can you feel my pain? I need you.

All my love, and your 'mate' forever,
Lily.

Langdon

The boys all stood in silence, mouths gaping in awe at what they had just read. 'We need to show this to Eric, it may be his uncle,' said Langdon.

Beau passed the letter to Langdon, then returned the stone block, and they all ran down the stairs, with Langdon calling Eric's name.

'Eric!' Langdon called out loudly.

Eric had been engrossed in his laptop but jumped up at the excitement he could feel from Langdon, he placed the laptop on the table. 'What is it?'

Langdon stood before him and passed him the letter.

Eric read the letter once, twice, his hand shaking as he looked up at the boys. 'Where did you find this?'

Beau was quick to respond, 'I was checking the toilet upstairs and one of those stone blocks was loose, so I gave it a tug and it moved and slid out easily.'

'Wow,' breathed Eric. 'This was my uncle, not the one I inherited this castle from, but another relative who must have lived here before him.' He stood holding the letter in his hand and stared into the distance. Once he recovered from his racing thoughts, he looked back at the boys.

'That's amazing, Beau, good searching!' Eric was clearly shocked by the find. He would do some research into that uncle and what 'claiming' and 'mate' meant.

'What does "claiming" mean? In the letter it said Ethan claimed Lily and what about the term "mate"?' asked Langdon, his curiosity piqued.

Eric shook his head, 'I don't know Langdon, I'll have to look into it. I'm guessing it has something to do with Ethan turning Lily. But biting her after she's been turned, I don't understand. Leave it with me, I'll go back to some of those diaries I found.'

'Okay, thanks, Eric.'

Eric turned his attention back to Tom and Beau, 'Why don't you boys come into the kitchen and grab a sandwich? I've made up some wraps and bread rolls, so just grab whatever you feel like.' Then he turned to Langdon, 'I'll bet your appetite has increased! Make sure you help yourself to as much as you need.'

Langdon raised his eyes in response, 'Yeah, it has actually, thanks, Eric.'

Eric grinned at him, nodding. 'We'll go sit out on the back patio.' He led the way into the kitchen and picked up two chicken and salad wraps, placed them on a plate that he had piled at the end of the table and headed out the back door, leaving it open for the boys to follow.

Langdon's stomach had been growling. *Wow, there's so much food here, Eric must get as hungry as me,* he thought as he picked up two wraps as well and headed outside.

Tom and Beau grabbed a plate and one wrap each and went out to join Eric and Langdon. It was beautiful and bright outside as they walked over and sat at the table with them.

Eric was sitting at a solid timber table with matching seating. The back patio was tiled in a dark stone pattern and opened onto the beautiful green garden. The grass was longer in some areas, and palm trees stood tall and full. Eucalyptus trees were abundant and could be seen for miles. The air was cool and fresh, the aroma of minty pine with a touch of honey gently soothing Tom and Beau's noses. They both looked around appreciatively at the undulating forest and the nearby foliage.

Eric and Langdon, however, could scent not only the powerful aroma of minty pine but also the woody tones of the surrounding trees. They could even pick up the scent of deer and other small animals nearby. Langdon sniffed and bunched his nose up at the scent of blood as the smell drifted past in the breeze. He glanced at Eric, who had a similar expression and knew that he'd picked up on it too. They both knew what was out there and that larger animals were always hunting the smaller ones. Eric shot him a knowing look, and Langdon understood that this was what they could now pick up on with their enhanced abilities.

They ate their lunch with mild chatter about the letter that Beau found, who asked Eric questions about his uncle as they tried to piece it all together. Eric told them he didn't really know his Uncle Ethan, as he had died when he was young. Although Eric remembered reading something about him when he was reading his other uncle's diary. *Uncle Darren. I'm going to research this further*, thought Eric.

'Boys, the papers and my uncle's diary I received with this estate only provided me with a general knowledge of the place. My uncle wrote that he searched the area for a cure, and he tried a couple of different plants, probably one of which killed him in the end,' his voice tapered off as he thought about his family's loss.

'Hey!' Beau exclaimed in excitement, 'Langdon and I did some research at the school library. I think we found something, I'll show you.' He pulled out his phone and showed it to Eric when he found the image of the plant he'd found that had healing properties. 'It's called an Anethum graveolens,' he said, pronouncing the words correctly, pointing to the picture. 'Have you seen a plant like this?' he asked Eric.

Eric looked at the picture, 'Yeah, I have seen some of them scattered throughout the area,' he said thoughtfully. He typed something into his own phone. His brow furrowed as he scrolled, then a smile tugged at the corner of his mouth as he looked up and around the table at the trio.

'Guys, you realise this is actually a herb? It's dill, it's used as a spice for flavouring food.' Eric chuckled to himself.

'Oh my God,' said Tom, laughing. 'A herb! Yeah, like that's a cure, I'm fairly sure my mum uses that in her cooking.' He laughed some more.

Langdon was smiling along, but he'd been there at the library with Beau. He knew the effort they both went to with their research. Beau had been so enthusiastic when he'd found what he thought might be a potential cure. Now, that option was blown away.

Langdon felt the weight of disappointment when he looked over at Beau. 'We'll just keep looking,' he said, looking directly at Beau.

Beau smiled and nodded.

After lunch, the boys helped Eric clean up. Langdon glanced at his watch and saw that it was already after 2 p.m. He was about to say that they needed to get going when Eric spoke up.

'Did you boys want to have a wander around the property? You never know what herbs you might find, and some could even turn out to be useful.'

Langdon stared at him, eyebrows raised, wondering if Eric was just taking the piss out of them.

Eric, sensing the miscommunication, quickly said, 'No, you never know what you might find, and I can look it up. There may be an actual herb or plant, perhaps combined that might be a cure.' He smiled in silent reassurance, showing them he wasn't mocking anyone.

Langdon looked over at Tom and Beau. They looked bored and like they wanted to get out of there. 'Nah, that's okay, we have to get going now, anyway.'

'Oh, okay then,' said Eric. 'Let me just grab my keys and I'll drive you boys back to the park entrance.'

Eric moved to the lounge room where he had placed his keys. The boys followed him through the castle and outside, and they climbed into the HiLux.

The drive was quiet and peaceful, lulling Tom and Beau to halfway fall asleep in the backseat so that when they arrived back at the park entrance, they both rubbed at their eyes to wake themselves up.

'So, Langdon, I'll pick you up at the park near your house on Thursday, the twelfth, yeah?'

'Yup, okay,' Langdon agreed as he stepped out of the HiLux.

Tom and Beau stepped onto the ground as well and, as they did, thanked Eric for lunch.

'Yeah, thanks for lunch and for letting us come out for a look around,' said Langdon.

'No worries at all, boys. See you again soon.'

The boys watched as Eric drove off onto the M4 highway to head back to Sydney.

'What are you doing now?' Tom asked Langdon.

Langdon stared back at Tom, a smile tugging at his lips, his eyes twinkling as he said, 'Seeing Finn.'

Tom rolled his eyes, 'Okay, fine, go and see your boyfriend,' he taunted light-heartedly.

Langdon said goodbye to Tom and Beau and rode off quicker than they could unchain their bikes.

Langdon rode his bike as fast as he could, straight to Finn's.

Arriving sweaty after the forty-minute ride, he wiped his brow before knocking on the door. He hadn't seen Finn in almost two weeks, and it had been incredibly difficult for him. Even though they had been talking on the phone and texting, it was not the same as being with him, touching him, and kissing him. Langdon needed the physical contact not just because he was a horny teenager, but because of the effects of his werewolf curse. Finn was his friend, partner, and life.

When Finn opened the door, Langdon scented him and breathed in his earthy vanilla aroma. He felt breathless at seeing Finn.

Finn smiled and his eyes lit up at seeing Langdon, 'Hey,' he said, eyes scrunching up in happiness.

'Hey,' Langdon replied.

They reached for one another and hugged before he stepped inside and kissed Finn gently on the lips. He quickly withdrew to look around the loungeroom. 'Where's your dad?' he asked.

'In his room, reading,' answered Finn as he stared deeply into Langdon's eyes. He reached for Langdon's hand and squeezed.

'I've missed you,' said Langdon, as he gazed at Finn. It had only been a few days since they'd seen each other, but it had felt like a lifetime.

'Mmm, same,' said Finn. He seemed just as reluctant to take his eyes off of Langdon. 'How was your morning? What did you get up to?'

'Jobs around the house, nothing interesting.' *God, I hate lying to him.* 'You?'

'Study, then went to the shops for dad. Now I need a distraction,' Finn said, raising his eyebrows suggestively.

'I need you right now,' whispered Langdon as he grabbed Finn's hand and placed it in front of his own bulge.

'Hmmm, I can feel that,' breathed Finn. 'Come on.' He linked his hand with Langdon's and pulled him gently back to his room.

As they walked down the hall, Langdon could hear a page-turning from the next room and knew they wouldn't be interrupted, going by Finn's dad's routine of afternoon reading and a nap.

Finn moved towards his phone and played music, connecting it to a small speaker — a good move to block out any noises they would no doubt be making.

***

Langdon arrived home by 6 p.m. just as he had promised his parents to keep them happy. He came home feeling pretty happy as well.

Chapter 25

Golden light streamed in through the small opening between the curtains, the bright rays falling directly on Langdon's face. He squished his eyes shut at the unwelcome wake-up call.

'Ugh,' he groaned, opening his eyes a fraction to look at his phone. He had woken up late. It was already 7.16 a.m. That was late for him. But it was Thursday, and he was on his exam block, so that made it okay. He wiped a hand over his face as he lay in bed. *Thursday,* he thought lazily. *Oh, what a crappy, intense week this has been.*

Since the end of the school term was approaching, he was enjoying the sleep-ins. He'd needed to go in for four exams, all of which had been scheduled for that week. General Math, General English, Science, and Health and Physical Education (HPE). They were tough, but at least he was almost done and still on exam block.

He'd studied late into the night, almost every night of the past fortnight. One good thing about exam block is that he only had to go in if he had an exam, otherwise, he was free to stay home… or see Finn.

Finn was on a similar schedule with his exam block, so they had seen each other more this week. A smile crept across Langdon's face as his morning arousal woke him up further, just thinking about Finn and the way he had kissed him, touched him, made his breathing quicker. His nerve endings, alert and sensitive, were vibrating a slow rhythmic hum throughout his body as he remembered every detail of Finn's touch. He groaned again, although this time for a different reason. *Ugh, I better go for a quick shower to freshen up,* he thought.

Slowly climbing out of bed, he made his way to the bathroom. He stripped his clothes off and stared down at himself, proud of his rippled stomach. He sucked it in, puffing out his chest and flexing his muscles, the corner of his mouth tugging up in a smirk. He showered, taking his time, and finally came out with a towel hugging his hips. After throwing on shorts and a shirt, he went downstairs for breakfast.

As he sipped some coffee and had a few bites of toast, his brain slowly woke up, more so since he'd woken himself up with a shower. He looked at the calendar; the date sparked his memory. Thursday, the twelfth of December. *Oh crap,* he thought, *the last month has gone so fast, and now it's the full moon again!*

Langdon was better prepared this time around. He had told his parents that he'd have dinner at Tom's because he had agreed to meet Eric at 3 p.m. Langdon had asked permission to stay overnight and because it was a weeknight, and after what happened last time, he needed to make sure this ran smoothly. He'd done so well studying for his exams that his parents had agreed. Langdon had shown that he was arriving home at reasonable hours, and he was focusing on his schoolwork—*that is only partly true*, thought Langdon. *I have been doing a lot of studying lately, but not just schoolwork.*

Thankfully, his karate classes had wrapped up for the year, and Langdon had earned his blue belt. The ceremony had been the previous week, and his family had come along for support. He was glad to have his Thursday afternoons free again.

Langdon had texted Eric to confirm picking him up from the park near where he lived. He didn't want to ride his bike and leave it overnight at that park, and with Eric driving him, it would save time. As it was a full moon, they would both be on edge.

After finishing his breakfast, he raced back up to his room and grabbed his phone. Langdon was already feeling on edge. He had to bite back his anger already this morning when talking to his mum.

He wanted to see Finn badly, feeling so aroused and needing Finn's touch. He had been with Finn earlier in the week and had told Finn they'd catch up on Thursday, because they both had the day free. But Langdon wondered if it was a good idea this close to his transformation. Realising he still had hours before it would happen, he texted Finn.

Hey x

Hey x Finn's response came through seconds later, making Langdon keener to see him.

Need to see you, Langdon bit his lip, eager for Finn's reply. He didn't know how he was going to make it through the day otherwise.

Sure, come over.

Well, that decided Langdon's plans. **Now?** He asked just to be sure.

Perfect x

C u soon xx

Langdon smiled and went to ask if he could borrow the car.

'Hey Mum,' he called as he walked down the stairs. Firstly, checking the lounge room, he saw she wasn't there. Then he went back to the kitchen to find her sitting at the breakfast bar, reading the paper.

'Mum?'

His mum looked up from the newspaper, holding a coffee cup in one hand, and glanced at her son, 'Yeah?'

'Could I please borrow the car for a bit?'

'Oh, where are you off to?'

'Just to catch up with a friend.'

'All right then, but can you be back by lunchtime? I want to head out and do the groceries.'

'Yeah, no worries, thanks, Mum.' Langdon walked over to where the keys were hanging and picked them off the hook. He made his way to the car and after selecting his favourite song, he was on his way to see Finn.

The drive to Finn's house was now familiar. Langdon drummed his fingers to the beat against the steering wheel, eager to see him. Touch him. Not only were his emotions running higher than normal, but so were his hormones.

On arriving, he didn't see Finn's dad's car in the carport which fuelled his excitement to see Finn. He bolted out of the car in his excitement he knocked loudly.

Finn opened the door in a matter of seconds, as though he had been waiting close by. Langdon stared at Finn's gorgeous face, his brown eyes appearing darker, his smooth jawline looking as though he'd shaved that morning. He couldn't stop himself when his eyes locked on Finn's lips, he bit his own lip unknowingly.

'Hey, you,' greeted Finn with a mischievous grin before stepping forward to grab Langdon's hand and pull him inside.

'Hey yourself. Is your dad home?' he asked. He quickly glanced around and listened intently for any noise confirming his presence.

'Nope, place to ourselves.' Finn still had a mischievous smile plastered on his face.

They were still standing just inside the door, fingers playing with each other as they stared into each other's eyes.

247

'Come and sit,' Finn led Langdon to the lounge. 'How's your exams going?'

'Not bad.' Langdon told him about the Math exam he'd had the day before and they compared questions they had to answer.

'I haven't been able to stop thinking about you,' Finn caught his eye and the heat between them grew.

'You're on my mind every waking minute,' Langdon bared his soul, his eyes penetrating Finn's.

Finn reached up to lock his hand behind Langdon's head and pulled him gently forward to press their lips together. It lasted only a second before he pulled back to stare into Langdon's eyes again.

'God, you're sexy,' Langdon breathed and leaned in to kiss along Finn's jawline, inhaling his scent all the way along his neck before heading back to Finn's lips.

'You never stop surprising me,' Finn whispered.

Langdon could feel Finn's smirk and pulled back from their heated kiss to see Finn's eyes glinting.

'What's that look?' Langdon smirked, searching Finn's face, knowing he was up to something.

'Want a game of cards?' Finn asked teasingly.

Langdon raised his eyebrows, and a smile tugged at his lips. 'Cards, hey? Only if you make it interesting.'

'Oh yes, I can make it interesting,' breathed Finn as he licked his bottom lip. Still holding Langdon's fingers, he pulled him up and led the way to his bedroom.

'Always keep a pack in here for occasions such as these.' The way Finn said those words was so seductive, he could have been saying, '*I'm going to touch every part of your body and make you moan.*'

Langdon's breathing intensified just listening to the tone of Finn's voice. It didn't help that his senses had picked up lust and desire. Langdon himself felt in overdrive, his senses were even more heightened than usual. The effect of the full moon grew more evident with each passing minute.

He sat on Finn's bed as he watched Finn bend over to reach into the back of his drawer. Langdon couldn't help but stare and admire the view.

'Okay, so strip poker, yeah?' Finn asked as he sat opposite Langdon and began shuffling the cards. Langdon watched Finn's hands and fingers as they expertly shuffled before swiftly dealing each of them a set of cards.

'Mmm,' Langdon responded. Mesmerised. Watching those skilful fingers.

In the first round, Langdon looked at an ace of spades and a seven of hearts. The remainder of his cards were not of any use for this round. Keeping his expression neutral, he took his time, not giving anything away.

Finn stared at his cards and looked deep in thought. He started the game by picking up three cards. He kept his poker face on to keep from betraying his hand as well.

Langdon, unsure how to play poker, followed Finn's lead and also picked up three cards and tried to keep his face from showing disappointment.

Finn placed two cards down and picked up another two cards. He looked up and locked eyes with Langdon. The heat in his gaze caused Langdon to gulp. He wanted to cross the distance between them, but he reluctantly turned his attention back to the game.

Other than the two previous cards he had drawn, Langdon now looked at the hand he was dealt. He saw the eight of hearts, nine of hearts, and a queen of hearts. *That must be good,* he thought as he stared at the set of three heart cards.

Finn licked his lips and displayed his cards, he had a king of clubs, two of hearts, five of clubs, five of diamonds and three of spades. 'I've got a two pair,' he pointed to the two fives. 'Reveal,' he quirked an eyebrow as he nodded at Langdon's hand.

Langdon displayed his cards to reveal that he, in fact, had won that round with his suite of seven, eight and nine of hearts. He looked at Finn as he smiled his victory and waggled his eyebrows at Finn.

Finn's mouth tugged into a smile as he removed his t-shirt, revealing a tanned and quite toned stomach and chest. Langdon's eyes wandered and checked out Finn's toned physique. He was intimately familiar with it, but that didn't mean he had tired of looking at Finn.

'Hey, eyes up here,' Finn teased as he dealt another hand.

This time, Finn won, and Langdon removed his shirt to find Finn happily taking in his fine form. Langdon tensed his chest to make his pecs move and rolled his shoulders to accentuate the flexed muscles.

Finn, watching Langdon's move, licked his bottom lip—in no way inclined to conceal his desire. Langdon's arousal piqued at the sight.

The next hand had Finn winning again, and Langdon had to remove either his socks or shorts. He went for his socks with a cheeky grin.

Finn was an experienced player and won the next round, leaving Langdon feeling exposed sitting in his jocks. Langdon sat confidently, side on, with one leg bent on the bed while the other foot bounced against the floor in anticipation.

He had one hand holding the next hand of cards and the other resting on his knee. Finn's gaze lowered to Langdon's jocks and couldn't help but notice Langdon's arousal. He feigned a loss and promptly removed his shorts, and to Langdon's surprise, Finn was *not* wearing any underwear.

Langdon sucked in a breath, his eyes widened before throwing the deck on the floor and then removing his jocks saying, 'We can play fifty-two pickup later.'

He leaned forward and kissed Finn hard on his lips, pushing his tongue in to play possessively with Finn's. Finn moaned, and his hands pulled Langdon closer. Langdon's heart was pounding hard in his chest with each touch of Finn's fingers. He could hear Finn's racing heart, his senses confirming what he already knew. Finn was highly aroused, and Langdon was unable to control his desire.

Finn took control. He knew where and how to touch. Langdon's breath hitched at the attention Finn was giving his body, voicing his pleasure in moans. His hands were exploring, touching, caressing every bit of Langdon's body that he could find. Langdon was so turned on.

'Don't stop,' Langdon pleaded.

Finn, hearing these words, didn't dare to. Langdon threw his head back as he unravelled under Finn's ministrations, his name a constant moan on his lips.

Later, as they lay in bed, Langdon felt so connected to Finn and held him close as long as he could until it was time for him to go.

Knowing he had to leave, Langdon let out a sigh, 'Oh Finn, I love holding you in my arms, but unfortunately, I have to get home.' He leaned in and pressed his lips softly against Finn's.

'Mmm,' Finn moaned, the sound muffled against their lips. As they pulled away slowly, unwillingly, Finn whispered, 'Langdon, what are you doing to me...'

Langdon stared back into Finn's deep brown eyes, knowing exactly how Finn felt because he felt it too. 'I know, I feel like I can't get enough of you.'

They smiled warmly at each other before Langdon reluctantly peeled himself from Finn's muscular arms. He brushed his lips over Finn's once more before slowly rising to grab his clothes.

Finn lay stretched out on the bed, in all his naked, fine glory, watching as Langdon fumbled with his clothes. Langdon had to focus intently on dressing - *left leg in, right leg in, look at the floor, don't look at Finn on the bed,* zip. He released the breath he had been holding and reached for his shirt.

Finn swung his legs off the bed and swiftly dressed, a smile playing on his lips. He walked Langdon to the door and grabbed him around the hips to draw him close. Langdon breathed in Finn's scent, a light, earthy fragrance mixed with vanilla. He ran his nose along Finn's neck and heard Finn's breathing slightly hitch. Langdon had to go. As much as he wanted to hold Finn longer, he really needed to go.

He gently held Finn's face between his large hands and kissed him again before taking a step back to his car, facing Finn. Their hands held on until they couldn't anymore. Finn stayed at the door, looking satisfied. Langdon could still see his dimple as he climbed into his car.

Arriving home, Langdon found his mum in the kitchen, making herself a salad sandwich for lunch. He could hear the knife on the chopping board and greeted her as he placed the keys back on the bench.

'Hey love, want some lunch?' she asked, her attention still devoted to her task.

'Yeah, starving.' Langdon gravitated toward the kitchen bench and slid onto a stool.

'There's chicken or ham in the fridge, and I bought wraps?' his mum suggested, looking in his direction.

'Hmmm, chicken, cheese, tomato on a wrap, thanks, Mum.'

He watched as she quickly threw together a wrap but screwed up his nose when she added avocado and spinach leaves. 'Ew, not avocado,' he whined.

'It's good for you,' she replied as she rolled the wrap and passed it to him.

Langdon ate hungrily and made himself another one before heading up to his room to pack an overnighter bag.

He was feeling a mix of nervousness and fear as he zipped up his bag. *This is it,* he thought, *I'll definitely be changing tonight, and there's nothing I can do to stop it.* Langdon felt as though he had the weight of the world on his shoulders as he thought about his curse.

He looked out the window. Across the road, he could see some of the park. As he had seen all week, more kids had come to the area with their phones, hoping to catch a glimpse of the wolf that everyone had been talking about.

What made it worse was the television crew that had frequented the area. They had visited the park for regular updates, cautioning the citizens to stay alert despite the fact that there had been no more sightings. Tonight, however, the media had ramped up, someone had claimed that they'd seen a wolf the previous night and so everyone was waiting with anticipation to catch the wolf in action. Animal Rescue had told the public they would monitor the streets in various vans, large enough to hold a wolf. They assured the public that they possessed tranquillizer guns and had advertised their mobile number everywhere, encouraging people to call if they saw anything and warning them not to get too close.

Trepidation increased in his body, causing him to tremble. Langdon tried to calm his breathing as he was rapidly going from unease to anger. Clenching his fists tightly, he glanced at his watch. It was only 1:20 p.m. He wanted to punch something or someone. Remembering that Eric told him he went for a run to ease these feelings, Langdon decided to change into gym shorts. He threw on a pair of socks and laced up his joggers, and before he ran out the door, picked up his phone and AirPods. He scrolled through and selected a song before calling out to whoever was listening that he was going for a run.

'Okay,' came the soft, harmonious voice that belonged to his mother.

With that, Langdon stepped outside, the sunshine instantly making him squint. He turned back inside and reached for his sunglasses. The light seemed to hurt his eyes, and he felt relief when his eyes had the protective cover of his Oakley's. Turning his music up and feeling the beat reverberating through his body, he began running.

He ran past the teenagers, joking about catching the wolf and skinning it. The way they were talking riled up Langdon, and he had to keep running to avoid a confrontation with them.

He ran for over an hour. That was all he had time for. The exercise only made a small dent in his growing tension. Now, he only had thirty minutes before meeting Eric. In a final attempt to ease his frustrations, Langdon ran around his block which usually took eight minutes to run, but tonight he sprinted and did it in five, arriving home drenched in sweat.

He walked into Hayley's room to return her iPad that he had borrowed to look up wolf behaviours and how to lift the curse, even though he had searched with Beau at the school library.

He made sure to clear his search history before returning it to her. His sister was sitting on her bed reading, one leg tucked under her, the other swinging gently, barely touching the floor. She looked up when he entered and screwed up her nose at him.

'Ugh, you stink, Langdon! Your shirt is soaked in sweat.'

Langdon looked down at his sweaty shirt that was sticking to him in places. 'Oh, smell good, don't I?' he taunted. 'Here's your iPad back, thanks, sis.'

She threw a pillow at him, but he twisted so that she missed. He gave her a wicked grin and strolled out, leaving the pillow on the floor.

To remove the stench — a build-up of sweat and anxiety he could smell on himself and that his sister had not so delicately pointed out — he decided to take a shower. By the time he left the bathroom, it was already 2:55 p.m. He quickly grabbed his overnight bag and ran downstairs.

He found his mother, feet up in the lounge room, watching a movie. Flicking her hair out of her eyes as she turned her head to Langdon, she asked, 'You off now, love?'

'Yeah, Tom's going to pick me up. I've got all my study books.'

'All right, love, have a good night and we'll see you tomorrow.' She turned her attention back to the TV.

'Okay, bye Mum. Where's Dad?'

'Oh, he's in the shed. I'll tell him you said hooray.'

Langdon walked outside and over to the park to wait for Eric. Sighing, he sat on the park swing and pulled out his phone.

Chapter 26

Earlier that day, Eric had been in his meeting with the Manager of the App Legend Dynamics (ALP) who had contacted his business for a quote on programming a new line of software. They were meeting to discuss the terms of the contract and to finalise the invoice. The manager of the company, Chris, was a young, tall, skinny man. Eric assumed Chis was in his late twenties, although he came across as much younger.

Eric stared assertively back at Chris as he tried to negotiate a lower price for the services. The manager was dragging out the meeting, trying to renegotiate the original bill, much to Eric's annoyance. *This was not a good time to go head-to-head with a client*, Eric thought to himself. He had been composing himself professionally up to this point, however, as time was ticking on, his emotions were unravelling, and he could feel himself becoming heated.

'This is the amount I originally quoted you, and as I said before, if I reduce it by 10%, I will be forced to withdraw the backup two-year service. It's your choice,' Eric stated defiantly.

Chris stared back at Eric and, as a new client, was silently impressed at the attention to detail of the contract and Eric's confident demeanour. He knew there was no knocking Eric down in price. 'Okay, fine. Set it up and I'll transfer a deposit this afternoon.'

Eric smiled in triumph. His tactics had worked successfully, winning him a new client. He shook Chris's hand, then closed his briefcase after adding the signed paperwork. He strode off purposefully, ready to leave all this behind to concentrate on his transformation.

Eric breathed a sigh of relief on his drive back to his apartment, feeling pleased that the meeting went well. His anger had subsided somewhat, however, his emotions were in overdrive. He had been feeling a mix of nervousness during the meeting, even though he looked as though he was cool, calm, and collected. As Eric's breathing relaxed, he thought of Summer back at the apartment. He still felt like he needed a release.

Striding into the apartment, he placed his briefcase on the kitchen table before looking around for his girlfriend.

'Hey Summer, where are you, babe?'

'Out here on the balcony,' she called out.

Eric strolled over to see Summer sitting at the small table on the balcony, one foot propped up on the chair beside her. The magazine she was reading crinkled as she turned to the next page. Eric stood in the doorway, taking her in. Her beautiful features stared intently at what she was reading. Her short denim shorts were so high, he could almost see her underwear with her leg raised. His eyes were drawn to her chest, her breasts swelling through her shirt. Eric's senses were becoming more intense as he scented her floral aroma.

He stepped onto the balcony and approached her, leaning in to kiss her neck, his lips lingering to assess her response. Eric left light, lingering kisses up and down her neck until she responded. Her breath heaving, she turned her head to place her mouth on his. She moaned as she kissed him, her tongue playing with his. He rose from his crouched position to lift her up and carry her to the couch inside, her legs wrapped around his waist.

He lay her down gently and covered her with his body, grinding his hips into the apex of her thighs. She smiled into his mouth upon feeling the hardness against her. His hands moved to her breasts, and she moaned her pleasure. He needed to feel her skin against his, and swiftly removed their shirts, his deft fingers flicking her bra open to allow him better access. Her breathing increased, and Eric could hear her heart pounding. He moved his fingers lower, past her stomach, even lower, to the top of her short denim shorts, and waited. She pushed her hips up to grind against him, needing to feel his hardness.

He kissed her more passionately, stroking her in places that made her moan. The anticipation of making love to her was now a physical ache. He ground himself down once more between her legs, as his fingers teased her breasts.

'Please,' she begged. Her hand reached down to push her shorts lower.

Eric, his heat rising, swiftly removed his shorts and hers, removing all the material between them both. He was breathing heavily, losing control, as he positioned himself so that their bodies became one, causing Summer to release a low moan. He was tender with his touch as they explored each other, moving, breathing, caressing. Eric listened to her pleasured sounds as they ignited him further, gradually rising to a crescendo as they came undone.

Later, they lay naked on the couch, bodies entwined, as they recovered their breaths.

'Do you have to go away this weekend? Couldn't you put off this trip?' Summer asked sweetly as she ran her fingers along Eric's muscular chest.

Eric had told her he was meeting with another client Sunday morning and needed to be in Melbourne by tonight, so he could be on time. As a computer programmer, he worked odd hours and sometimes had to take the work when he could get it.

'Sorry, baby, I can't put this one off, but I'm all yours next weekend,' he promised, as he ran his fingers gently up and down her bare stomach. She had her head tucked under his arm so he couldn't see her expression, but she moved now to look up into his deep brown eyes. She leaned up and kissed him on the mouth before slowly rising to get dressed. He watched her lovingly as she finished putting on her top. Eric thought she had the sexiest body.

'You're really beautiful,' he said.

'So are you, lying there naked on that couch,' she stood back to admire the view.

'Oh, really?' he asked seductively. He swung his legs off the couch and leapt up to grab her and pull her back down....

*

Later, when Eric saw it was nearly 2:00 p.m. he knew he had to get going. He peeled himself away from Summer and dressed quickly.

She saw him off from the balcony, waving as he drove his HiLux down the road.

Eric glanced at the time again and sighed. 'Siri,' he called out, 'text Langdon, Sorry, runny half an hour late.' Eric couldn't help it due to the full moon influencing his arousal.

A minute later, Eric received a response from Langdon, and he chuckled: S-OK

It took an hour and twenty minutes for Eric to drive from Sydney CBD to Wentworth Falls. The early afternoon traffic had been hectic, with people finishing work early.

As he approached his destination, he called out, 'Hey Siri.' As Siri responded, he added, 'Text Langdon, I'm five minutes away.' Siri responded, and the message was sent. A minute later, his computerised screen indicated a new message.

K texted Langdon.

Eric shook his head and chuckled. *Oh, the language used these days by teenagers.* He knew that 'K' meant okay. The funny thing was, since hanging out with these teenagers, Eric himself had started abbreviating his own text messages.

In a little while, Eric arrived at Wheeler Street, near the park, and was surprised to see a few cameramen and reporters. Some teenagers were also hanging out there, holding their phones close.

Eric saw that Langdon was already waiting for him. As soon as Langdon entered the vehicle, he picked up on Langdon's heightened emotions. The waves of nervousness, anxiety and fear radiating off him were troubling.

'Hey,' Langdon greeted Eric abruptly.

'Hey. Sorry, I'm a bit late. How are you feeling, kid?' Eric asked sympathetically.

Langdon made a whining noise, unable to voice what was going on inside him.

Eric thought it would be a good idea to distract him. 'Gee, these news reporters are relentless,' Eric commented.

'Yeah, I know, I saw them before when I went out for a run.'

'Oh well, we'll be right, we'll stay within the perimeter of my property tonight,' assured Eric, assessing the situation. He hoped no one would be stupid enough to wander through the woods looking for "the wolf".

As Eric drove, he tried to take Langdon's mind off the inevitable transformation that was to occur later that evening.

'So, what did you get up to today?' Eric asked casually.

'Not much, went to … um, a friend's house,' Langdon stumbled over his words, thinking of Finn and if he should tell Eric about his relationship.

Eric glanced sideways at him. *Hmm, something going on there,* he thought. 'A friend, hey? A girlfriend?'

'Not a girlfriend, no,' answered Langdon quietly.

Eric waited patiently, not wanting to pry too much into Langdon's private life. It was up to him if he wanted to share. 'You don't have to tell me if you don't want to.'

'That's okay. His name is Finn. We've been together for a few months now.'

Eric raised his eyebrows and quickly adjusted his features to not show judgment. He hummed noncommittally, wanting to ease Langdon's worries.

But Langdon had been staring straight ahead, having quietened down after his admission. Soon, they turned onto the dirt track near the park where he and his friends were normally picked up. Both of them were shocked to see people with their phones out, waiting to capture something. *Is that a TV reporter?* thought Eric as he saw the large camera stand. *Shit, they're really out here this afternoon!*

'Langdon, we're going to have to be careful tonight. There may be hikers and stupid people trying to get footage on their phones in the woods. But if we stay inside our perimeter, we should be fine.'

Langdon nodded. He knew that if he stayed with Eric in wolf form, Eric would look after him.

Eric continued driving ahead, and the vehicle jostled on the uneven dirt road. But with the sudden silence, and the reporters out of their sight, Langdon turned his head to look at Eric,

Eric, sensing Langdon's mood, had first thought that Langdon wasn't that keen to discuss his relationship. But given the anxious waves rolling off the boy, he thought he should perhaps show some interest. He was getting to know the kid, after all. He was feeling like an older brother towards Langdon, so he asked, 'Finn, hey? Where'd you two meet?'

Langdon swallowed his fear, and his breathing regulated steadily, calming himself down as he thought about his answer. 'I met Finn when I was taking my younger sister to her dance class. It's an open-age class, so he was part of it too. He's the same age as me. It's not ballet or anything that he does. It's actually really cool. He does flips and spins, and he's a fantastic dancer.'

'Oh, that sounds cool.' Eric offered. He didn't want to go saying anything about Langdon's sexuality. He wanted to avoid anything that might upset him. They were both on edge as they drove closer to the castle.

'You have a girlfriend, don't you?' asked Langdon.

'Yeah, that's right. Her name is Summer. We've been dating for about eight months, and we moved in together a few months ago.' Eric remembered he had mentioned Summer to Langdon, but figured that the kid had a lot on his mind.

'Wow, you must really like her then.'

'Yeah, I do. I feel like she gets me, you know?'

'Yeah. That's how it is with me and Finn. I never dated guys before, Finn, you know, but it's different with him. I've fallen for him.' Langdon said these words with such conviction.

Eric smiled because he could scent lust coming off Langdon as he spoke about his male partner. *Oh well,* he thought, *these days, anything goes.*

Eric just hummed in agreement.

It was nearing 5 p.m. when they walked into the castle.

'Okay, mate, just drop your overnight bag near the couch. You won't be needing it until the morning, anyway. How are you feeling?' Eric could hear Langdon's rapid heart rate and picked up on his fear.

This was all becoming too real for Langdon. He didn't want to admit that he felt afraid, so he said, 'Bit on edge.'

'That's to be expected. Look, the best advice I can give you is that for the next couple of hours, we'll just sit outside and relax. It's peaceful, and being close to nature can have a calming effect.'

Langdon nodded and followed Eric outside to sit on the back patio. Eric grabbed a beer for himself and a Coke for Langdon on his way past the kitchen.

Settling into the soft comfortable chair, Langdon relaxed slightly. He felt safe there with Eric.

Soon the two settled into easy conversation and watched the moon slowly rising through the eucalyptus trees. They could smell the pungent notes of woody pine, eucalyptus, and honey. Even though they were both on edge, they were in a comfortable setting.

Eric sat comfortably, thinking about what Langdon had confided in him about his relationship with Finn. There were a few things that Eric had learnt and felt he should share with Langdon. 'Hey Langdon, I just thought I should mention a couple of things. First though, your relationship with Finn — how serious is it?' He glanced across in the darkness and could see Langdon clearly with his enhanced vision.

'Fairly serious, why?'

'Well, I don't know how far you've gone, and I don't want you to tell me, but you need to be careful when being intimate. Even in human form, you can still turn someone. All it would take is for you to break the human's skin, either by your teeth or fingernails. I keep my nails short for that reason.'

Langdon was silent for a minute, thinking about what Eric had just told him. He thought back to all the times he would bite Finn's lip or nibble here and there. He had never bitten so hard as to hurt Finn, and he thought that he never would. 'I'd never hurt Finn,' said Langdon defensively.

Eric could pick up Langdon's emotions, his silent interjection of fear and anger. 'I know you wouldn't mean to, mate. The only reason I brought it up is because I read in my uncle's diary that he had a girlfriend whom he bit in human form, and the next month she turned. The girl ended up ending her life, unable to cope with what was happening to her, and there was nothing my uncle could do to help. He wrote pages and pages on the grief he felt. I just don't want that happening to you.'

'Shit.' Langdon could not even think of that happening to Finn.

'Sorry, buddy, I'm not trying to scare you, it's just that for you and me, we need to make sure we don't pass this curse on.'

'Yup,' mumbled Langdon.

'Hey, how about some dinner?' Eric rose out of his chair.

'Yeah, I'm starving.' Langdon rose as well.

'Brought some steak. How do burgers sound?'

'Yeah, good. Can I help?'

'Sure. Grab the meat from the fridge and I'll start the grill.'

Twenty minutes later, they were sitting back outside eating.

Eric had learned Langdon was interested in karate and had gained his blue belt. He also listened to him talk about rugby.

They'd been talking for about two hours and found out more about one another. It had been slow going though because Langdon was quite succinct with his answers. Eric had felt like he was pulling teeth.

They had both finished their drinks and were feeling more and more on edge. Langdon's foot was bouncing up and down, feeling quite riled up. Eric, knowing the signs, took action.

'Okay, mate, I think it's time. I usually walk out into those trees,' he pointed north to a condensed group of eucalyptus trees. 'I leave my clothes there and go for a wander around until the change overtakes me. I've found that if I try to stay calm and focus on the image of the wolf I am about to become, it happens quicker and is less painful.'

Eric rose to his feet then and gestured for Langdon to follow him to the tree line. 'I'll go there,' he nodded in the direction he pointed to earlier, 'and you go there. If you strip now, you'll save yourself from tearing up your clothes.'

The darkness concealed Langdon as he undressed, yanking his shirt over his head, followed by his shorts and jocks which he placed in a neat pile under a tree. He could hear Eric rustling his clothes and knew now that they were both naked. His heart rate quickened at the thought of the imminent transformation.

Langdon breathed in long and deep, his hands resting on his hips, and looked up at the moon. The brightness illuminated his face and surrounding area as if someone had a flashlight. The minutes ticked on, and he could feel the change happening within him. His skin felt heated, and his breathing became heavier. At first, he felt afraid, and panic rose in his chest.

'Settle down, Langdon,' Eric called out. 'Remember to breathe, just breathe, don't try to stop it. Surrender yourself and visualise yourself as a wolf. Want it. Embrace it. It will happen easier and quicker.'

So, Langdon did. He changed his focus and his thoughts to allow the transformation to happen quickly and easily. The next few minutes comprised quick rapid breaths, then dry retching, then a flash of light, and he was in his wolf form. He howled, loud and terrifying. The sound travelled far and wide.

Eric, also now in wolf form, responded with his own disciplinary howl. He padded over to Langdon, sensing exactly where he was. The grass and leaves underfoot crunched softly as he walked. Once in front of Langdon, he stood erect, with his tail held higher. He was the dark wolf, the wolf who had dominated the area for miles. Although now he was aware a younger, lighter-haired wolf depended on him, submissive to him by the way he slouched to the ground.

The dark wolf made a small noise in his throat, and the light wolf stood taller, approaching to lick the dark wolf's face, cementing his position as the younger, dependent wolf. The dark wolf responded by putting his nose on the light-haired wolf as if to say, 'Hello.'

We hunt now, the dark wolf projected his thought to his companion, who agreed with a nod.

The two wolves travelled as a pack through the mountains, hunting together, and exploring together, and later, when finally satisfied, they slept side by side in the open near the castle.

Chapter 27

The evocative calls of cockatoos startled Langdon awake. Lying on the forest floor, his ears picked up on the morning birdsong of honeyeaters and silvereyes, singing ebulliently in the distance. He was aware of the hard earth beneath his skin, sharp leaves digging into his side and hips. Bright sunshine loomed across the open land as he blinked a few times against the brightness.

Looking around at his surroundings, he noticed the intently bright green ferns, shrubs, and their intricate detail. Never before had he seen such detail of each stem, root, and complex leaf; the characteristics were mind-blowing and majestic!

When he drew his eyes away from all the plant life, he looked at the low trees that were scattered nearby, and the dense forest followed. Waking up was surreal. A forest. A castle, he was now a wolf shifter.

Langdon wiped a hand over his face, continuing to wake up. The smell of eucalyptus hung strongly in the cool, crisp air. He ran a hand through his blonde locks, and his fingers caught on a leaf that was entangled, so he yanked it out and ran his hand to sort through the mess again.

He moved slightly to look over his shoulder and could see Eric lying close, his muscled back and bottom exposed. Langdon quickly looked away, knowing full well he was just as naked. He moved to rest on his left elbow to scan which tree he had left his clothes by. Spotting the blue shirt, he rose slowly so he didn't wake Eric, treading lightly over to a tree far enough away to relieve himself. Then he walked quietly, *crunch,* or as quietly as he could over to where his clothes were lying and quickly dressed himself.

When Langdon came back, Eric was not in his spot. Although some telling noises told Langdon exactly where he was. Moments later, Eric walked into view, fully dressed. His face looking tired, he ran a hand through his messy hair, then back down over his face, pausing to scratch at the dark shadow of stubble along his jawline.

'Morning, Langdon,' he greeted tiredly, covering his mouth as he yawned.

'Hey, Eric. Hey, last night wasn't so bad, from what I remember.'

'Yeah, see, I told you it gets easier.'

'So much better being out here, thank you.'

'No worries at all, Langdon,' he paused. 'I feel like an older brother to you now.'

Langdon smiled. He felt a brotherly connection as well.

'Come on, let's get inside and have some breakfast, I'm starving and in need of a strong coffee.'

'Same,' agreed Langdon.

***

Sometime later, Eric drove Langdon back home and dropped him off. Langdon felt like he had learnt so much about Eric and the castle while they had sat and talked. Eric was now on his way back into the city, back to Summer.

It was still early, just after eight o'clock. As it was Friday, his father had already left for work, and his mother was either still in bed or in the kitchen. She had started her long service leave a week before school finished. And Hayley would be getting ready for her last day of school unless she had talked their mum into letting her have the day off.

Langdon made it inside quietly, seeing no sign of his family. He raced up to his room to grab some fresh clothes and slipped into the bathroom. He quickly showered and had to scrub at the dried blood underneath his fingernails. The smell was putrid to his sensitive nostrils, so he added more soap, pleased with the vanilla aroma, reminding him of a certain someone. Standing under the shower, enjoying the water cascading down his back, with the water pressure perfect, he looked closely at his fingernails, examining their length. *My nails are short,* he tested their sharpness up his thigh to see if they would break the skin. However, it only left a white streak. Happy with that result, he finished washing and stepped out to dry himself.

He rubbed his forearm across the foggy mirror to be able to see and looked back at his reflection. Slight stubble sprinkled his jawline like sand, he ran his hand across it and decided to have a quick shave.

His hair was a tangled mess, so he hurriedly ran a comb through it, sprayed deodorant, and threw on the clothes he had brought in with him.

'Hayley, are you going to school today?' He knew she could hear him through their interconnecting bathroom door.

'No, Mum said I can stay home.'

Langdon went down the stairs and into the kitchen. He saw his mother there, ingredients out and nose close to a recipe book. She glanced up and saw Langdon, 'Oh, hi love, how was your night?'

'Yeah, good thanks.'

Pleased with his response, she went back to baking.

After grabbing a bite to eat, Langdon turned and went back up to his bedroom. He checked the time and waited an hour before texting Finn. It was still early, and considered Finn could be sleeping in. Langdon picked up his phone and scrolled through Instagram, looking at photos he'd taken, some of him and Finn. He'd saved those to a special file and lay back on his bed to look through them. After a while of mindless scrolling, he placed his phone back on his bedside table.

Once he noticed his watch was reading past 9 a.m. he went straight for his phone again. Picking it up off the bedside table, he swiped it open, face recognition allowing him access. His fingers swiped and tapped as he messaged Finn.

Hey. He sat on his bed waiting to see the dots that would indicate Finn typing his response.

... Oh good, he's replying.

Hey, how's things?

Good, what u doin? Langdon placed one arm behind his head, anxious to receive Finn's reply.

Washing my car.

I'm all wet. Finn added to his text. Langdon knew he was trying to rile him up on purpose, but he took the bait.

Oh, is that so? Need any help? I'm good with my hands!

You better get over here then!

Be there in 10. Langdon shook his head at his own eagerness, reading Finn's reply before getting ready to see him.

Chapter 28

Saturday morning, he woke up thinking back to his visit to Finn's the previous day. His visit had been shorter than he would have liked due to his mum wanting the car. They'd still had a good time together playing cards and messing around but being careful because Finn's dad was there.

Finn, he thought. He was seeing Finn today. He ran down the stairs and ate a quick breakfast before heading up to his room to dress. He'd arranged to go around 10 a.m. so he had time to go for a run.

*

When Langdon returned, he showered and dressed again, keen to get to his boyfriend's place.

After grabbing his phone, he ran down the stairs, following the smell of chocolate cake that his mum had in the oven. Looking around once he walked in, he found her with her head in the pantry. She took a step back with her arms full of the ingredients for her next recipe. On looking up and seeing Langdon walking towards her, she jolted and dropped the bag of flour.

'Oh, darn it!' she complained, hurrying to place the items on the bench before picking up the bag. She sighed when she saw that a small amount had spilled. Rising to her feet to look at her son, she exclaimed, 'Langdon, I didn't hear you coming!' She put the flour down to clutch her chest, accidentally wiping flour on her loose-fitting F.R.I.E.N.D.S t-shirt.

'Sorry, Mum, I just wanted to know if I could borrow the car?'

'Oh, sure love, where are you off to?'

'Ah, just visiting a mate.' *My partner, my boyfriend, the guy who has stolen my heart* — the words rattled silently in his head.

'Right-o, keys are on the bench,' she pointed to the middle section.

'Thanks, Mum,' Langdon grabbed the keys and strode to the carport.

Langdon drove, wishing he had his own vehicle. To come and go as he pleased would have been awesome.

Arriving at Finn's, he waited at the door for someone to answer. He couldn't wait to see Finn, he had missed him last night.

The door opened, and Finn's dad answered. 'Hi Langdon, come on in.'

'Hi Mr Romano,' Langdon greeted as he followed Finn's dad inside.

'Finlay,' his dad called out.

'Coming!'

Finn walked out of his bedroom and into the loungeroom smiling at Langdon. 'Hey,' he greeted with a huge grin.

'Hey,' Langdon said absently, thoughts a little scattered at his boyfriend's appearance. *Oh, he looks hot!* Finn was wearing black running shorts that went to his mid-thigh and a dark blue Nike t-shirt. Langdon couldn't help but run his eyes up and down Finn's body.

Langdon could see Finn's eyes roaming his body, too. Glancing to the side, Finn's dad wasn't moving. He knew Finn liked to show affection, and they had done nothing since he had arrived. *Wish Finn's dad would leave us.* Langdon waited a beat, unsure whether he should suggest going to Finn's room.

'Wanna go for a walk to the shop?' Finn asked. 'We can get a drink and go sit at the park?'

Finn lived in an estate where there was a beautiful park of hedges, flowers, and manicured lawns for people to play cricket and another section with a children's playground. There was a small corner shop only a ten-minute walk up the road.

'Yeah, sure,' agreed Langdon, grateful they could get out of there.

Finn walked over to the doorway and slipped on a pair of joggers. His black Adidas shorts were clinging to his toned backside as he bent over. Langdon had to avert his eyes quickly, as he had been staring and felt like Finn's dad was glaring a hole in him.

Langdon swung his eyes to Finn's dad and noticed that he was, in fact, staring at him. Langdon smiled and put his hands in his pockets. Nervousness grew in the pit of his stomach. He hoped that Finn's dad didn't think less of him.

'All right, let's go,' said Finn.

Langdon followed Finn out the door, and they walked up the road. Once they had walked past a few houses, Finn linked his fingers with Langdon, drawing circles with his thumb. They continued until they turned the corner, when Finn suddenly stopped. When Langdon turned to look at him in question, Finn leaned over and gently kissed him on the lips.

'I've been wanting to do that since you walked in the front door,' breathed Finn.

Langdon, wanting to be closer, grabbed Finn around his firm muscled back, pulled him closer and kissed him back harder, pushing his tongue into Finn's mouth. Finn moaned and placed his hands on Langdon's hips. Langdon drew the kiss out, tasting him, caressing him with his tongue before finally pulling away and grinning back at Finn, looking into his heated brown eyes.

Finn's sexy, dimpled smile deepened as he intertwined their fingers once more, and they kept walking. Looking around, Langdon noticed a young group of girls paused to watch them. Langdon didn't care, but he glanced at Finn, knowing that he'd seen them too. They smiled at each other, and Finn squeezed Langdon's hand, a silent agreement to ignore them as they concentrated on each other.

'So, what did you get up to last night after going home?' asked Finn.

'Oh, nothing really, I was tired, so had an early night.' He was still catching up on sleep from the night of the full moon. His thoughts took him back to his energetic night. *Turning into a wolf and running with another wolf through the overgrown woods takes its toll. We hunted and ran the entire forest of the Blue Mountains.* But he couldn't tell Finn any of this.

'Gee, that's boring,' teased Finn.

'I'll give you boring,' challenged Langdon as he unlinked their fingers and threw his arm around Finn's side to tickle him. Finn yelped and stepped away, looking back with a grin. When he came back to Langdon's side, Langdon put his arm around him again, and then lowered his hand to caress his bottom, to which Finn gave a surprised "oh".

Laughing, Langdon moved his arm back to Finn's side and linked their fingers again.

Finn chuckled at his antics. Langdon loved it when Finn laughed, the sound lifted him up inside.

'So,' Langdon began, 'your dad seemed weird back there.' He waited for Finn to respond. *Am I just overthinking this?* he wondered.

'Oh, I didn't take much notice. But I think my dad is suspecting something. I've only brought one boyfriend home before, last year. And he sees us spending a lot of time together. I think he's just putting two and two together.'

'Oh shit, really? Are you okay with that?'

'Yeah, I mean, this is who I am.'

'Yeah, I guess.' Langdon squeezed Finn's hand in support.

By now, they had reached the small convenience store and walked inside.

'What do you feel like?' asked Finn.

Langdon smiled and winked.

Finn laughed, 'No, really, come on let's get something to drink and some chips and go sit at the park.'

Langdon walked over to the cold fridge and looked at all the soft drinks. He opened the door and reached in for a Coke. He looked sideways at Finn and raised his eyebrows in question. Finn nodded, so Langdon grabbed another can.

Finn then walked over to the selection of chips. 'Doritos?' he asked.

'Yeah, okay,' agreed Langdon. He watched as Finn picked up the largest packet.

They walked over to the counter and just like the first time they met each other, Langdon pulled out his wallet and handed Finn a ten-dollar note, but Finn had already pulled out his money and paid. Langdon shook his head in disagreement until Finn's offer made him stop.

'You can get it next time.'

Langdon sighed but agreed and picked up the chips to walk out with Finn. Finn passed him a can, and they cracked their Cokes open, taking long sips as they walked. It took another fifteen minutes before they reached the park.

As it was early afternoon, Finn and Langdon wandered over to the jungle gym which had a hard-plastic square that was used to connect the monkey bars. They sat together on the flat stepping crossroads joiner. They relaxed, leaning back against the metal pole and sharing the small area. It was so small they were sitting hip to hip. Langdon hung his long legs over the edge, his feet touching the sand beneath.

They shared the chips, both reaching in at the same time and conveniently made contact. The cold, refreshing Coke soothed Langdon's throat as he looked around at the park.

There were a few teenagers down further kicking a soccer ball around, he could hear them talking to each other if he focused his attention, but his senses were drawn back to Finn beside him. Finn always smelled like vanilla, earthy, musky–his body aroma was both warm and sweet. Heck, he always smelled so damn good.

They spent the next half an hour talking about cars, the gym, and their programs. Finn told Langdon about his job at the gymnastics centre, recalling funny stories that had Langdon in stitches.

Once they had finished their drinks and chips, they sat close. Finn began caressing Langdon's hand gently with his thumb. Langdon, looking to see that no one was around, used his other hand to reach across himself to Finn's thigh, and he ran his fingers gently up and down, in slow circles, caressing Finn's knee then back up to his thigh as far as was appropriate.

Finn leaned closer, brushing his lips over Langdon's. The simple kiss sent electric pulses racing through Langdon's body, all the way down to his toes. Finn's lips were impossibly soft against his own, the gentle press lingering just long enough to make Langdon crave more. He pressed his lips harder, then, moving a hand behind Finn's head, he traced Finn's bottom lip, feeling Finn edge closer.

Then the sound of children's laughter broke the spell as a group of kids rode past on their bikes, squealing and calling to each other as they headed for the playground.

Langdon pulled back reluctantly, smirking. 'Figures. We're never alone, are we?'

'Guess not,' Finn replied with a mischievous glint. In the next second, he snatched up the chip bag and bolted across the grass.

'Hey!' Langdon shouted, leaping to his feet. He chased after Finn, who weaved around a hedge and sprinted toward the open lawns. Their laughter echoed through the park, Finn throwing quick glances over his shoulder as Langdon closed the gap.

Finn sprinted.

Shit! He can run! Langdon increased his speed, following Finn around the wide trunk of a huge gum tree.

Finally, Langdon lunged, tackling Finn around the waist. They tumbled into the grass, both breathless and laughing so hard neither could speak.

'You're insane,' Langdon gasped, brushing grass off his arm.

'Still got the chips, though,' Finn said between laughs, holding the bag aloft like a trophy.

'Competitive much!' Langdon joked, reaching across to tickle his side.

Finn yelped and squirmed, pushing Langdon's hand away until he stopped. 'Well, I do hold the Sydney West Regional floor and vault title, thank you very much.'

Langdon raised his eyebrows, 'Ooh, not just a pretty face,' he said smiling and reached across to caress Finn's chiselled jawline.

'Oh, stop,' Finn blushed, pushing his hand away and looking away.

'Nah, really, I think you're fucking gorgeous.'

'Yeah, well, I think you're pretty handsome too,' Finn spoke seriously as he turned to lock eyes with Langdon.

They lay there for a moment, side by side in the grass, hearts still pounding as they stared at each other. Langdon reached out, his fingers brushing the inside of Finn's arm in a slow, gentle caress.

Finn shivered under his touch, a smile tugging his lips. 'Your touch gives me tingles,' he murmured.

The air seemed to hum between them, but before either could say more, the jingle of dog collars and the murmur of voices drifted their way. A couple of dog walkers were strolling toward them along the path.

Langdon groaned, removing his hand from Finn's arm and pressing it to the earth. 'Come on, before we get trampled.'

He got to his feet and offered Finn a hand up. Together, they brushed themselves off and fell into step along the path, shoulders bumping now and then as the laughter faded into something gentler.

After a pause, Langdon glanced sideways. 'Hey… can I ask you something?'

'Sure,' Finn glanced across at him.

'Your mum — she lives in Orange, right? How come she and your dad split?'

Finn's smile softened but dimmed. 'Dad worked away a lot. Mum got tired of it — said she felt like she didn't have a husband half the time. They argued. A lot. Eventually, she just left. Said she couldn't do it anymore.'

Langdon nodded slowly. 'That sucks. But I get it. Families can be messy.'

'Tell me something I don't already know about you?' Finn prompted.

Langdon shoved his hands into his pockets. 'I wasn't exactly the model student. Got into fights, lost my temper — suspended a couple of times. And I wagged school more than I should've.'

Finn raised his brows, half-amused. 'Seriously? You?'

Langdon gave him a look, though a smile tugged at his lips. 'Don't sound so shocked.'

'Why'd you do it?'

'I guess when Hayley came along, she could do no wrong. She was the golden child. Then Mum started studying to be a teacher when I was ten, and for those five years Dad leaned on me more. I was always babysitting Hayley so Mum could study, and when Dad got home late from work, he still expected dinner ready and the house spotless. Hayley would run havoc, and no matter what I did, I couldn't do anything right in his eyes. She was the princess, and I guess I didn't handle my frustration too well.'

Finn squeezed his hand, 'That's rough…no wonder you acted out.'

'Hmm,' Langdon hummed, thinking back. Yet inside, he felt lighter. Somehow, talking with Finn — about the messy stuff as much as the fun — made him feel seen in a way he never had before.

Time slipped away without them noticing. Eventually, they wandered back to Finn's house. They went back to Finn's room just to lie together on Finn's firm bed, feeling each other's warmth.

They talked and shared, opening up more about themselves until Langdon looked at his watch and saw it was time to go.

Chapter 29

The next week went by quickly. Exams were finally over, it was finally time for the Christmas school holidays. The Core family had talked about going away for a couple of weeks. Mitchell was considering taking the family to Byron Bay.

The lively beach town offered stunning beaches and opportunities for kayaking, surfing, and snorkelling. They had been there many times, taking advantage of the beaches that they normally don't have a chance to get to. The family had relished the time spent there, exploring, relaxing, and being active in the many activities on offer.

When Mitchell had suggested it just two days ago, Hayley and Leah had jumped at the idea; however, Langdon had seemed to recoil and showed little enthusiasm. His blue eyes had gone wide, and he stuttered out a response by saying something about preferring to hang out with his friends here.

Something or someone was keeping him here.

Mid-morning, Langdon sat having a late breakfast. Sitting at the breakfast bar alongside his father, his father continued drinking a coffee. Langdon glanced up because he could feel his father's eyes on him, but his dad looked away. He looked deep in thought.

Langdon returned his attention to his phone until minutes later when his dad spoke.

'Hey Langdon, can you give me a hand fixing the car this afternoon?' Mitchell looked over at his son for his reaction.

Langdon glanced up from his phone to look at his father. 'Uh, yeah, sure Dad, what time?'

'Four o'clock would suit me, a bit cooler then, and we can work in the shade.'

'Okay,' Langdon went back to his phone.

Netflix, Finn had texted, continuing their conversation about what they had done last night.

Langdon hadn't seen him for a few days because his exams were finishing up and Finn's dad had said 'no' to visitors Friday night because his aunt and uncle were coming over for dinner. Finn had wanted to head out later to see Langdon, even if it was 10 p.m. But the dinner had gone on and on, until finally, they had sat in the lounge watching Netflix with cups of coffee. Finn had endured the whole evening and by 11 p.m. he had been so tired that he had gone to bed.

Finn had just texted to ask Langdon to come over after lunch and stay for dinner. Langdon responded by telling him he had to help his dad with something in the afternoon and wasn't sure how long that would take. He looked at his watch and saw it was nearly eleven o'clock.

What u doin now? Langdon tested.

Nothin, Finn replied.

Come over now if u want, Finn's suggestion came through moments later.

Langdon texted his assent, and he looked up at his dad. He was engrossed in reading the newspaper, holding the page delicately between his thumb and forefinger. A loud crinkle sounded as he turned the page, made even louder with Langdon's enhanced hearing.

'Hey Dad, can I borrow the Subaru for a few hours? I'll be back by four to give you a hand.'

'Sure, son, where are you off to?'

'Ah, just a friend's.'

'Friend?' Mitchell questioned.

'Ah, yeah.' Langdon responded as he lurched across the bench for the keys.

Mitchell chuckled, 'Wouldn't be a girl that has you all smitten, is it?'

Langdon ignored him and was out the door before his dad could ask any more questions.

Langdon drove carefully to Finn's, following the speed limits, his excitement growing as he drove closer to his destination. The radio blared out the song *Blinding Lights*, and Langdon sang along to his favourite part, 'No, I can't sleep until I feel your touch.' He belted out the word 'touch', nodding along to the beat.

He arrived at Finn's and found himself in the familiar routine of knocking on Finn's door. Langdon heard heavy footsteps coming, *not Finn,* he thought. As he suspected, Daniel opened the door and smiled at him.

'Hi Langdon, how are you today?' he asked as he stepped aside and motioned for him to enter.

Langdon smiled back and walked in. 'Yeah, good, thanks. You?'

Daniel chuckled, 'I'm well, lad. Finlay is in his room,' he pointed down the hall.

'Okay, thanks,' Langdon said as he strode towards Finn's room.

As he entered, he saw Finn sitting on his bed, one leg tucked underneath him, looking curiously at the writing on the iPad in front of him. Hearing Langdon enter, Finn smiled and stood, walking the three steps to close the distance between them. He linked his fingers with Langdon and leaned in to kiss him. Langdon responded by kissing back, and soon their tongues were gently caressing each other. Finn moaned into Langdon's mouth.

'Ahem,' a voice cleared its throat to proclaim their presence, and the two sprang apart, turning to the noise.

Finn's dad stood with his arms folded in the doorway, staring intently at his son and then at Langdon. His mouth was in a thin line, pressed together.

Langdon immediately tensed and fought the colour rising to his cheeks.

Finn just smiled and said, 'Hey Dad, what's up?'

Finn's dad seemed to relax and responded, 'I was just going to ask if I could make you boys some lunch?' He tried hiding a smile.

'Ah, yeah, thanks, Dad, that'd be great.'

'I'll get started soon and let you know when it's ready.'

Langdon couldn't speak, they'd been caught!

As Finn's dad was leaving, he said, 'Oh, and Finn, the door stays open, please.'

'Okay,' called Finn, rolling his eyes.

Finn looked back at Langdon and grinned. 'Don't look so worried, it's okay.' He leaned over and gently kissed Langdon on the mouth, then linked his fingers once more to pull him over to sit on the bed.

Facing each other now, Langdon grimaced, 'Oh, shit,' his features showed his concern.

Finn laughed softly, replying, 'It's okay, my dad knows.'

'What?!' asked Langdon, shocked.

'Yeah, um, a week ago, Dad said to me he knew we were dating because you were over here so often and he said he's seen us holding hands and looking, well he used the words, "lovey-dovey",' Finn rolled his eyes. 'So, yeah, it's all good. Although he said that he'd prefer if we kept the door open and didn't get up to too much mischief.' Finn laughed again at his father's words and leaned forward to grab Langdon's hands to rub and caress them.

Oh, Langdon loved the feel of Finn's hands. It sent tingles throughout his body and always seemed to build his arousal.

Finn stared affectionately into Langdon's widened ocean-blue eyes. He still loved looking into Langdon's eyes, they were such a deep blue strong colour. Langdon's stare often appeared to have a sharpness to them, and Finn felt as though Langdon was staring straight into his soul, it's like he could pick up other people's vibes just with his stare. Finn smiled back at Langdon, who now appeared more relaxed.

Langdon breathed out a soft exhale, the air rushing through his lips. 'So, Finn, what can we do?' And he didn't just mean sexual things.

Finn ran his hand along Langdon's arm and responded, 'Well, Dad doesn't mind about the kissing and holding hands, but while he's around, that's about it.' He looked to see that Langdon looked like his question wasn't fully answered, so continued by saying, 'Otherwise, we can play my PlayStation. I can kick your arse at cards,' he winked, 'go for a walk, or um, just hang out, I guess.'

'Yeah, that's cool, I don't mind what we do. Just as long as I'm with you.' Langdon smiled back at Finn.

So that's exactly what they did until lunch. They hung out in Finn's room talking. Now and then, Finn or Langdon would lean over and steal a kiss. Mostly, they lay facing each other, with Finn caressing Langdon's hand. Langdon just enjoyed being so close to Finn, having him caress his skin the way he did.

'Oh, by the way, Dad's talking about us going away for a couple of weeks to Byron Bay.' Langdon cringed.

'Oh, then I won't get to see you!' exclaimed Finn sadly.

'Is your family planning on going anywhere?' Langdon asked.

'Nah, Mum and Dad don't really get together over the holidays except for Christmas Day when we all come together and they're amiable.'

'I wish you could come with us.'

'Well, why not?' asked Finn. 'I mean, you could talk to your parents about us. They might be understanding.'

'No way,' Langdon shook his head. 'I wouldn't even know how to bring it up.'

'Langdon.' Finn spoke seriously, 'We've been dating for four months now. You haven't told anyone we're dating.'

'I've told Tom and Beau!' Langdon rebutted.

'Yeah, but you haven't introduced me to them and you still haven't told your parents.'

'I…' Langdon stammered. 'I will introduce you to them. When the time is right. Just,' Langdon paused and ran a hand over his face in frustration. 'Not yet.'

Finn huffed, but then asked, 'Why won't you tell your family? Is it because you don't see we are in a serious relationship?'

Langdon didn't know how to respond. It wasn't that at all. But putting into words how he felt eluded him.

When Langdon didn't respond, just stared down at their joined hands, Finn pulled away. He sat up and folded his arms. 'I can't be a hidden boyfriend, Langdon. If you only want to do things in private and not have me in your life, then that's not the sort of relationship I want to be in.'

Oh shit! Langdon suddenly feared that Finn was breaking up with him. Sensing Finn's emotions, Langdon felt his heart ache. His entire chest felt as though someone was ripping his heart out, and it caused a sob to break through his throat.

'Finn, no! Please!' Langdon begged, sitting up to face Finn.

Oh, Finn's words pulled at something deep inside Langdon's heart, and he couldn't lose him. 'I've fallen for you,' Langdon responded, his voice breaking. 'Please,' he reached out and gripped Finn's hand, clinging to it, he continued. 'I promise I'll introduce you to my friends soon. And as for my family…' Langdon glanced down at their entwined fingers, 'I'll get there…'

'So, will you talk to your parents?' Finn pushed. 'Just try testing the waters, you don't have to come right out and say it, just hint at it and gauge their response. Maybe try talking to your dad this afternoon when you're helping him with whatever job he's working on?'

'Yeah, you're right. I mean, they haven't even met you yet, so I will try, this afternoon, I'll try. For you.'

Langdon didn't know why he felt this strongly about Finn. He stopped to analyse it. He remembered Eric telling him that since being bitten, his feelings had felt more intense.

'Oh, Langdon,' Finn breathed. as he lunged forward and pinned Langdon to the bed. 'I've fallen for you too,' he whispered, his brown eyes telling Langdon he spoke from the heart. Then Finn kissed him so fervently that Langdon couldn't stop himself from moaning loudly. Finn's touch, his scent, and the way he kissed built a fever in him, a desire to want more. Finn slowed down the kiss, smiling as he pulled away and pulled Langdon up into a sitting position. He glanced down at Langdon's shorts, smiling at his growing arousal. Finn had to adjust his own shorts, he was just as turned on. Langdon noticed and smiled.

'Need help with that?' Langdon asked suggestively.

Finn only smiled sexily back and linked his fingers with Langdon's before whispering, 'Later.'

They sat quietly for a minute, recovering.

They were just leaning in to kiss again when Daniel called out, 'Lunch is ready.'

'Come on,' Finn groaned as he pulled on Langdon's hand to follow him out to the kitchen.

The boys sat with Finn's dad out on the patio. He had made them ham and salad sandwiches, but Daniel had used a delicious soft sourdough loaf he had cut thickly. Langdon's mouth was watering, all the flavours he could smell were making his stomach growl.

'Hmmm,' the sound came out of Langdon before he realised. He'd just taken a huge bite, and the flavours had exploded in his mouth.

Finn and his dad laughed.

'Glad you're enjoying it, Langdon.' Finn's dad smiled across at him.

Finn's dad asked Langdon if he and his family had any plans for the Christmas break. So Langdon told him they might go to Byron Bay for a couple of weeks. Finn's dad had taken Finn and his mum years ago and smiled at the memory. He asked Langdon a few more questions, trying to get to know him, and found that he had a younger sister who also learnt to dance.

The rest of his time with Finn was spent in his room talking and playing cards, the nonsexual kind, much to Langdon's disappointment.

When it was time for Langdon to leave, he thanked Finn's dad for lunch on his way out, and then Finn walked him out to the front of the house.

They stood staring into each other's eyes once outside until Langdon said, 'I really have to go now,' and he leaned over and brushed his lips softly over Finn's.

Finn held Langdon close, his hands resting on his boyfriend's broad shoulders as he deepened the kiss. Langdon breathed heavily, a low moan escaping him. Finn moaned as well, but reluctantly pulled away and ran his fingers down Langdon's biceps.

'I'm catching up with Tom and Beau tonight,' he paused, staring into Finn's eyes, 'why don't you come with me, it'll give you a chance to meet them.'

'All right, if you're okay with that.'

'Yeah, definitely, I've told them heaps about you.'

Finn laughed, 'Only the good stuff, I hope!'

'Obviously,' grinned Langdon. 'I'll pick you up at six, or maybe a bit later if I'm still helping my dad. The guys usually order a pizza, and we just chill out on the X-box. He's got heaps of good games.'

'Oh cool, I love *Halo* and *Call of Duty*,' exclaimed Finn.

'Great, see you soon,' Langdon breathed as he turned to walk back to his car.

***

Langdon walked outside to find his father. He could hear him in the shed, so he walked in that direction.

'Hey Dad,' greeted Langdon.

'Oh, hey Langdon.'

His dad was still organising tools and, after grabbing his toolbox, walked over to his car that was parked at the side of the house.

The car's hood was lifted, and Mitchell stuck his head in to look around the engine compartment, and also to check the oil. He poked around for a minute, pausing, his brow furrowed as he stared inside the engine.

Langdon folded his arms, staring at his dad. Waiting.

Soon, his dad's features relaxed. 'Yup, that's all good. Okay, just need to change the back tyre, Langdon.'

Langdon squatted down beside his father to watch and help where he was needed.

Mitchell set up the jack and began loosening the wheel nuts. 'Here, Langdon, this will be a good experience for you.' He pointed to the jack and waited for him to place it in position and watched as he slowly raised the car.

Langdon followed his father's instructions and turned the handle attached to the jack, raising the vehicle up.

'Whoa, stop there,' Mitchell said, making sure there was at least a five-centimetre gap.

Mitchell continued talking Langdon through each step until the new tyre was in place.

Now and then Mitchell would ask Langdon about what he had been doing on the holidays and what his plans were for the upcoming weeks.

Langdon said that he was 'just going to be hanging with friends and chillin'.'

Mitchell checked the tyre pressure on the other wheels and asked, 'Got a girlfriend?'

'Nah,' Langdon answered, his heart now beating harder. Warning bells started going off in his head as he watched his father working.

'You know you can tell me if you are dating someone, son. I'm interested in who's been grabbing your attention of late. I can tell there is someone special in your life. A father knows these things,' he turned and winked at Langdon.

Shit. This is it. Finn's words played in his head, "I won't be a secret boyfriend, Langdon." *I have to tell him.*

Langdon shuffled his feet, 'Well, there is someone,' he replied slowly, his heart pounding out of his chest.

'Oh, that's good lad, now are you using protection? Or need me to get you some?' Mitchell stopped to turn around and look at his son. 'I'm well aware of how teenagers go, son. I was one myself, you know.'

Langdon suddenly felt dizzy, *what? Oh, fuck! Here we go*, thought Langdon. His mind struggled to say the right words.

'Um… Dad,' he paused, *oh, how am I going to say this…*

Mitchell saw the hesitation and obvious unease in Langdon's eyes.

'Son?' he asked cautiously, 'she's not pregnant, is she?' The concern on his dad's face was extreme, his eyebrows were furrowed, and his face looked contorted. He waited for Langdon to respond. Mitchell swallowed nervously.

'No, Dad! Of course not!' cried Langdon.

'Oh, that's a relief, son.' Mitchell relaxed.

'But Dad, there is something I need to tell you about the person I'm seeing.'

His dad relaxed his features and looked over his shoulder at Langdon's expression.

Langdon stared back, his nerves getting the better of him. He thought of Finn again and how Finn had asked him to try.

For him.

For Finn, he would try.

So, he took a deep breath and, staring into his father's eyes, he said, 'I'm dating a guy.'

'What?' asked Langdon's dad, dropping the tool that was in his hand. It landed on the ground with a thump, just missing his foot. Confusion increased the dent between his eyebrows.

'His name is Finn,' continued Langdon. 'We've been together for about over four months now.'

Mitchell stared at his son. His strong athletic son who played football and was good at karate. 'What?' he repeated in a disbelief whisper.

Langdon nodded, then looked at the ground, fearing what his dad would say. When his dad said nothing for a beat, Langdon looked up.

His dad frowned as though he were trying to process what he was hearing. The words were out of his mouth before he could think it through; he didn't mean for it to sound harsh. 'Langdon, are you telling me you're gay?' asked his father, his voice barely a whisper.

'No,' Langdon took a deep breath. 'But I can't help what I feel for Finn.'

Langdon felt so overwhelmed with emotion just then. 'He's my partner, and I don't see myself as gay, and I can't help that I've fallen for a guy. To me, it's a relationship, I don't want to put a label on it,' he paused. 'It just is what it is. I can't explain it better than that,' said Langdon, his palms out in front of him, open, honest. He felt so exposed before his father right now and hoped, really hoped, that his dad could try to understand him. Not judge him, just understand. Langdon felt he was close to tears. He *needed* his father to understand.

Mitchell stared at his son, noticing how he looked so vulnerable, so young, and impressionable. At that moment, he knew that his reaction could make or break his relationship with his only son. If he tried to make Langdon stop seeing this boy, he'd no doubt sneak out and see him anyway. With these thoughts whirling through his head, he leaned forward and patted Langdon on the shoulder, 'It's okay, son. If this boy makes you happy, then you're right, it is what it is.' He took a deep breath. 'So, are we going to meet this Finn?'

'Yeah, I guess, but, um, we have to tell Mum as well.' Langdon cringed at the thought.

'Don't you worry about your mother,' crooned Mitchell, 'I'll have a chat with her.'

'Okay,' replied Langdon, glad that he wouldn't have to go through this again. *Although I probably should mention it to Hayley*, he thought to himself.

Langdon continued to help his father with the job he was working on, although Langdon noticed he wasn't doing much other than tinkering here and there, checking the oil, and after changing the tyre, he wondered if this was just an excuse to get him out here for this conversation.

He put the thought out of his head, grateful that he had this time with his dad and that he had been so okay with what he told him. He expected his father to yell and tell him he was too young to understand what he wanted, but the opposite had happened. Langdon was grateful.

The sun was going down, and everything that Mitchell wanted to achieve had been done, so he said to his son, 'All right, thanks for your help, son. You can go on in and get washed up, I'll finish up here.'

'Okay, Oh, and Dad, remember I'm headed over to Tom's tonight, so I won't be home for dinner.'

'All right, just make sure you remind your mother.'

'I will,' replied Langdon as he walked away, towards the house.

When he went inside, he found his mother in the lounge room reading a magazine, feet propped up on the couch.

'Hey Mum, I'm off to Tom's soon, I'm having dinner there, remember?'

Leah looked up at her son, 'No worries, Langdon, don't be home too late.'

'Okay,' Langdon said as he walked up to his room. He could hear Hayley in her room jumping around, *she must be playing music*. He walked straight past his room and knocked on her door.

'Hayls,' he called out.

No answer.

He knocked louder, 'HAYLEY.'

The door opened, and he was greeted by a cranky, sweaty face. 'What!' she grumbled. She had been dancing around her room, her breathing sounded heavy.

'Ah, I was just going to have a quick chat with you about something… but if you're busy,' he trailed off, taking a step away.

Her features relaxed, and her pink face softened, 'No, wait. Langdon, sorry, come into my abode,' she took a step back and lowered her arm into a half bow.

Langdon chuckled and wandered in to sit on her bed.

She followed and sat on her office chair that was in front of her desk, slowly swivelling by gently pushing off with her toes. She leaned back and looked at her brother. He seemed relaxed, but not his usual cocky self; she noted. His face was serious. She looked into his eyes to figure out what he wanted to tell her.

'So Hayls, there's something I should probably tell you,' he began, watching her expressions.

She sat waiting and gestured with her hand for him to go on.

'I'm seeing Finn,' Langdon blurted out.

'And?' she asked, waiting for more.

'And …he's my partner… We're in a relationship.' Langdon raised his eyebrows. *Was she getting this? How much clearer could he explain this?* Hayley's response surprised him.

'Well duh! I knew that already,' she said, a grin forming on her lips.

'What? How could you know?'

'Oh please,' she said. 'I've got eyes. I've known for months.' She leaned back in her chair, looking smug, a smile playing on the corner of her mouth. 'I saw you two gazing at each other back that time he brought us drinks after dance class, and then he was here that day, and you two were sitting *very* close. And,' she added, dragging out the word, 'you're like, never here, always going to a "friend's" house,' using her pointer fingers to emphasise the word.

'Oh, well, right then,' Langdon struggled to maintain his composure.

'Have you told Mum and Dad yet?' asked Hayley.

'Told Dad this afternoon.'

'What'd he say?'

'Not much.'

'And Mum?'

'He's going to talk to her.' Hayley nodded.

'All right then, Hayls.' He threw a small pillow at her as he stood, 'I'm off to see friends,' he smiled cheekily as he walked out of her room, barely missing the pillow she tossed back at him.

After showering, Langdon dressed quickly, checking the time. 5:33 p.m. *Better head to Finn's now to pick him up,* he thought. He reached for his phone on the bedside table, stopping to text him.

Told Dad, Langdon texted.

Finn exhibited his surprise and elation with an emoji. Then Langdon saw—*And?*

Went well.

Good, Finn's response came through a second later.

Well, that was that. He informed Finn that he was leaving to pick him up soon. Smiling, he headed downstairs to grab the keys.

'Bye Mum,' Langdon called out.

'See you, love,' his mum replied.

A few minutes later, Mitchell strolled back into the house, wiping grease off his hands onto his pants. 'Hey Leah, are you there, love?'

'In the lounge,' she called out.

Mitchell continued to the lounge room and sat beside her. 'Hey love, we need to talk about Langdon.'

'What?' She turned to face him, a worried look on her face. 'What's happened?'

'Well, you know how I was getting him to help with the car and I was going to ask about the girlfriend?'

'Yeah,' Leah said tentatively as she looked into her husband's deep blue eyes.

'Well,' Mitchell paused. 'It turns out he's been seeing a boy.'

Leah raised her eyebrows, 'What?'

'Mmm,' confirmed Mitchell.

'Oh, I did not expect that,' said Leah as she tried to process what she was hearing.

'Me neither,' agreed Mitchell as he leaned back into the couch.

'So… did he tell you he's gay? Is he "coming out"?' She moved her fingers to make speech marks.

'No, that's the strange part,' mused Mitchell. 'He said that he's not gay, just something about liking this boy and "It is what it is".' Mitchell air quoted the words that Langdon had said.

'Well, did you try to explain to him he's just confused?'

'Nah, Leah, you should have seen his face,' Mitchell sighed at the memory. 'Oh, love, he just looked so pained at telling me. Geez, we're lucky he did. He could have just kept this to himself.'

'Yeah, but come on, Mitchell, dating another boy! That's not right, that's not like Langdon at all. I think we should put a stop to this.' Leah stared closely at her husband's features, trying to gauge how he thought about this news.

'Leah, he's seventeen. He'll be eighteen in four months and free to do what he likes.'

'Yes, I know, but while he's under our roof…'

'Leah, do you want him sneaking out again? He's going to see this boy whether we like it or not.'

Leah sighed, 'I never thought our Langdon…' she trailed off. 'Oh, Mitch,' she leaned into his brawny chest.

Mitchell put his arm around her. 'I know, love, but I think at this point we should support him, otherwise, he will just keep everything from us. Look, it could just be a phase, let's just take it day by day, hey?'

'Mmm,' Leah agreed, thinking about her son. She thought for a minute before saying, 'Well, we should invite…what's his name?'

'Finn, apparently.'

'Okay, we should invite Finn over for dinner and meet this boy.' She looked up into Mitchell's eyes.

'Sure, sounds good, love,' he leaned down and kissed her softly on the lips.

When he pulled away, Mitchell smirked, 'Well, I guess we'll be staying here this Christmas.'

Leah just sighed and nodded.

***

Langdon arrived at Finn's, finding him standing out the front. He left the car running and waited for Finn to climb into the seat beside him. Finn took two giant strides and jumped in, leaning over to kiss him. Langdon kissed him back, his hand moving to the back of Finn's head to hold him close.

They kissed long and deep until Langdon sighed and said, 'We should probably get over to Tom's.' If they didn't leave now, he feared he'd undress Finn, right there in the car.

Langdon told Finn more about Tom and Beau on the drive over. Finn was looking forward to meeting Langdon's friends - slightly nervous, but excited.

They arrived at Tom's fifteen minutes later and knocked on the door. Tom answered and grinned at Langdon and then Finn.

'Hi, I'm Tom,' he stuck out his hand to shake Finn's.

Finn nodded and replied, 'Finn,' shaking the offered hand.

'Come on in, guys. Beau's already here.'

They followed Tom up to his bedroom. Finn noticed how spacious it was, especially with a double bed. There was an open window looking out onto the street, the dark blue curtains were pinned back to allow light in. Now that it was getting darker, Tom had put his light on.

Beau was sitting in Tom's office chair. Langdon saw Beau's eyes widen and roam over Finn's body before landing on him with his eyebrows slightly raised.

Langdon glared at Beau. *Is Beau going to speak or just sit there staring?*

Finally, Beau seemed to gather himself, and he rose out of his chair. 'Hi, I'm Beau, it's nice to meet you.'

Finn walked confidently over to Beau and held out his hand, 'Hi, I'm Finn, it's nice to finally meet you and Tom,' he smiled at Beau and then looked over at Tom as he said his name.

At that moment, Langdon's heart swelled, feeling proud of him.

'Take a seat anywhere, Finn, before Langdon hogs the bed,' Tom grinned.

Finn smiled and sat on the end of the bed nearest Beau. Langdon came up beside him on the bed to sit right next to him. He shifted across the bed further, tugging Finn's hand to join him.

'So, I'm ordering pizza, what's everyone want?' asked Tom.

'Meat lovers,' called out Langdon.

'Bacon and egg,' Beau answered.

'Ew,' said Langdon. 'Not bacon and egg, egg doesn't belong on a pizza.'

Tom rolled his eyes, 'See what I have to put up with?' he looked at Finn.

Finn chuckled.

'What sort do you like, Finn? You can be the deciding vote,' suggested Tom.

'Oh, I like meat lovers and also super supreme,' said Finn.

'Yeah,' Langdon cheered.

'All right, I'll get two meat lovers, and one half and half of bacon and egg with super supreme on the other side. Happy?' Tom asked as he looked around the room.

Seeing nods all around, he picked up his phone and dialled the number. While Tom was on the phone ordering, Langdon told Finn about their usual pizza and X-box nights and how they disagreed over everything.

Tom, now off the phone, came over to sit on the bed at the other end of the couple. 'So, Finn, tell us about yourself.' Tom lazed back comfortably and looked at Finn.

'Um, well, I'm into gymnastics, and I've been dancing for about five years now. I work out at the gym a bit to gain upper body strength for my gymnastics.' He glanced from Beau to Tom with an eager expression.

'Yeah, Langdon told us you did a dance class with Hayley. He even said you're the best in the class.' Tom glanced at Langdon, smiling, then back at Finn. He could see the muscles of Finn's shoulders and arms through his t-shirt.

Finn blushed, glancing at Langdon beside him, smiling. He looked back over at Tom, 'So Langdon told me you guys do karate?'

Tom told Finn how he had met Langdon at karate, and how they had just gained their blue belts. He told Finn about the funnier moments that had happened at karate, like the one time when Tom and Langdon mimicked the Sensei behind his back, and they both got caught out and had to spar with him. They both ended up with bruised backsides after having their legs pulled out from underneath them. They'd worn bruises for a week. Langdon laughed at the memory.

Then the chatter went loud, between the mocking criticism from Langdon to Beau's claim of being an expert gamer, especially at the game *Fortnight* and finding that Finn was a novice *Fortnight* gamer and keen to get better scores, Beau liked Finn straight away. The two talked about gaming strategies and the best places to land in the game until Tom and Langdon both put an end to it.

Finn and Beau smiled at each other. Langdon was pleased that Finn was fitting in so well with his mates.

They sat back, squabbling among themselves about which game to play. Tom had called out the titles of the X-box games he owned. They argued over which game was better, and Beau said he wanted to be paid to play video games, he was up to almost 1,000 viewers.

Finn was impressed.

Langdon surprised Beau by saying, 'He's actually pretty good.'

Beau smiled at Langdon - that was the nicest thing he'd ever said about him. He watched as Finn subtly squeezed Langdon's fingers and the smile that played on Langdon's lips.

Soon after the pizza arrived, and they all grabbed a slice and hungrily devoured it, focussing all their attention on the food before them.

In between slices of pizza, Tom slipped off the bed to the floor to look inside his small TV cabinet, pulling out three games to show his friends. 'How about Call of Duty: Advanced Warfare?' he suggested. 'At least this way, we can all play.' He pulled out four controllers and passed them around. He set the X-box up to select a competitive multiplayer and sat back to enjoy his pizza as the game loaded.

The boys ate quickly to begin their first mission in the game.

By the time Langdon dropped Finn home and arrived home himself, it was almost 11 p.m. He was so tired that he went straight to bed, falling asleep the moment his head hit the pillow.

Chapter 30

By the twenty-fourth of December, Christmas Eve, Langdon and Finn had spent as much time together as they could. As they were both on holidays, they spent time at the Aquatic Centre and going to the movies, where they would sit in the dark and hold hands. They had privacy at Finn's house when Daniel was at work, so they made the most of their time alone.

Finn had even been over for dinner to meet Langdon's parents. It had been an awkward evening for Langdon, but his parents had been very welcoming. His mum was surprised to learn that she knew Finn. She'd seen him dance for the past three years. Leah had supported her son and made Finn feel welcome. She knew Finn was a nice boy. He'd helped Hayley out with learning the end-of-year dance the previous year. It had been Hayley's first year in the open hip-hop, and it had been a difficult transition with the older kids. But

Finn had always been kind and helpful to her. Leah was grateful for this.

Langdon wanted to wake up next to Finn on Christmas morning. They had planned to spend the evening together at Finn's house, and Langdon would slip home early the next morning. He hoped his parents were none the wiser, as he had become quite resourceful and found a way to scale the side of the house to get inside. He just had to remember to leave the window open.

Finn's dad had welcomed Langdon for a BBQ dinner and afterwards was heading out himself. He was not even aware that Langdon was staying the night. Langdon had snuck out after he left and shifted his car down the road under a tree, out of sight. That way, when Daniel arrived home, Langdon's car wouldn't be in the driveway.

Finn and Langdon were now alone, finally, after days of only brief touches, kisses, and whispers of something more. When Finn's dad was home, they needed to keep the door open. At the park, kids were everywhere. But now, in the privacy of Finn's bedroom, no one and nothing was in their way.

Finn and Langdon stood opposite each other, the desire mounting as anticipation built in their gazes. Langdon stepped forward and lifted Finn's shirt over his head. He kissed Finn's chest, moving his mouth across to each nipple, flicking his tongue, gripping Finn's hips tighter. Finn moaned, his head tilted back, and his breathing turned heavier as he ran his fingers through Langdon's hair.

They undressed each other, kissing, licking, teasing. Now, both stood naked as they looked at one another, a slow smile curling Langdon's lips. He liked what he saw. His eyes travelled over every inch of Finn. His gorgeous, chiselled face, his well-built curves, his hips, his arousal.

Finn had similar thoughts as he grabbed Langdon's fingers to put them into his mouth, sucking and licking. He then stepped closer to caress Langdon, who groaned into Finn's mouth, his arousal peaking. Finn's lips, his fingers, the way they caused every nerve ending in his body to light up—it was intoxicating. His breathing became heavier, he felt like he would lose control.

Making their way over to the bed, they lay together, side by side. Langdon caressed the side of Finn's face, feeling the subtle spike of his stubble while Finn gazed into his eyes. Finn's eyes seemed darker with desire with every stroke of his fingers. 'I'm in love with you,' whispered Langdon.

'I'm in love with you too,' whispered Finn as he gazed back into his boyfriend's eyes which were so open with honesty that Finn could feel his intensity.

Langdon leaned in and kissed Finn gently at first, just focussing on his lips. He pulled back and looked into Finn's eyes again before leaning in again. First, he ran his tongue along Finn's upper lip, then the bottom lip before Finn opened his mouth to take Langdon's tongue and massage it with his own. Their kiss deepened, becoming more sensual and urgent. Langdon moaned into Finn's mouth. Finn responded with his own sounds of pleasure.

Finn trailed his mouth to nuzzle his face into Langdon's neck, nibbling, his hand gently snaking its way down, making his intentions clear. Langdon took a quick inhale of air, *oh yes,* he thought. Fingers grabbing, mouths exploring, the heat between them grew stronger. Desire flooded through them, every touch pushing them higher to their climax. Finn groaned his release loudly. Their hearts were beating fast, their breaths coming quicker. Langdon, with a feeling of ecstasy rushing down his spine, gripped Finn's back and groaned loudly as he let himself go under and enjoy what Finn was doing to him.

Finn pushed Langdon towards his undoing, and Langdon groaned loudly again and dug his fingernails into Finn's back, gripping, dragging his nails harder down Finn's strong, muscled back, claiming him. For a moment, Langdon forgot where he was, forgot he possessed a curse so terrible that it overtook his body every month. He held Finn close in the aftermath of their sexual intimacy. Their breathing slowly recovered as sweat dripped down Finn's face. They fell asleep holding each other close, both of them naked, skin to skin.

***

Langdon woke to the soft light streaming in through Finn's blinds. He was aware of Finn's warm body beside him and opened his eyes to see that Finn's back was to him. Langdon had been spooning him. A slow smile spread across Langdon's lips as he recalled the intense and awakening experience he and Finn had last night.

He was still pressed up against Finn's back, his arm resting on Finn's torso. The skin-to-skin contact instantly caused arousal and desire to course through Langdon. *Hmmm,* he thought, *might have time for a quickie before I have to head home.*

He rolled himself back slightly to look at Finn's muscled, smooth back. He was first considering waking him slowly by gently running his fingers across his back. But his eyes fell upon Finn's back, making every fibre of his being freeze. He held his breath, his heart started racing as he took in the sight before him.

For what he saw were deep scratches down Finn's back that had bled, pronounced by the dry clotted blood. Langdon's mouth dropped open as he looked down at himself, there was dried blood on his chest. He looked at his fingernails in disbelief as he saw more dried blood. The wounds inflicted on Finn's back had mostly healed, but the evidence was still there.

What have I done? Langdon thought fearfully. Shock reverberated through him as his mind caught up with his careless actions.

To be continued… in Book 2: **Rogue Blue Mountain Wolves.**

This book continues with Langdon and Finn's story:
Book 2—Blue Mountain Wolves - Rogue.
   Book 2 will have you on the edge of your seat! This book is full of steamy, mature references.

Blue Mountain Wolves - Rogue.
Out 2021.

Find out what happens to Finn.

If you enjoyed reading **Blue Mountain Wolves - Awakening**, please leave a review on the place where you found the book—Amazon, Goodreads, Kobo.

I want to thank all of my readers for coming on this journey with Langdon and Finn. I wish you all well.
You can also ask questions or add comments on my Blue Mountain Wolves Facebook page.
Thank you.
S.C. Macklin

Langdon's playlist when he has energy to burn close to the full moon.

- Whatever it Takes—by Imagine Dragons
- Wishing Well—by Juice WRLD
- Only Human—by Jonas Brothers
- Sweet Dreams (Techno version)—by The Eurythmics
- Big World—by Conrad Sewell
- Connection—by One Republic
- Wasted—by Peking Duck
- Sweat—by Snoop Dog vs. David Guetta
- Youngblood—by 5 Seconds of Summer
- Natural—by Imagine Dragons
- Thunderstruck—AC/DC

www.ingramcontent.com/pod-product-compliance
Lightning Source LLC
Chambersburg PA
CBHW030543190726
48283CB00006B/2003